WOLF DECEPTION

The Cause Book II

By DAN KLASING

Publisher, Copyright, and Additional Information

Wolf Deception – The Cause Book II

Copyright © 2022 by Dan Klasing

For permissions contact: danklasing@gmail.com.

ISBN – 9798988149828

Cover design and interior design by Rafael Andres

PROLOGUE

Nobody leaves a nuclear bomb on a beach, at least not on purpose. And the United States Air Force didn't intend to leave one there either. But they did.

At 2:30 a.m. on a cold February night in 1958, Captain A.J. "Sparks" McClosky climbed into his B-47 Stratojet bomber using a slim ladder lowered from the open bomb bay doors. The other two members of his crew, co-pilot Lieutenant "Slim" Jim Falco, and navigator/bombardier Warrant Officer Rex Wilson, were already on board.

"What's the course outline tonight, Rex?" the captain asked as he shuffled through the narrow crew-access passageway next to the navigator's position.

"Very exciting," Rex said, sarcastically. "The exact same route we've done the past twenty missions. Up the east coast, over lovely Greenland, and along the frozen Russian border. Then it's only another twelve exciting hours retracing our path back here. But, as a special treat, we have roast beef sandwiches tonight instead of ham."

Sparks slapped Rex on the back. "It sounds like you might be a little bored with protecting democracy from the Communist hordes."

Despite their casual banter, both men knew that their job, though monotonous, was critical to the defense of the United States. As part of Operation Chrome Dome, if the Soviet Union launched a surprise nuclear attack, Sparks and his crew would immediately fly into Soviet airspace and drop their Mark 15 nuclear weapon on Leningrad, one of Russia's major cities.

For their part, the Russians knew the United States Air Force kept nuclear-armed bombers near their borders twenty-four hours a day, seven days a week. If they attacked, the U.S. would respond in kind, assuring mutual destruction of both countries.

The world stood on a knife's edge. One nuclear explosion, even an accident, could ignite a full atomic exchange. If such a thing actually occurred, humanity would instantly become an endangered species.

"Don't worry, sir. I'd be perfectly happy to vaporize some Commies if needed," Rex said, turning back to his instruments. "We're all set. Weapon is secure. Plot laid in."

Sparks had every confidence in his crew. They had flown together for almost a year without a single incident. As always, he paused before climbing into the pilot's position to pray for a quiet, peaceful mission.

"Alright, Slim," Sparks said to his copilot as he climbed into the cockpit. "I'll take the first leg."

After buckling into his ejection seat, Sparks pushed the throttles forward. The massive plane gathered speed slowly, its six engines ejecting thick plumes of black smoke from under long, swept wings. Runway lights flashed across the polished aluminum skin faster and faster until the giant bomber finally clawed its way into the air.

Sparks and Slim enjoyed a magnificent view of the night sky and Florida coast from under the bubble canopy mounted atop the nose of the aircraft. When they reached ten thousand feet, Sparks engaged the autopilot and sat back to enjoy the ride.

Just as they swung north for the initial leg of the flight, two F-102 Delta Dagger fighters climbed away from their base in North Carolina. The Daggers' training mission that night called for them to locate Spark's aircraft and simulate a missile attack. If all went well, the Stratojet bomber crew would have no idea the Daggers had approached their aircraft – or pretended to blow them out of the air.

The Air Force chose the sleek delta-winged fighter, the world's first supersonic, all-weather interceptor, to hunt down and destroy approaching enemy aircraft. The Dagger's new radar system could not only locate enemy planes but could automatically place the aircraft into firing position. As soon as the radar detected it was within range of its target, an array of air-to-air rockets and missiles would blow the enemy aircraft out of the sky.

As expected, the two fighters located Spark's plane's radar signature almost as soon as they reached cruising altitude. Both fighter pilots engaged the radar's automated functions and waited for their planes to swing around into firing position behind the bomber. As they got closer, the bright yellow exhaust from the bomber's General Electric jet engines seemed to fill their windscreens. On their instrument displays, small lights appeared, indicating the computer had successfully fired four non-existent missiles at Sparks' aircraft. With the simulated attack a success, the pilots switched back to manual flight mode and prepared to break away from the bomber and return home.

Then something went wrong. One of the fighter's radar systems malfunctioned, unexpectedly punching the fighter's engine into afterburner. The little plane shot forward, directly at the bomber's tail. The startled fighter pilot instantly pulled his stick hard right, but it was too late. The Dagger's pointed nose clipped the bomber's right wingtip, sending the fighter into a wild spin.

Without warning, two of the Stratojet's three right-side engines burst into flames causing the big bomber to snap into a right roll. Sparks grabbed the control yoke and desperately fought to keep the plane from plunging into the sea.

Even while fighting for their lives, the crew knew that if the plane smashed into the black water below, the impact could detonate the four hundred pounds of high explosives surrounding the bomb's nuclear core. In the next millisecond, one hundred and fifty pounds of enriched uranium would go critical, releasing enough energy to disintegrate everything within two miles of the crash site. The nuclear flash would expand outward from there, its fire consuming the city of Savannah.

In a supreme show of airmanship, Sparks managed to level his aircraft just a few thousand feet above the ocean. He could see the lights of Savannah off his left wing and the outline of Tybee Island directly ahead. But he could barely keep his plane flying. And with two of his six engines out of action, the rest screamed in protest at having to produce enough thrust to keep the enormous aircraft and three-ton bomb in the air.

Realizing they had to lighten the plane, Sparks ordered Rex to radio for permission to eject their payload over water. Yet, even as his navigator tried to contact their base, Sparks knew they didn't have time to wait. Either they dropped the bomb with its safety mechanisms fully engaged or die hoping they didn't take tens of thousands of innocent people with them into a nuclear hell.

"Sir, shouldn't we eject?" Slim asked over the radio.

"Too low!" Sparks called back. "We can't risk an uncontrolled crash!"

Out of options, Sparks made a fateful decision. He flipped up a red cover on the instrument panel, revealing a simple toggle marked DROP.

"God forgive me," Sparks prayed as he threw the switch.

Under the fuselage, two doors opened. A second later, the bomb fell serenely away from the plane, its nose slowly tipping over toward the water.

Nobody had ever ejected a live nuke, and none of the crew knew with certainty whether or not the safety devices would hold. All they could do was wait for the bomb to hit the water. Seconds in the cockpit turned into hours.

Slim twisted in his seat and craned his neck around to see what happened next.

"It's in the water! I saw the splash! No detonation! No detonation!"

"Note the position!" Sparks shouted into his intercom.

"Got it," Rex responded immediately.

"She's responding better already," Sparks said, relief in his voice. "Maybe, just maybe, we'll get home."

While Sparks nursed his wounded plane toward the nearest military airbase, the bomb settled onto the seafloor completely intact, its metal casing slightly cracked, but its uranium core undamaged. In a few million years, the uranium's radioactivity would fade away.

But it wouldn't be left alone that long.

For months afterward, the Air Force mounted a desperate search for the lost weapon, but they were looking in the wrong place. In the confusion of the mid-air collision, the crew mistakenly indicated the bomb release point almost seven miles north and three miles east of where it actually hit the shallow water. Eventually, the military stopped looking altogether.

Over the ensuing decades, the lost nuclear bomb of Tybee Island became something of a legend. Locals regaled tourists with stories of a lost nuke, and from time to time, intrepid treasure hunters and thrill-seekers combed the waters around the island — all without success.

The 'broken arrow,' as the military describes a lost nuclear weapon, rested undisturbed for almost exactly sixty years, not at all near Tybee Island, but just off a mostly deserted beach several miles to the south.

ONE

Wassaw National Wildlife Refuge, Georgia
Present Time

When Hurricane Florence finally exited the area, its record-setting wind, rain, and storm surge left behind destruction up and down the eastern seaboard. The combination of heavy precipitation inland and storm surge caused significant erosion of several beaches along the Georgia coast, particularly those close to rivers that emptied into the Atlantic. One such beach lays at the edge of the Wassaw National Wildlife Refuge.

Located twenty or so miles southeast of Savannah, Wassaw is a vast wilderness area of pine forest and coastal marshes. No roads lead to the refuge, so it is only accessible by boat. The usually deserted coastline has few visitors, but those that take the time to pull up onto the soft sand find it extraordinarily beautiful — both undiscovered and undeveloped. One such family would discover more than they ever expected.

John Stillman was a despicable husband and father. In fact, he regularly beat and abused his third wife and two young boys during prolonged cycles of binge drinking. Afterward, Stillman would swear off alcohol for a few weeks, apologize vehemently, go to church, and try to make up for his drunken, sadistic flare-ups. During one of these remorseful periods, he decided to take the boys out on his boat for a day of fishing.

As a pawnbroker, Stillman's income varied widely, sometimes making windfalls from selling pawned merchandise, but more often barely making enough money to survive. It didn't help that he usually drank and gambled away the vast majority of his profits. Stillman managed to acquire his twenty-five-foot off-shore fishing boat after the previous owner failed to redeem it from the pawnshop. While he should have sold the boat for a big profit, he selfishly decided to keep the Cobia 217 for himself. Anyway, he deserved it. Or so he told himself.

Early on Saturday morning, Stillman loaded up a cooler with sandwiches and soft drinks and took ten-year-old Jason and twelve-year-old Joshua out into the Atlantic to troll along the coast. The sea was flat, as it often is after a storm, but the boys soon grew bored. The fish weren't biting, and Stillman got aggravated when the boys became restless and began wrestling each other on the narrow deck. When Stillman's yelling didn't stop their horseplay, he turned the boat toward Wassaw's beach, thinking that maybe he could find some peace while the brats ran around on their own. He knew a few beers would help, but he didn't have any, a fact he regretted more and more as the day wore on.

The pawnbroker gently eased the boat onto the sandy beach as the boys jumped into the surf and ran off along the water's edge.

Grabbing the cooler, he looked for a spot near the tree line where he could kick back in the shade and enjoy the quiet.

Finding a log where he could rest his back, Stillman eased his five-foot-eight-inch frame onto the sand. After flipping off a pair of old sandals, he pulled his stained sleeveless t-shirt over his head, revealing a narrow chest over a soft round belly that bulged over cut-off jean shorts. Rubbing a hand across his dirty-blonde hair, Stillman actually began to enjoy the day. At least a little.

Stillman had just finished a sandwich and was closing his eyes for a nap when his younger son came charging toward him, his feet throwing up little clouds of sand behind skinny legs.

"Daddy, you gotta come see this!" the youngster said, resting his hands on boney kneecaps.

"What the hell! Can't you see I'm sleepin' goddammit!" Stillman shouted without even opening his eyes.

"Sorry, Daddy, but Joshua says he found a bomb down there!"

"Right. I bet he did!" Stillman replied sarcastically. "Y'all bring that bomb up here and let me see it!"

"Can't, Daddy. It's too big. And it says, uh, yeah, I remember, 'USAF.'"

At this, Stillman sat up and looked at his son. The shirtless boy stood there, so thin through the chest that Stillman could see his ribs moving up and down as he panted with excitement. The kid's face was dead earnest.

"Where?" Stillman asked.

"Down there," Jason said, sticking one arm straight out and pointing up the beach. "You wanna see it? It's huge and black and everything!"

A thought flashed through the pawnbroker's mind. *Could it be? Wasn't that supposed to be up off Tybee Island?*

"Alright. Show me where it's at," Stillman responded, trying to dismiss the wild idea that this could be the bomb he'd heard about his whole life.

Jason scampered ahead, looking back to make sure his father was following.

After several hundred yards, Stillman found Joshua squatting in the water next to what appeared to be a rock sticking out of the sand. *If this is a joke...*

Joshua exclaimed, "Look what me and Jason found. I think it's a real bomb!"

Stillman pulled his son back by the arm.

Even though three-quarters buried, Stillman could see this was no rock. On the side of the black metal object, he could make out "USAF," clearly stenciled in fading white paint. Leaning down, he splashed some water onto the metal casing revealing more stenciling. It read: "Mark 15."

"Holy shit! You boys know what this thing is?" Stillman exclaimed.

"Is it a bomb, Daddy?" Jason asked, wide-eyed.

Stillman stood and looked out at the ocean, his mind already churning through profit-making possibilities.

"Is it a bomb, really? Is it dangerous or something?" Joshua said, fear evident in his young voice.

Stillman shook off his dreams of profit long enough to quickly backtrack. "Uh, no boys. It's just an old gas tank. Probably fell off some plane a long time ago. It's just junk."

"Aw, man! You sure it ain't a bomb? That would be cool!" Jason complained.

"Yeah, just junk," Stillman lied. "Let's get home. It's getting late."

The pawnbroker didn't pay any attention to his boys' moaning about having to leave so soon. Instead, he worked on his next move. Obviously, the first thing he had to do was find a way to get the monstrous device somewhere safe – and do it quietly.

As a testament to Stillman's faultless self-interest, he never even considered reporting the discovery to the authorities.

TWO

John Stillman did not possess what most people would call a keen intellect, but he had enough sense to realize he had no idea how to handle a nuclear bomb. The fact that it weighed three and a half tons complicated matters even more. If he was going to make a play to get the device off the beach, he knew two things. First, it had to happen soon. If he found it by accident, odds were someone else would eventually stumble across it as well. Second, he needed someone to help him move the bomb to a safe place.

Luckily, Stillman's profession often brought him into contact with certain individuals who tended to make a living at the edges of the law. While carefully avoiding actually purchasing anything that might have been illegally acquired through his pawn shop, Stillman often acted as a middleman of sorts, brokering sales of stolen valuables between sellers and willing buyers. While the police kept half an eye on his business, often suspecting him of shady dealings, they could never pin anything on him. They eventually labeled the pawnbroker a small-time fence and generally not worth their trouble.

It didn't take long for Stillman to figure out who to call first. One of his usual customers owned a boat salvage yard. Much like a junkyard for cars, this guy recovered and stockpiled old boats, motors, and parts. More importantly, he had the necessary equipment to pull sunken or grounded boats out of the water.

The day after finding the bomb, Stillman called his old friend Tommy Roberts, known locally as "Torp," short for Torpedo because he claimed to have been in the Navy. Torp appeared older than his fifty-eight years. Gray hair circled his head like a monk, revealing a scalp so sun-damaged it looked like a lunar landscape. His usual dress was limited to stained cut-off sweatpants held up by a pair of old suspenders that flared around the sides of an impressively round beer belly. Most of the year he didn't bother wearing a shirt. More gray hairs sprung sporadically from his shoulders and down two ape-like arms. Everyone in Garden City, Georgia knew Torp, but most avoided his unapologetically gruff manner, less than concealing clothing and questionable personal hygiene.

At first, Torp didn't believe Stillman's story. Having plied the waters off the Georgia coast for decades salvaging wrecks, he was well acquainted with the legend of the lost nuke. From time to time, treasure hunters tried to hire his recovery barges as research platforms. Torp had thrown every single one off his property. So, when Stillman came to his salvage yard with a wild story about finding the nuclear bomb, Torp laughed in his face.

"Now look, Torp, I know it sounds a little crazy. But I've seen this thing with my own eyes," Stillman pleaded, sitting in Torp's cluttered office.

Torp leaned forward on his desk, his tattooed forearms resting on piles of ignored paperwork, and looked Stillman in the eye.

"You got a picture or something to prove it?"

Stillman had intentionally left his cell phone behind to avoid constant calls from his old lady.

"How long have we known each other Torp? In all those years have I ever screwed you over? No. We've made a few bucks. But all those deals ain't nothin' compared to this. I'm telling you this thing is real! It's an Air Force bomb and has 'Mark 15' stenciled right on the side. I looked it up and that's the exact kind of bomb lost back in '58," Stillman argued.

Torp sat back. In truth, Stillman hadn't ever lied to him and they had cooperated on a couple of fairly profitable deals.

"Who else have you told about this?" Torp wanted to know.

"My boys saw it, but they don't know what it is. I haven't told another soul," Stillman said, hopefully.

"I want fifty percent," Torp said simply.

"Done," Stillman agreed before Torp could change his mind. "But we have to get it quick, before someone else finds it."

"Be here tonight. We'll take my flat bottom with a crane. But if it's not what you say, or where you say, I'm going to take it out on your ass. Understand?"

"I'll be here tonight," Stillman said, sticking out his hand.

That night, Stillman guided Torp along Wassaw's beach, jumping into shallow water at the spot his son had first found the device. After searching for only a few minutes, he breathed a sigh of relief to find the huge black object exactly where he first saw it the day before.

Torp carefully approached the beach until the bow of the barge slid onto the sand next to the bomb. Walking out of the pilothouse and onto the deck, the salvage man pointed his flashlight at the object laying half-covered in sand and water. Torp's equipment could pull entire boats off the bottom of the ocean, so hoisting the bomb out of the sand would be child's play.

"Well, I'll be damned, Stillman. You was right all along!"

"Can we get it out?" Stillman asked.

"Oh, yeah. I'll swing the crane over. Just hook the chains into those metal attachment points. Holler out when you got it and I'll bring her on board," Torp replied.

"Don't drop it," Stillman half-joked.

"No shit," Torp snorted, turning to walk back to the controls.

Thankfully, plucking the huge bomb off the beach and hoisting it onto Torp's boat went without a hitch. After carefully concealing their treasure under several old tarps, Torp backed off the beach and turned the rusty salvage vessel back toward town.

The smooth ocean and moonless night made for an easy cruise. Torp left the boathouse several times to check on the straps securing the bomb to the deck. At least that's what he told Stillman. It wasn't in Torp's nature to trust another human being, and he certainly wasn't going to trust a lowlife huckster like Stillman. The salvage hunter had no idea whatsoever just how much money the bomb could bring, but he was certain this score was too big to share.

Stillman had been drinking beer ever since they had successfully hoisted the bomb on board. The pawnbroker now stood leaning on the crane, enjoying the cool sea air, and dreaming of how he was going to spend all his new found money. With enough dough, he could finally dump his old lady and ungrateful kids, move to Vegas, and have the life he truly deserved. Expensive strippers already danced in his head.

Torp watched Stillman closely. When he looked half plastered and happy as hell, Torp made his move. Walking out on deck, he carefully checked in all directions for navigation lights from other vessels. Other than some big transports at least three miles away, the sea was empty.

"Hey, Buddy!" Torp called cheerfully as he approached Stillman. "We should be back in about two hours. Your wife gonna notice if you're out late?"

"Hell no!" Stillman replied, raising his beer. "Sometimes I stay loose for days, you know, chasing tail, partying and shit."

"That's good. She doesn't know where you are, right?"

"Nope. Why would I tell her? Or anyone? We ain't sharing our baby!" Stillman called back.

"Yeah, that's just what I wanted to hear," Torp said, pulling a forty-five-caliber automatic out of the back of his sweatpants.

At that moment, Stillman turned around and saw the gun.

"What's the gun for?"

"Gotta keep our secret," Torp said simply.

Stillman didn't understand what was happening until the big salvage expert raised the weapon. Sweat broke out on Stillman's forehead and his hands started to shake so badly he dropped his beer on the metal deck. The bottle shattered, the last of the beer foaming around bits of glass. Neither man noticed.

"Look, Torp, you ain't got to do this. We can, you know, talk about this thing! I got a wife and kids!" Stillman pleaded.

Torp raised the pistol and pulled the trigger, the sound from the shot disappearing quickly across the empty ocean.

The back of Stillman's skull exploded backward, blood, brains, and chunks of skull rained onto the deck and spattered into the water.

"I have a wife and kids!" Torp mocked, looking down at the body.

Working slowly and carefully, Torp wrapped the body in a heavy chain and rolled it over the side, kicking some pieces of skull in after it.

When he got back to the salvage yard, Torp stashed the nuclear weapon in one of his many old metal buildings. Fluorescent bulbs cast a dim, dirty light, illuminating only a small portion of the old marine parts that threatened to overflow rickety shelves. Like Torp himself, the space smelled of sweat, junk metal, and motor oil.

After securing the bomb to a sturdy metal frame meant to support boats while being repaired, he stood back, admiring his biggest find to date. He didn't fully appreciate that he was looking at a real nuke, one capable of destroying the entire city. Instead, he focused solely on the potential riches it represented.

Like Stillman, Torp never considered turning the bomb over to the Air Force or other authorities. The very thought made him chuckle to himself. For all he knew, he could end up in jail for just touching the damn thing. What he needed was a buyer. A rich buyer. The problem would be finding one.

Torp stood resting one massive arm on top of the bomb and rubbing his stubbled chin while he mulled over his options. Every so often he reached around and pulled up the back of his cutoff sweatpants. He knew guys who knew other guys. Maybe one of them might have a connection to some rich Arab or crazy dictator who would be willing to pay millions for an honest-to-God nuke. Torp didn't particularly like Arabs or dictators. He was an *American* after all!

Then again, isn't getting filthy rich the only real American dream?

THREE

Two weeks later
Big Bend State Park, Texas

Torp wrestled with the steering wheel, trying to keep his big four-wheel-drive pickup and camper trailer on the narrow dirt and sand path. The well-compacted unpaved road had disappeared twenty-five miles ago when he passed through the tiny desert ghost town of Terlingua. Since then, coaxing the truck and trailer rig deep into the remote Big Bend State Park became more and more difficult every minute. Now near exhaustion from his hurried drive from the Georgia coast to the Texas desert, Torp continuously checked his GPS receiver and maps for the exact delivery location. He was close, but not there yet.

Estimating he had another mile to travel, Torp nervously checked his watch. His five-million-dollar payday depended on him having the old nuclear bomb at the exact GPS coordinates no later than 5:00 that afternoon.

The day before, one of Torp's contacts had put him in touch with an unnamed interested party. In exchange for pictures of the bomb and its serial number, the potential buyer dropped a $100,000 down-payment into an offshore account Torp kept for off-the-book transactions. Torp and the buyer quickly agreed on a final sales price. However, the mysterious buyer insisted on delivery in just over twenty-four hours in the middle of the Texas desert.

Loading the bomb into his old camper trailer had required welding some bracing into the frame, cutting away the roof, and lowering the deadly black weapon inside using an overhead crane. Once secured over the trailer's axles, Torp replaced the flimsy roof using nothing more than duct tape. After hanging a "closed" sign at his salvage yard, he headed west.

Now, the road led uphill. Around the next tight hairpin turn, he found himself on the edge of a high mesa. Just ahead, the road dipped sharply into what looked like an abandoned strip mine. Torp took a deep breath and began a slow descent. If anything, the road got worse, and the trailer jumped and skidded back and forth on the rocky old road that once carried truckloads of cinnabar ore up from deep within the earth.

With only ten minutes to spare, Torp finally stopped the truck at the bottom of the mine. All around, steep walls climbed back toward the surface. Thankfully, his GPS unit displayed the exact coordinates specified by the buyer.

Torp slowly climbed out of the truck, stretching his legs and back that ached from almost twenty-four hours of hard driving. He didn't have any further instructions, but somehow, he felt like he wasn't alone. Reaching under the driver's seat, the salvage hunter found his .45 caliber revolver and stuck it in the back of his pants.

Now ready for anything, the salvage man called out.

"I'm here! Show yourself!"

"You won't need that gun, my friend," a voice said from deepening shadows somewhere to Torp's left.

"Well, good!" Torp responded sarcastically. "Then I'm sure you don't have a weapon with you either?"

"I don't. But my friends do," the voice responded. "Shall we finish this transaction or remain out here posturing all night? I'm sure you would prefer we transfer the money so you can be on your way."

"I would, at that," Torp replied warily, walking to the back of his trailer and opening the door. "You can inspect the merchandise inside. And don't worry. I came alone just as you said."

"Yes. We know."

Two men stepped from behind a boulder wedged against the mine wall and approached the camper with their hands in plain sight. One of the men wore a white lab coat and carried what Torp assumed was a Geiger counter. The other, wearing chinos and a light jacket, held a cell phone.

Without asking further permission, the lab-coated man ducked into the camper. Torp could hear the distinctive clicks of the Geiger counter being passed over the bomb.

After less than a minute, the technician reappeared and nodded at his partner.

"Excellent," the jacketed man said, making a few entries into his phone. "Payment has been made."

Still cautious, Torp checked his bank balance on his own telephone. Over five million dollars!

"It's there," Torp confirmed.

"Then our business is complete. Thank you, Mr. Roberts."

"I'll just unhook the trailer and be on my way," Torp said, turning to go.

"Oh, that won't be necessary," the jacketed man replied. "We'll keep the truck too."

"Now, I admit I got enough money, so the truck don't mean much to me. But I can't exactly walk twenty-five miles back through the desert," Torp replied.

"Yes, well, I'm afraid that won't be necessary either," the other man said, turning his back and walking away. Torp didn't see him entering the codes to reverse the multi-million-dollar transfer.

Before Torp could react, a single gunshot rang out from somewhere above. The eccentric old man who made his living scavenging from the sea never heard the shot that ended his life in the dry Texas desert.

The dead man's still open eyes didn't see a thirty-foot-wide door slide open in the mine's wall. Inside, high-intensity photoelectric lights illuminated a smooth concrete road leading down into the earth.

Stepping over Torp's body, the technician climbed into the truck and drove it inside. Fifteen seconds later, the door closed again, indistinguishable from the rest of the mine's rough walls.

The new owners of the thermonuclear device just left Torp's body where it fell, leaving its final disposal to the vultures and coyotes – just as Torp had left John Stillman's body for the sharks and crabs.

FOUR

Torp's truck and trailer rolled through the wide tunnel for several miles before emerging into a massive laboratory buried deep underground. Pulling under one of the industrial cranes that crisscrossed the ceiling, several lab technicians jumped into the trailer, attached lifting straps, and guided the bomb onto a pre-assembled support frame.

Even as the old truck pulled away, another team of experts began inspecting and disassembling the weapon. To one side, Dr. Dave Knox and the former governor of Texas, Margie Franks, watched the procedure carefully.

"Is that thing safe?" Franks asked in her gravely Texas accent.

"We'll know in a minute, Madam Director," Dave replied. "If it's not, we won't care for more than a few milliseconds."

Dave could have told Franks the truth. An antiquated bomb like the one sitting twenty feet away required a complex manual arming procedure. Until that happened, the weapon was no more harmful than a gun with no bullets. He didn't try to assuage Frank's anxiety, enjoying the fact that the often abusive and overconfident woman needed his expertise. With a Ph.D. in aeronautical engineering, Dave previously worked at Area 51 for the U.S. government, eventually becoming one of the world's leading innovators in the aerospace industry. Franks needed him, and Dave knew it.

Franks looked up at Dave's self-satisfied expression. While she stood only five-foot-four-inches tall and wore her hair in a short but stylish haircut, Franks would never be mistaken for a wealthy country club grandmother. She dominated women and men alike with her fierce, unbending, and often cruel personality. Franks had brawled her way to the governorship, ruthlessly destroying her all-male opponents. Now, as one of the Directors of a powerful hidden organization, she had no intention of letting Dave talk down to her.

"Well, you know why I feel perfectly safe?" Franks asked, a sneer appearing on her lips.

"Why?" Dave replied, feeling he may have overstepped.

"Because a cowardly prick like yourself would be a hundred miles away if our new acquisition there posed any danger whatsoever."

Dave just laughed. "I can't argue with your impeccable logic. When it comes to nuclear weapons, everyone should be, shall we say, cautious. Right now, my men are opening the outer forged aluminum casing. They will then check to see if the steel trap door preventing the plutonium capsule from falling into what they called 'the pit' is intact. If the door corroded after fifty years submerged in seawater, and the plutonium capsule is indeed in the pit, the weapon will have armed itself. We'll know in a minute."

Franks looked less confident. "And if it's armed?"

"It's still safe. Nothing happens until the TNT shell around the pit is ignited," Dave answered without any concern in his voice. "Retrieving the plutonium capsule will just take a bit more time."

"Just explain how it works to me. In layman's terms. Leave out the egghead bullshit," Franks demanded.

Trying not to be exasperated, Dave explained: "The Mark 15 is a thermonuclear device – meaning it has two stages. First, when the plutonium capsule enters the pit, it sits inside a solid ball of uranium. This arms the device. The uranium is encased in a hollow basketball-shaped sphere of TNT. When the TNT explodes, it compresses the uranium, causing a fission reaction. That explosion ignites the fusion stage made of a plutonium spark plug inside a lithium casing. All this happens in, like I said, milliseconds. This particular weapon has a yield of 1.5 to 2 megatons. Enough to evaporate a medium sized city."

"Damn. That's the simple explanation?" Franks asked.

"Yep. And this particular device, while advanced for its time, it's childishly simple next to today's weaponry. But it's perfect for our purposes," Dave replied, confidently.

The two Directors of The Cause stood quietly for a few minutes watching Dave's team examine the interior of the Mark 15. The tense atmosphere remained unabated until a man dressed in a heavy hazmat suit reached inside the case and removed a long metal tube. When it was free of the bomb's frame, he moved the tube to a worktable and unscrewed the back plate. Carefully lifting the tube at an angle, a sliver-looking capsule of metal about six inches wide and a foot long slid out onto the table.

Dave breathed an audible sigh of relief. Despite his earlier bravado, taking a nuclear weapon apart was never without risk. But the plutonium capsule had not fallen into the pit. The bomb was disarmed.

For now.

FIVE

MI5 Headquarters
London, England

Sir Gregory Fender's assistant ushered FBI Special Agents Frank Deal and Stella Sims into the head of MI5's plush London office. Both agents were somewhat surprised by the sleek, modern decor. Floor to ceiling windows revealed expansive views of the Thames and East London. Black leather and chrome furniture flanked a massive glass table that served as Sir Gregory's desk.

The head of MI5, Great Britain's security service, stepped from behind his desk and offered his hand to both agents. A rather short, balding man of seventy, Sir Gregory's tweed jacket, school tie, and tan trousers seemed out of place and out of time, especially in the ultra-fashionable office atmosphere.

"Well, Frank, you look fit! Thank you for coming on such short notice!" Gregory said with friendly warmth.

"Sir Gregory, this is Special Agent Stella Sims, my number two," Deal said, introducing his partner.

"My pleasure, Agent. Won't you both sit down?" Gregory said, indicating a more intimate grouping of several chairs tucked in the corner of his office. "I so hate sitting behind my desk with friends."

They each chose a seat and Deal said, "It's been a while since Afghanistan, Sir Gregory. But I don't expect your urgent request for our help will leave much time for reminiscing."

"Indeed not, I'm sorry to say, Frank. Although it's the very expertise you acquired during our time there that my government has requested."

While serving as a Major in the JAG Corps of the United States Army, Deal led a special task force. With a hand-picked unit of specialists, he had crisscrossed Afghanistan and Iraq hunting down chemical, biological, and sometimes nuclear weapons and their makers. Deal's methods and tactics had proven extremely effective. Then, several years ago, Deal had been recruited to perform much the same work for the FBI. He was given wide latitude to choose his own team and utilize his own unique practices – tactics that often set him at odds with the more traditional elements of the agency.

Now recognized as a world-wide expert in tracking down rogue weapons of mass destruction, allies of the United States often requested his team's assistance.

"As you and I discussed earlier, we have intelligence from a reliable source that something big is in the works. Perhaps even bigger than 9-11," Sir Gregory explained.

"And you are confident of your source?" Deal asked.

"Quite. The source's identity is the one item I can't reveal. But all our data points to a terrorist cell in the United Kingdom that has acquired the resources to conduct a strike against us like the world has never seen before. We now believe that they may have access to some advanced technology originating from one of our top universities. Perhaps even people inside the university itself."

"Which university?" Sims asked.

"Oxford," Sir Gregory replied, simply.

"Sir Gregory, how much leeway will your government afford my team? We can be most effective if we have near complete authority to operate in the UK," Deal asked.

"I've already spoken to the Prime Minister about just that. Given the danger this threat poses to our nation, and perhaps others, you and your team are clear to conduct operations as you see fit. You'll report only to me, personally. Should you run into trouble from local authorities, or require assistance, give them this number to call," Sir Gregory said, handing over a business card with a hand-written number.

"And we'll have access to all your data?" Sims asked.

"I'm afraid there's not much to share, Agent Sims. But I'll let our people know to cooperate in every way possible."

"Then my team will fly in tonight. We'll set up shop in Oxford and be operational here in eighteen hours," Deal responded.

"Will you require facilities?" Sir Gregory asked. "The last time we worked together, I recall you had several technical types and a quite talented bunch of field operators."

"We'll be fine, thank you. I'll keep you informed," Deal answered, rising.

"Yes, please do," Sir Gregory said, looking Deal in the eye. "Once you have reviewed the intelligence, you'll see just how critical this is."

As Deal and Sims left the building, Sims turned to her boss.

"He seemed scared," she observed.

"I agree. I've known Gregory a long time, and I've never seen him frightened like this."

"You didn't tell him about our, uh, undercover operatives," Sims said, smiling to herself.

"I'm not sure he would have understood. When are they scheduled to arrive?"

Sims looked briefly at her phone. "They should be landing at Heathrow about now."

SIX

"What's 'bangers and mash'?" Bubba Adcock asked with a deep Southern United States accent. "Sounds sorta dirty to me."

"God, Bubba! It's just sausage and mashed potatoes," Zach Self replied from his somewhat cramped position on the inside of their booth at one of Heathrow Airport's many restaurants.

"Well, we've been flying all night and I need a real breakfast," Bubba replied, grumpily.

Bubba and Zach's two best friends, Michael King and Sarah Marshall, sat across from them. While they all battled a case of jet lag from their overnight flight from Atlanta to London, Michael and Sarah couldn't help being amused by Bubba's reaction to his first trip out of the United States. They chuckled at his struggle to find breakfast and at Zach's futile attempts to come to Bubba's aid.

"Alright. Alright. I'll get the bangers, but England better have good food or I'm goin' home!" Bubba announced.

Michael and Sarah looked at Zach with raised eyebrows, but decided to let Zach try to ease Bubba's concerns.

"Don't worry big guy. The beer over here is outstanding!" Zach replied.

"I don't suppose I should try out one or three of them English beers now?" Bubba asked, pulling his six-foot-three-inch frame higher in his seat.

"Bubba, it's only nine in the morning here and we have to catch the train up to Oxford in less than an hour," Sarah scolded, tapping the face of her watch.

"Alright, alright, I'll just eat my bangers and wait on the brews for later. Who would have thought all this globe-trotting secret agent crap would be so hard on the body!" Bubba complained.

None of them could believe they were actually in London working for Agent Deal and the FBI once again, instead of back home completing their sophomore years of college. Just weeks before, the four friends had been instrumental in assisting Agents Deal and Sims track down a clandestine secret organization that had stolen highly classified government plans for a completely new type of aircraft. It was their actions that led directly to the group's failure when it attempted to use the weapon in a treasonous plot against the U.S. Government. The college students had proved extremely valuable to the FBI, providing intelligence they uncovered on their own while students at a major southern university. Deal had invited all four to do much the same for him in the United Kingdom – at Oxford University.

"You've been to England before, right Zach?" Sarah asked while they waited for their food.

"Yeah. A couple of times with my family when I was younger. My father used to fly here on business and he brought us along a couple of times," Zach replied, obviously not remembering the trips fondly.

The overworked waitress brought their orders a few minutes later. Bubba found himself staring at two fatty sausages, perched on top of a mound of lumpy mashed potatoes in the center of a white plate. A small army of green peas surrounded the central pile while drowning in a sea of thin, brown, greasy gravy.

"Aw, come on!" Bubba exclaimed, poking at the unfamiliar food with his fork.

After breakfast, Michael couldn't help being just a little bit excited by their upcoming trip to Oxford by train.

Sarah read her long-time boyfriend's mood and smiled to herself. She enjoyed watching him peer under the cars and jog ahead to take a look at the engine. Michael loved all things mechanical, particularly if they were fast and powerful. Back in the States, he and his father restored old muscle cars to their original beauty. As a result, he became a skilled mechanic and expert driver.

Sarah watched as Michael asked questions of one of the conductors several yards down the long train platform. Sarah was the more practical and cautious of the young couple and kept them both on schedule and often out of trouble.

When it was time to board the train, Sarah called out to her boyfriend. Recognizing Sarah's 'serious voice,' Michael excused himself and ran back to join his group.

"Did you know we'll hit nearly two hundred miles per hour on this trip?" Michael asked, not trying to hide his enthusiasm.

"Yeah, well, you have to get on the train first, you big dummy," Sarah kidded as she climbed into the car behind Michael.

They found their seats across from Bubba and Zach. Bubba already had his laptop open and appeared deeply engrossed. Zach, sitting next to the aisle, chatted up a fair-skinned redhead sitting just across from him. Michael and Sarah just shook their heads knowing that Zach could make friends with anyone, anywhere, any time. They wouldn't be at all surprised if he got a date before they were in the country for twenty-four hours.

The car was brightly lit and modern in every respect. The seats were arranged in sets of four, with two leather chairs facing two others. Michael guessed the car could hold eighty people, transporting them across the country quickly and in comfort, especially relative to the cramped seating he had endured during the almost ten-hour flight across the Atlantic. He should have been tired and jet-lagged, but the thrill of international travel kept him wide awake. Unlike most of the other passengers, who probably commuted like this every day, he didn't want to miss anything and couldn't wait for the train to get underway.

Sarah curled up in her seat and began texting her parents about the trip, what they were doing, and where they were going. Sarah told her mother everything – except the fact she would be working with the FBI.

The train left the station and traveled slowly through the populated outskirts of London. As the urban sprawl disappeared, the train quickly gained speed. Michael watched the pastoral landscape fly past his window. Despite the speedometer mounted on the front of the car indicating over a hundred and fifty miles per hour, the ride was smooth and quiet, almost disappointing in its lack of drama.

After checking in with her parents, Sarah snuggled up against Michael's shoulder. He thought she had fallen asleep when she unexpectedly asked, "What's that smell?"

"We've been traveling for fourteen hours, so I might not smell like a daisy!" Michael responded.

Sarah sat up.

"It's not you. It smells really weird," Sarah said, sniffing at the air.

"Huh? I don't..." Michael began to say. "Wait. Yeah, I smell it too."

Bubba, who had been reading up on the latest missile technology in various engineering publications also noticed. "That doesn't smell like an electrical fire to me."

"Or burning brake pads," Michael offered.

Without waiting, Bubba heaved his extra-large body out of the seat and looked back along the car's interior. Long tendrils of white smoke poured through ventilation vents in the ceiling.

"Oh, crap!"

SEVEN

As soon as he sat down again, an alarm sounded and a series of red overhead lights began to blink. Then, without further warning, the train suddenly and violently decelerated, throwing Sarah and Michael forward. Sarah came completely out of her seat, landing directly in Bubba's lap. Michael just managed to hold on, keeping himself from flying bodily into Zach.

Bubba wrapped his huge arms protectively around Sarah as the force from the train's unexpected deceleration tapered off. Within a minute, they came to a complete stop. Before they could fully recover, a conductor appeared at one end of the car ordering everyone off the train. While outwardly calm and professional, his words were clearly not to be questioned.

"Let's go!" Michael urged, pulling Sarah to her feet.

"I'm right behind you," Zach announced as he got up and moved into the aisle.

"Zach! Come on!" Michael yelled at his friend's back.

The activity in the car became frenetic. Passengers hurried toward the exits at either end of the car. Some delayed, trying to grab their luggage from overhead wracks, blocking the way out. While the conductor literally shoved people toward the door, smoke began to fill the car, burning their eyes and causing fits of uncontrollable coughing. They had to get out!

Michael lost sight of Zach in the confusion. He, Sarah, and Bubba had no choice but to make their way quickly through the car and outside. Zach would have to look out for himself.

Stepping off the train, they followed other passengers into a nearby field. Guided by railroad personnel, they moved awkwardly, stumbling across dirt furrows, finally stopping on a small road at the far side. Looking back, they saw lines of passengers emerging from the other train cars to their left and right, coughing and crying, making their way to safety. Zach had not reappeared.

Despite his own hacking cough and tears streaming from his eyes, Michael turned back toward the train to find his friend, but was almost immediately confronted by the conductor who had ordered the evacuation.

Michael tried to push past, demanding to look for Zach.

"Look, mate. I can't let you back there. We don't know what's happened, and it's my job to keep you lot safe and *off* the train. Now, be a good lad and go back over there with the others. Don't worry, your friend will turn up. Probably just went out the other exit."

Michael wasn't satisfied and he wasn't going to let a train cop, or whatever this guy was, keep him from finding Zach.

Michael walked quickly back to Sarah and Bubba. "You guys alright?" he asked.

"Yeah, but my eyes are burning in their sockets!" Sarah replied, sniffling and crying. "What was that?"

"Lachrymator. Otherwise known as tear gas," Bubba replied, wiping the constant stream of tears running down his face. "It will stop burning in a minute or two. We weren't exposed to a big dose."

"What did the conductor say?" Sarah wanted to know.

"He politely told me to shove off," Michael responded. "Zach couldn't have gone too far. He didn't have time to even get to the next car! I'm going to find a way around this guy."

"Bad idea, bro," Bubba announced, pointing over Michael's shoulder.

Michael turned around to see a squad of extremely serious look-ing police, dressed in black assault gear and carrying automatic weapons surrounding the train. Within moments, three other peo-ple dressed in hazardous material suits appeared, obviously prepar-ing to investigate the train cars.

"That ain't good," Michael said, stating the obvious.

"Nope," Bubba agreed.

Zach was struggling. His eyes streamed tears, blurring his vision while stinging smoke filled his lungs. He would have bounced him-self off the train right then – if it wasn't for the two hundred pound plus unconscious woman in his arms.

As soon as the train began its emergency stop, Zach remem-bered the overweight lady sitting three seats behind him and across the aisle. While chatting up the redhead, he had noticed the large woman was asleep, holding an enormous and expensive looking purse in both hands on her lap. He hadn't given it much thought at the time, other than to wonder why a woman holding a Prada purse and sporting several gaudy diamond rings would be traveling alone in a second-class train seat.

Jumping to his feet to evacuate with Michael, Sarah, and Bubba, Zach glanced back in the woman's direction. She wasn't in her seat. He almost turned to leave when he saw two feet in high heels and the lady's purse laying on the floor beside where she had been sitting. Without thinking further, Zach pushed his way through the panicked passengers in her direction.

He found the woman unconscious on the floor with a bleeding gash on her forehead. Trying desperately to revive her, he didn't notice that the entire car had been abandoned. Nobody had seen him crouching between the seats in the dense smoke and confusion.

Zach weighed his options. He couldn't just leave the woman there. But his eyes were beginning to water heavily and his lungs burned for some reason. Zach yelled for help, hoping somebody would be making a sweep for stragglers. No response.

"Okay, lady," Zach said pretty much to himself. "Let's get out of here."

Knowing he wouldn't be able to lift that much weight, Zach stood, lifted the woman under the shoulders and tried to drag her through the car. Zach weighed a hundred and fifty pounds soaking wet, and with the smoke quickly sapping his strength, he was soon forced to sit down and use his legs to slowly pull the woman backward toward the exit. With each pull, his strength ebbed a little more, until he was only moving a few inches at a time.

Time seemed to slow down and Zach's entire world became pulling the woman with his back, pushing with his legs and dragging the woman the next few inches. Sweat poured from his head, adding to the pain in his eyes from the smoke. Pull, push, drag. Pull, push, drag.

Finally, and near total exhaustion, Zach reached the stairs leading outside. Thankfully, the door was open, allowing some of the smoke to escape up and out. The ever so slightly fresher air revived him enough to pull the woman down one step at a time. His last act before passing out was to make one last mighty heave, causing him to fall backward – the woman's body landing on top of his own outside the car.

"Hey, look! Is that Zach?" Sarah cried, pointing to the door on the other end of the car from where they emerged.

"What's he doing? Is he dragging something?" Bubba asked.

As they watched, Zach fell backward, the body of a large woman in his arms.

Michael, Bubba, and Sarah began yelling and pointing, trying to get the attention of the black-clad police. But they didn't need to worry. As soon as Zach fell out of the car, several officers began running in his direction.

Zach came to unable to move. He almost panicked, as an immovable weight pinned him against the ground and forced the air from his chest. The incredibly strong smell of perfume brought the last few minutes back into focus.

Zach tried to push the woman's body off his own, but he simply didn't have the strength left in his arms to lift the woman's torso off his chest. All he could manage was to move her hair away from his face so he could look around.

Moments later, two men in yellow hazmat suits finally relieved the smothering weight.

"Well, what have we here?" one of the rescuers said, noticing Zach for the first time.

Zach rolled onto his side and coughed loudly, his lungs still burning from the smoke.

"Come on, mate. Let's get you up," the fireman said, pulling him up by one arm.

Zach stood and looked through the plastic faceplate on the hazmat suit.

"Oh, crap," he managed between coughs.

"It's not that bad, boyo," the massive fireman said in a distinct Irish accent. "You'll be fine. We think some idiot set off a few tear gas grenades on the train. The suits are just a precaution. Come along, let's get you checked out."

Zach followed slowly as the rescue team loaded the woman onto a gurney and pushed her across the field to a fleet of ambulances. Zach did as he was told and sat down in another of the ambulances while someone pulled an oxygen mask over his face.

All Michael, Sarah and Bubba could do was watch from a distance as Zach emerged from beneath the large woman's body. They were relieved beyond belief when they finally saw him up and walking on his own.

"They'll take him over to those ambulances. Let's head over there," Michael suggested pointing off to his left.

"Good thinking. Let's go!" Bubba agreed, already walking quickly in that direction.

Skirting the police, they finally found Zach wrapped in a blanket, still looking a bit shell-shocked and unsteady. He brightened considerably when he saw his friends approaching.

"Hey," Zach said, weakly.

"Dude, what happened? Where did you go? We lost you getting off the train!" Michael asked.

Zach coughed. "I, you know, saw that lady on the floor and…"

"And you had to see if she needed help. Right?" Sarah said, finishing Zach's sentence when another coughing fit got in the way of Zach's answer.

"I guess. If I'd known she weighed that much, I might have reconsidered!" Zach explained.

"You mean you dragged her out alone?" Bubba asked, incredulously.

"I suppose so," Zach replied. "But damn, it hurt when she landed on top of me."

Bubba laughed. "I bet it did! You looked like a little old dog trying to drag a dead cow!"

"Bubba!" Sarah said, punching the big man's upper arm.

"Ow!"

"She's small, but she hits like a hammer!" Michael said, chuckling.

Sarah turned and rewarded Michael's comment with a punch to his arm.

"Hey!" Michael cried.

"That's for laughing," Sarah said.

Turning to Zach, Sarah said, "And don't you think you're not in trouble for disappearing like that!"

Zach raised both hands and put his oxygen mask back over his face. "You can't hit me, I'm injured!" he mockingly pleaded.

"Well, you're fine now, young man," an elderly emergency medical technician said, sticking his head out of the ambulance. "Good job, my boy! Jolly well done indeed!"

"Thanks," Zach replied. "Do you know if the lady is okay?"

"They took her to hospital a few minutes ago. The laceration on her head looked bad and we were worried she might have had a cardiac event," the EMS tech replied.

"We sure hope she'll be alright," Sarah added.

"Yeah. Sure do. Do you think we can go now?" Zach asked.

"Medically you're fine. But I suspect the police will want a word."

"Why?" Zach asked.

"Because this might have been a terrorist incident."

"Oh, great. That's just great!" Zach moaned, looking to his friends for support.

"And it looks like there's a lot of other people that might want a word as well," the EMS tech added, pointing to the edge of the field.

They could all see several media vans discharging reporters and camera crews. It wouldn't be long before they started filming and interviewing victims of the train incident, railroad employees, and law enforcement personnel. On top of that, police were already walking in Zach's direction.

Michael understood his friend's anxiety, but he knew they had to consider what Agent Deal would want them to do.

"We better get out of here before we all get caught up in a media frenzy," Michael suggested. "I'm pretty sure Deal wouldn't want us on television."

Bubba and Sarah agreed.

"What do you think I should do?" Zach asked, already knowing the answer wouldn't make him happy.

Michael put his hand on Zach's shoulder. "Sorry, buddy. Your disappearance now would draw too much attention. I think you'll just have to ride this thing out."

"Crap," Zach muttered.

"Sorry, hero. Get back to Oxford as soon as you can," Michael said, leading Bubba and Sarah as quickly as possible away from the throng of media.

EIGHT

Michael called Deal and filled him in on the tear gas attack and how Zach rescued a lady injured during the incident.

"Okay. Look, you, Sarah, and Bubba get on the next train or bus or whatever and get up here to Oxford. I'll send Agent Sims down there to keep an eye on Zach. Hopefully, the locals will be done with him soon."

"I don't think it will be that simple," Michael replied.

"Why the hell not?" Deal demanded.

"It seems young Zach Self has become kinda popular with the press," Michael answered, somewhat sheepishly.

"The press! Why is he talking to the press?" Deal demanded.

"They must think Zach is a hero or something. But from the looks of things, I'd guess you could get more information watching the news," Michael explained. "There's even helicopters overhead."

"You were supposed to be flying *under* the radar," Deal said, not masking his irritation.

"Yes, sir. We know. But we didn't exactly set off the tear gas," Michael replied into his cell.

"Is anyone paying attention to you?" Deal wanted to know.

"No. We checked on Zach and disappeared into the crowd before his heroics attracted any attention."

"Good. Keep it that way and report to me when you get to town. And for God's sake, keep your heads down."

At first, Zach had no idea why he was suddenly surrounded by police and reporters. He could understand law enforcement would want a statement. He was a witness after all. But reporters? All he did was help one woman out of the train! Despite thinking that all the attention would dissipate quickly, it only got worse.

Zach was still standing next to the ambulance where he received first aid. The good-natured EMS technician remained nearby, making sure Zach didn't have any lingering reaction from what the police now confirmed to be a tear gas attack.

As Zach watched, a ring of blue-clad police formed a circle round him, a human fence against what was becoming an increasingly insistent gaggle of reporters yelling out questions. Zach normally had no problem being the center of attention, *but really?*

"Looks as though you've become something of a phenomenon, Mr. Self," the medical tech commented over Zach's shoulder.

"Yeah, but I don't get it. There were a lot of other people on the train," Zach answered.

"You've got me stumped, mate. Maybe one of these tossers will sort this," the tech suggested, gesturing at the police.

"Huh?" Zach didn't understand the British slang.

"Ask one of the coppers," the medical tech explained.

Just as Zach was about to do just that, a woman dressed in a fashionable but conservative business suit pushed her way through the crowd. Flashing a badge and identification card, she made a bee-line for Zach.

The woman held the badge in Zach's face and said, "I'm Officer Eva McWilkinson. I'm in charge of the investigation into this incident."

Zach had to look up at the tall, gorgeous black woman. Like most males, Zach became immediately entranced by Eva McWilkinson. Standing six feet tall with straight shoulder-length silky black hair, McWilkinson looked far more like a Milan-based fashion model than a police officer.

"You are Mr. Zachary Self?"

The question came out more like a statement than a question.

McWilkinson's tone snapped Zach back to reality. "Yes. Uh, yes, ma'am," Zach managed to blurt.

"Your passport, please," the officer asked, all business.

Zach fished in his pocket and passed it to the MI5 officer. He waited as she opened it, used her phone to take a picture of the page bearing his photo and passport number. After a moment, she nodded and handed the document back to Zach.

"Come with me, please," McWilkinson ordered without explanation.

"Where? I didn't do anything wrong. I'm supposed to meet my friends in Oxford," Zach protested.

"Best not argue, mate," the tech whispered into Zach's ear. "These blokes are serious business."

"Indeed, we are," McWilkinson said, flatly. "Mr. Self, we know you have done nothing illegal. In fact, just the opposite. We just need to speak with you about this incident. You can contact your friends shortly, but for now, we need to get you away from the press."

Zach just shrugged and followed the MI5 officer, who was already instructing the police to keep the press back so they could exit the area unmolested.

Clearing the ever-growing crowd of news people, Zach asked again, "Officer, where are we going, really?"

"Back to London. MI5 headquarters. Then over to the palace, I imagine," McWilkinson replied without emotion.

"What do you mean by 'the palace'?" Zach asked, honestly confused.

McWilkinson stopped long enough to turn and face Zach. "You don't have any idea, do you? Zachary, you saved the life of Lady Carol, the Duchess of Cambridge, the Queen's cousin and closest confidant ever since the Queen Mother's death."

"Oh, crap," Zach replied, his eyes as wide as dinner plates.

"Too right."

NINE

On the outskirts of London, three men sat on the floor engrossed with their cell phones. Their apartment, or flat as the English call it, was located on the third floor in one of the cluster of buildings Americans might call a housing project. Thousands of identical apartments stacked into ugly brick twenty-story towers covered hundreds of acres known as the East End. The apartment was spotlessly clean and the three Arabs wore traditional white robes instead of the western clothes they donned whenever they ventured outside.

Three men living together in a small flat went largely unnoticed in the neighborhood. Within the huge housing complex, people minded their own business, assuming the three men were bachelors trying to save expenses. As in many low-income areas, drug sales run by youth gangs constituted the bulk of the crime. And, while the police patrolled the area regularly, they rarely interacted with the mostly Muslim residents.

One of the men smoked a sweet tobacco mixture, called Shisha, from a gilded hookah while sitting on several oversized ornate pillows. The smoggy air added to the tension that had been building in the room for several hours.

These men were terrorists. They were not citizens of Great Britain and no legitimate country would have claimed them. Two were Palestinian by birth. The other came from the slums of Cairo. Hardened by lives of poverty, violence, and political upheaval, they had been the perfect recruits for terrorist organizations. After complete indoctrination into radical Islam, they all served time as simple soldiers, honing their combat skills against Americans in Iraq and Afghanistan. Just before receiving their assignment in London, they had fought Russians and Syrians as part of ISIS.

Based on their innate intelligence and leadership capabilities, each had moved up quickly through the ranks. Their reputations grew steadily until they finally came to the attention of the Kataih Hezbollah and were chosen for any terrorist's most coveted assignment — operations deep within an enemy country.

The infamous leader of Kataih had only one name — Wolf. Although sought for decades by intelligence agencies around the world, his identity remained a complete mystery. So much so that CIA and MI5 counter-terrorism agents gave him a nickname, the Werewolf, because they couldn't prove that he existed at all. Without so much as a blurry black and white photo of his face, some believed he was a myth, simply a name conjured up to confuse western intelligence agencies.

But the Wolf did exist. And no natural wolf could match his savage violence, ruthless cunning and thirst for blood.

The three terrorists anxiously awaited word on the status of their current operation. They had conceived their plan after a news report that one of the lesser-known members of the royal family insisted on taking all forms of public transportation. The press, usually quick to report extensively on any royal scandal, extolled the Duchess of Cambridge for her willingness to mingle with the common people, unwittingly making the aging royal a perfect target.

The terrorists' operation on the train carrying the Duchess had several objectives. The most important of which was to run a live test using their latest remotely-operated drone. The possibility of killing or injuring a member of the royal family would be a welcome bonus. They realized they only had an outside chance of killing the old lady using only tear gas, but everyone knew the Duchess's advanced age and weight made her health quite fragile.

After what seemed to be hours, reports from field operatives confirmed that the attack had been a complete success. The long-range drone, powered by eight small but powerful electric motors and controlled from twelve miles to the north by one man, had carried a payload of six tear gas canisters to the intercept point. Upon contact with the train, a computer program took over, precisely guiding the drone and instructing it to insert two explosive canisters into ventilation ducts on the roofs of each of the first three passenger cars. Simple magnets held the gas charges in place until the drone could exit the area. Then, the operator simply pushed one button to ignite the charges, sending the gas flowing into the passenger spaces.

Pleased, the three terrorist leaders nodded and smiled, their stoic nature preventing any more celebration.

After waiting several minutes, during which reports came in about the reaction of the train personnel, passengers, and emergency services, they finally got the news they wanted. An unconscious woman matching the description of the Duchess had been removed from the train bleeding from the head. The news would later confirm that the Duchess of Cambridge had been injured in the suspected terrorist attack. Television news reports quickly added that she had suffered serious injuries and a heart attack. The reports also included a description of her rescue by a young American student, who was credited with saving her life.

"I believe we can report success to the Wolf," the terrorist who went by Simon said, looking up from his telephone. Simon served as the group's technical expert.

For the sake of cover and to protect their identity, the three men had taken western names and spoke fluent English with very little accent, easily passing as natural citizens raised in the majority Muslim areas of London. By affecting western dress, avoiding Mosques and political protests, and even socializing with neighbors, they succeeded in staying well off law enforcement radar.

John, the oldest of the group at thirty-three, held overall responsibility for in-country operations. Tony, the youngest at just twenty-four, spoke the most fluent English and knew the most about current western society, including popular culture, and social media.

"I agree. We have proven our capability to strike at the heart of this infidel country with impunity from afar," John said. "Our objectives have been met. Tony, please convey our news to Wolf in the usual manner."

"Absolutely. I'll put together a post on our social media pages, according to our approved codes, of course," Tony replied.

Simon added, "And I'll meet with our young genius engineer tonight in Oxford."

TEN

Zach had been given no choice but to accompany Officer McWilkinson to MI5 headquarters. Yet, he desperately needed to contact Agent Deal in Oxford. Since leaving the site of the train accident, he hadn't been left alone for a second. While he knew that Michael would report everything that happened, he needed help to extricate himself from the tidal wave of attention flowing over him from law enforcement and the media.

In any other circumstance, Zach would revel in his current situation. He had every intention of eventually attending law school and becoming a politician. His effusive personality, engaging smile, and ability to instantly make friends made him a natural fit for a career in politics. But that would have to wait. For the moment, he found himself stuck inside a modern and very comfortable conference room deep within MI5. With few options, Zach decided to wait it out while maintaining his story that he was merely an international student on his way to continuing his study of history at Oxford. He would let Deal decide whether or not to intervene with MI5.

Arriving at MI5's headquarters, Zach had been scanned and thoroughly searched. He didn't know it, but the entire contents of his cell phone had been downloaded, even while it remained tucked in the pocket of his jeans. Officer McWilkinson had disappeared almost immediately, replaced by a mountainous uniformed officer who escorted him into the conference room. The same officer now stood silently at the only door.

After fidgeting in his seat for thirty minutes, Zach decided to at least try to reach Michael.

"Excuse me, officer," Zach said, attracting the large man's attention. "I'd like to make a call to my friends. They don't really know where I am and I don't want them to, you know, worry."

The officer slowly looked down at Zach. "Best not until Officer McWilkinson returns."

"Yeah, sure. Any idea how long I'll be here?" Zach asked, politely.

"Not long, Zachary," a voice said from behind him, startling the young man.

Turning quickly in his chair, Zach caught sight of a panel in the back wall sliding closed as Eva McWilkinson moved smoothly into the room.

"Wow. That was awesome!" Zach blurted.

"Yes. Quite," McWilkinson replied coolly.

Zach sat nervously while McWilkinson's fingers flew over a small computer pad.

"Zachary. May I call you Zachary?" she asked.

"Sure, but everyone but my grandmother calls me Zach," he replied.

"Zach," McWilkinson said, smiling for the first time. "Can you tell me what happened on the train? Let's start with when you first thought something was wrong."

Zach described how they had noticed a strange smell, the train's emergency stop, the confusion while the passengers evacuated, and how he tried to help the unconscious woman. He intentionally minimized his actions, hoping to avoid as much attention as possible.

"I see," McWilkinson replied. "You did more than just assist the Duchess from the train, didn't you?"

"I don't think so," Zach answered.

"Well, the Duchess was unconscious, and she is not a small woman by any measure, now, is she? In comparison, and I mean no disrespect at all, but I imagine you weigh sixty or seventy pounds less than she does. I also imagine that moving her by yourself through a cloud of tear gas couldn't have been easy, could it?" McWilkinson observed, lifting one eyebrow.

Zach replied simply. "I guess I managed alright. Can I give my friends a call now? Like I told the big guy over there, they're probably wondering where I am."

"We should have you back at the university tomorrow afternoon," McWilkinson replied looking back at her pad.

"I'd rather return tonight," Zach objected.

"And miss an audience with Her Majesty? Don't be a pillock," McWilkinson laughed, chiding Zach with English slang. "She has a state dinner tonight. The president of Ecuador, or some such. She wishes to thank you in person afterward."

"Well," Zach answered quickly, "I wouldn't want to be impolite, would I?"

"I'd think not. The royal family has insisted you be their guest for the night at The Lanesborough. They have arranged for a suite. Quite posh. Also, the media would like a chance to ask you a few questions. So, we've set up a press conference at the hotel," McWilkinson replied, looking down at her pad.

"I'm not exactly dressed for any of this," Zach objected, looking down at his jeans, short sleeved shirt, and sneakers. "Even if I had my luggage, I didn't bring along a suit and tie."

"No worries, Zach. We gathered your sizes during your security scans. Proper attire will be waiting at the hotel as well as everything else you need," McWilkinson said with a grin. "The royal family can be exceedingly appreciative."

"Okay, I guess. Will I be doing all this great stuff alone? Can I invite my friends?" Zach asked.

"The answer to both questions is 'no.' Sorry, your friends are not invited. But I'm sure they'll be able to watch on the telly. I'll be accompanying you to the audience," McWilkinson answered.

While disappointed his friends wouldn't be with him, he couldn't believe his luck at having the incredibly beautiful MI5 officer at his side to meet *the queen*!

"Awesome! I'm a lucky guy!" Zach blurted.

"It's not a date, Zach," McWilkinson replied, a serious edge in her voice. "I'll be there to protect you. You foiled a terrorist plot today. And they are still about somewhere, and probably quite unhappy with you. You know, personally."

If one is to meet the Queen of England, staying at The Lanesborough provides a glimpse of the opulence to expect at Buckingham Palace. Guests are personally welcomed into a lobby fit for royalty and billionaires. Each room and suite has access to twenty-four hour a day butler service and is uniquely decorated and furnished.

The hotel is the very definition of five-star luxury. And, it sits just across Hyde Park from the Queen's home.

Later that afternoon, Zach stood comfortably behind a podium facing reporters standing six deep in one of the Lanesborough's impeccably appointed meeting rooms. Television cameras stood on stout tripods behind the reporters. Flashes from still cameras danced across the mirrors and gilt furniture of the meeting room. And Zach loved it all.

Zach's clothes, still rumpled from his transatlantic flight that morning, also bore a few rips, tears, and stains from the train accident. But he didn't care. If someone wanted him to shower and change before meeting the press, they should have said so. He suspected that whoever set up the press conference wanted him to appear a bit ragged from the accident.

Zach answered the press mob's fast-paced questions with considerable skill. Both the British government representatives and a high consular official from the U.S. Embassy found themselves impressed and relieved by Zach's articulate and humble responses.

After being congratulated and thanked over and over, Zach was led by McWilkinson up to his suite. The same huge uniformed officer from MI5 headquarters stood at the door, this time dressed in a black suit. As Zach approached, the guard nodded at McWilkinson but said nothing. McWilkinson nodded back and the huge man reached down and opened the door. Zach's friendly 'Hi!' elicited no response.

As the door closed, Zach commented, "He's not a chatty guy, is he?"

McWilkinson laughed. "His job is to be intimidating. He doesn't have to be eloquent for that. In fact, just the opposite is usually best."

"Yeah, well he scares the crap out of me," Zach replied absently as he gazed around the impressive three-room suite.

"Everyone, including our enemies, calls him The Bear. He's actually a big teddy with his friends and family. But you wouldn't want to mess with him in the field. What he does to people threatening our country isn't pretty," McWilkinson explained.

"Okay. Then I guess I'm glad he's here," Zach muttered, dropping onto the couch.

For the first time that day, the full weight of what had happened during the train incident and afterward crashed down on Zach all at once. His hands began to shake and his breathing quickened. He felt his heart racing out of control. He put his face in his hands and sat for a moment, trying to pull himself together.

"Are you alright, Zach?" the MI5 officer asked with genuine concern.

Zach didn't answer. He was afraid if he spoke, the pressure of the emotions welling up inside of him would burst out in an embarrassing cascade of tears.

"It's alright. Truly it is," McWilkinson said, sitting down next to the young man and placing a hand on his shoulder. "You've been through a traumatic event. Not only at the train, but being plucked up by me, and then speaking to the national media. Your body and mind are simply releasing all the fear and anxiety that you have had to control up to now. Believe me. You are safe here."

Zach took several deep breaths, calmed his breathing, and got up from the couch, still hugging himself with both arms. He paced the room until he felt some level of calm return.

"I think I'm okay now. Thanks," Zach announced after several minutes.

"Good. Nothing to be ashamed of. Happens to me from time to time. Sort of comes with the job," McWilkinson explained.

"I suppose. I wasn't exactly raised to be a cry baby," Zach said.

"Ah. Tough dad?" McWilkinson asked.

"You could say that. He's a rich asshole. Pardon the language. He probably wouldn't have approved of anything I did today."

"That seems a bit unlikely. You saved a person's life. He wouldn't have approved of *that*?" McWilkinson asked.

Zach looked up at the ceiling. "He never approved of anything I ever did. Long story, but he threw me out of the family. Won't even let me contact my mom. And except for worrying about her, I couldn't be happier."

McWilkinson could see Zach's torment and wanted to help.

"Well, the 'asshole,' as you put it, will certainly get his come-uppance when he finds out you met with the Queen of England," McWilkinson suggested.

"You'd think so. But I doubt it."

ELEVEN

Back in the dingy housing complex flat, the terrorists continued to scan the news for reports on the train attack and the condition of the Duchess of Cambridge. They learned their attack was being treated as a terrorist incident, but the use of tear gas confused the authorities. The police had no answer for why terrorists would use non-lethal tear gas in an otherwise well-planned and executed terrorist operation — if that's what it was. Experts estimated that had the perpetrators used sarin gas, the casualties would have been in the hundreds. The police and MI5 went on to speculate that the terrorists placed tear gas canisters in the ventilation intakes while the train was stopped and undergoing maintenance. But they expressed confidence that the devices used remote detonators.

The news then cut to a shot from outside King Edward VII Hospital, the fifty-six-bed hospital used by the royal family for many years, including for Queen Elizabeth II's recent knee replacement. Standing in front of the six-story brick building, two doctors faced the press and explained that the Duchess of Cambridge had suffered a concussion and a significant heart attack but that she was expected to make a full recovery. They credited a young American student, who had quickly extricated the unconscious Duchess from the train, with saving her life.

While slightly disappointed the old lady hadn't died, the three terrorists considered the operation a complete success. Now, the fact that their target had been rescued by an American student caught their attention. Television stations aired Zach's hotel press conference nearly continuously, allowing John, Simon, and Tony to watch it several times. Apparently, the student arrived in England to study at Oxford through some kind of overseas study program. He looked like every other American to them — smug and overconfident.

"Infidel," Simon snarled at the television screen.

"I must observe that he makes quite an excellent impression. To the western press, of course. He will be a very public figure for at least several days. I would not be surprised if he is invited to Buckingham Palace," Tony observed, carefully objective with his judgment.

"Hmmm," John said, stroking his chin. "Perhaps we have identified our next target? Allah willing, perhaps we might even inflict the prophet's wrath upon him."

Simon agreed. "If we are to make a move, we must do it quickly. Media coverage in the West is fleeting, and the infidels care only about what is before their eyes at any one moment. Tomorrow, they will once again be more concerned about some sinful rock and roll singer's illegitimate child or purposeless football match than their own souls," Simon stated.

"Then it must happen now," Tony said. "But should we not first get Wolf's approval?"

John's open hand slapped the side of Tony's face, knocking him to the floor.

"I, and I alone, lead us! I am confident Wolf would trust my judgment in this," the older man hissed. "Simon, you will contact the nearest action team and task them with killing the American. Instruct them that they have permission to martyr themselves only if it is necessary to take out the target."

"It shall be done."

Tony wiped a drop of blood from the corner of his mouth. Although hand-picked by Wolf himself to be part of his most valuable team inside the United Kingdom, he was still subject to John's orders. In the two years they had been in the country, John's leadership, while sometimes brutal, had certainly been successful. But he didn't like being pushed around.

"Shall I begin arranging a set of post-action denials and acceptances of responsibility in anticipation of the American's death, my sheik?" Tony asked John while rising from the floor.

"Yes. And transmit our plans to Wolf in two hours. Not before," John ordered. "By then, the matter shall be concluded. Allahu Akbar!"

And you shall reap glory for yourself alone, Tony thought ruefully.

TWELVE

While Zach reveled in all the attention from the media and his truly luxurious hotel room, his friends Michael, Sarah, and Bubba found themselves subjected to Agent Frank Deal's scrutiny. The three young people were exhausted from their overseas travel and harrowing train ride. Now, sitting in a small conference room on the first floor of the American Consulate in Oxford, their prospects of a hot meal and warm bed seemed to dim with each passing minute.

Upon their arrival in the university town an hour earlier, Deal personally whisked them away from the bus station to avoid any media that might have connected them to Zach. His original plan called for all four college students to remain indistinguishable from the thousands of others from all over the world studying at the famous university. Deal hoped that as ordinary students, the four Americans could uncover a lead to the suspected terrorist activity on campus. But Zach's heroic actions had attracted national media attention. While irritated, Deal couldn't help but be impressed with Zach's actions — but he kept that to strictly himself.

After Michael, Sarah, and Bubba described the train attack in excruciating detail, as well as absolutely everything else that happened since their arrival in England, Deal asked, "Have you been in contact with Zach?"

Michael responded. "We got a text from him. He's fine and in London."

Zach had finally convinced McWilkinson to let him send a short text message to Michael, but only after she had him safely secured in the hotel room.

"He's hanging out in that fancy hotel where he gave the press conference," Bubba added. "He surely is one silver-tongued devil."

"You've seen the interview?" Deal asked. "I thought you were stuck on a bus for the past few hours."

Bubba just held up his cell phone. "Miracles of human ingenuity," he said with a hint of sarcasm.

Deal ignored him.

"This is important. Do you think the media identified any of you as Zach's friends?" Deal asked.

"No," Sarah answered flatly. "After Zach separated from us on the train, we were hustled off a hundred yards or so from the action. The news people were focused entirely on the train — at least until Zach and the Duchess or whomever came tumbling out the door. We talked to him for a minute after they took him to the paramedics, but we left before the media got to him."

"Miss Sarah is right as rain about that. Nobody so much as turned a head in our direction," Bubba agreed.

"Okay. Good. Keep it that way for now. Don't mention that you were on that train to anyone. And none of you know Zach Self. Understood?"

Michael looked concerned. "Sure. But it's going to be hard to deny knowing Zach when we're supposed to be roommates."

"We can fix that," Deal responded. "Bubba has a flat just off campus. You move in with him. Maybe you and Zach can become friends again later. But for now, it's best that you don't know him from Adam. You happen to be from the same university in the states, but that doesn't mean you know each other."

"Fine. But Bubba's a slob," Michael complained.

"Oh, now, we'll get along just fine!" Bubba exclaimed, slapping Michael on the back. "We'll drink us a bunch of this fancy English beer I keep hearing about and eat us some bangers and mush."

"Maybe we can actually use Zach's fame to our advantage," Sarah suggested, ignoring Bubba and Michael's antics.

"How?" Michael wanted to know.

"All this attention and everything plays right into Zach's strengths. If anyone can handle himself in the public eye, it's Zach," Sarah explained, excitement in her voice. "Being famous will absolutely open doors for him and allow him to meet more people."

"Yeah, mostly girls," Bubba joked.

Deal thought about Sarah's comment a moment. "Okay. Maybe Sarah's right. In the meantime, go get some food. You missed today's check-in at the school, so bunk up at Bubba's apartment. I'll meet you here in the morning. We have a lot to discuss, so get some sleep. I'll get in touch with Sims in London and have her explain all this to Zach as soon as she sees him."

THIRTEEN

Outside the Lanesborough Hotel
London

The lovely girl's smile had the desired effect — completely capturing the young police officer's attention. Straight white teeth flashed brilliantly behind full lips, while dark, wide set eyes looked up at him with an irresistible mix of innocence and suggestive allure.

The officer had been ordered to keep one side of the hotel clear of traffic. An hour earlier, his sergeant had pulled him off his usual beat around St. James's Park to help with security at the hotel, which had become the epicenter of today's stunning news of the terrorist attack on Lady Carol. But he quickly became bored. All the action was taking place around the corner at the front of the hotel, where excited media and onlookers still jockeyed for position, hoping to catch a glimpse of the good-looking American hero. He couldn't believe his luck when the pretty girl with long dark hair flowing over the collar of a red raincoat stopped to ask directions.

As she flirted with the officer, asking questions about his uniform, touching the material of his coat, and absently flipping her hair, her two accomplices slipped behind the couple, deftly climbing to a low balcony above their heads. Without a sound, the two men expertly picked the lock on the double glass door and disappeared inside.

Her job distracting the besotted young officer finished, the girl apologized for having to leave but promised to meet him in a few hours at a local pub. As she walked casually up the street, she had to keep from giggling at how easily she could manipulate men.

Now inside, the two terrorists, slim, fit, and well-trained men in their twenties, found themselves in the sitting area of a vast empty hotel room. If necessary, they would have quietly dispatched any guests they encountered. With the space to themselves, they stripped off the black bodysuits, revealing white shirts, black bow ties, and pressed black slacks that matched the hotel service staff's uniform.

Both men pulled nine-millimeter Sig Sauer P938s from their waistbands, attached noise suppressors, and chambered a round. Though rushed into action only an hour before, they were both ready and willing to carry out their mission. Their orders had been simple — enter the hotel, and find and kill the American Zach Self. After whispering a quick prayer, they opened the door and walked down a long hall, chatting casually, their weapons concealed under white linen napkins.

Making their way to the basement via a service elevator, they arrived in the bustling heart of the Lanesborough. Waiters dodged around one another with trays held high in the air, cooks shouted out the status of orders, and sweaty dishwashers scrubbed at all kinds of cookware. After passing through the kitchen completely unnoticed, they located their objective — the laundry.

Large canvas carts overflowed with used white sheets, robes, tablecloths and other linens. The busy crew didn't even look up while the two men loaded a chrome delivery cart with freshly folded towels, slipped their guns into the pile, and rolled it out the door.

"Hey, mate!" one of the terrorists called to a passing waiter in perfect English. "What floor's the American on? He wants more bloody towels!"

"Four. I just took up a plate of sandwiches. Watch out up there, though. The hall is full of serious blokes with black suits and bad attitudes."

The terrorists gave each other a knowing smile. They both had the same deluded dream. By killing the American, they would gain glory for themselves and their families, die as martyrs, and earn honored places in paradise.

Once inside the service elevator, they withdrew their weapons from between the towels, checked their ammunition loads, and waited patiently for the doors to open.

Fifteen seconds later, the elevator doors parted, revealing an MI5 officer standing at the door, his hands folded in front of him. "Excuse me ..."

He didn't have time to utter another word. Two quick shots to the chest sent him reeling backward into the wall.

The two terrorists stepped out and swung their weapons in opposite directions down the long hall.

Two alert MI5 officers stationed at double doors to a nearby suite saw the agent fall, blood smearing the wallpaper as he collapsed to the floor. Instantly retrieving their Heckler & Koch MP5-4A submachine guns from under their jackets, they sent a hail of 9x19mm rounds down the hall.

The first killer caught several rounds in the stomach, dying before his bloody body landed with a thump on the expensive carpet. The second, shielded briefly by his partner, managed to return fire, emptying the remainder of his clip.

One of the MI5 officers took a round in the shoulder, spinning him around and knocking him out of the fight.

But any hope the remaining attacker had disappeared in the blink of an eye. A second volley from the other officer's HK blew the proud young terrorist off his feet and into whatever afterlife awaited him.

The wounded MI5 officer reached for his shoulder-mounted radio, even while keeping his gun trained down the hall.

"Code red! Code red! Fourth floor! Officer down! Two, repeat two, Tangos down."

One floor below, Eva McWilkinson took a call on her cell phone, while standing in Zach's actual hotel room.

FOURTEEN

Zach didn't understand. After being in the dreamlike opulence of his room for only an hour, he watched Agent Eva McWilkinson's entire body visibly stiffen as she listened intently to a call on her cell phone. Zach couldn't hear either side of the short conversation, but from the agent's reaction, he knew the news wasn't good.

"What's going on?" Zach asked, when McWilkinson ended the call.

"No need to dance around it, is there? We need to move you to another location right away," she answered tensely.

"Okay, I guess. But what's going on? Where are we going?" Zach wanted to know.

"Zach, I'm not trying to be difficult. But there's not much I can tell you. I will say that you made quite the splash on the telly. You apparently attracted the attention of the wrong sort of people. We're moving in fifteen seconds."

Now visibly shaken, Zach asked, "What? What does that mean? What people?"

"No time to explain right now, we have to go," McWilkinson replied, as she withdrew a frighteningly large black automatic weapon from her purse. "It's all fine. I promise."

"Yeah, sure it is," Zach replied, sweat beginning to appear on his forehead.

"Just a precaution, love," McWilkinson said, obviously forcing a smile.

The MI5 officer pulled an earpiece from her pocket and stuck it in her ear. "McWilkinson. I'm on comms."

After listening intently for a moment, she looked at Zach and motioned for him to join her at the door. "Good. Right. Off we go, then."

Leaving the suite, Zach noticed that the big officer McWilkinson called 'The Bear' had been replaced by a female agent dressed in a form-fitting black suit and dark sunglasses. While not as overtly frightening as the giant MI5 officer, this woman appeared every bit as dangerous. With a savage looking submachine gun scanning ahead of the group, the female officer led Zach and McWilkinson down the hall and into a nearby stairwell.

As they descended, McWilkinson took point, with Zac following. She moved like a cat, smooth, quiet and fast. It was all Zach could do to keep up with the rangy officer. He had been one of the best base runners on his high school baseball team, but he found himself panting heavily as they reached the ground floor.

McWilkinson paused before opening the door to the basement, looking quickly through its small smudged window. After checking both directions, she opened the door and stepped through. Zach was about to follow when the second agent pulled him back by the shoulder. Whatever bravado he had vanished during the frightening rush out of the hotel room and scramble down the stairway.

A low rap on the door signaled the agent to bring Zach out. They found McWilkinson standing with her weapon pointing down, but still intensely scanning the hallway. Bright fluorescent lights revealed a long empty service corridor with stainless steel swinging double doors lining the walls. They could hear the faint tinkling of someone washing dishes and pans somewhere in the distance.

With the other agent pointing her weapon down the long hallway, McWilkinson turned in the opposite direction, moving to another thick metal door. She motioned for Zach to follow. Speaking softly into her radio, she momentarily glanced out the door's window.

"The car's just outside. We'll be going down four stairs and ducking in. *Don't dawdle*," McWilkinson ordered. While she kept a fake smile on her face, her words were clearly a command, and not a suggestion.

Trying to at least appear calm, Zach just nodded.

McWilkinson opened the door, took Zach by the upper arm, and hustled him down the steps. The door of a black Range Rover was already open, and McWilkinson pushed Zach unceremoniously inside before jumping in after him. The big SUV shot forward, throwing Zach backward into his seat. He found himself pinned between McWilkinson and The Bear while the driver mercilessly wheeled the car around the tight streets of central London. The wild ride, claustrophobic conditions, and the fear that someone may have threatened his life crystallized into a ball of nausea in the pit of Zach's stomach.

"I'm gonna puke," he managed to announce, just before actually doing so on the floor in front of him.

"Hang tight, Zach. We're almost there," McWilkinson said, putting her arm around Zach's shoulders.

More humiliated than anything, Zach put his head in his hands and squeezed his eyes shut. He felt sick as hell. *This isn't happening!*

Just then, a big hand took Zach by the back of the collar and pulled him up straight in the seat. Another hand appeared with a clean handkerchief.

"You'll feel better if you sit up," The Bear growled, not looking down at Zach. "And you might consider refraining from vomiting on my new shoes again."

Zach gratefully took the cloth and wiped his nose and mouth.

"Will you all, *for God's sake*, tell me what the hell is going on here?" Zach demanded. He had had enough. One moment he's the toast of London and the next he's being pushed and pulled by people with guns, puking in an expensive car, and being manhandled by someone called Bear.

"Zach," McWilkinson said, causing Zach to look her in the eyes. "You deserve answers and you'll get them. Everything is fine now, but we had to get you out of the hotel for your own safety."

"What you're saying is that someone wants to, like, cause me harm?" Zach asked unsteadily, already suspecting he knew the answer.

"No, mate. Someone, like, wants you *dead*," The Bear corrected.

FIFTEEN

Special Agent Stella Sims stood fuming outside the Lanesborough. Four unmoving London police officers dressed in black assault gear had denied her any access to the hotel, even after showing her FBI credentials. A police lieutenant curtly informed her that the hotel was under lockdown and that they had strict orders not to allow anyone inside without permission from MI5 – and that included the FBI. To make matters worse, London's famous misting rain had nearly soaked through her suit jacket. She had no overcoat or umbrella, a mistake no Londoner would have made.

Before attempting to see Zach in person, Sims had tried to call him several times on his cell phone with no response. Either he had turned the phone off, or he no longer had it with him. Calls to the hotel asking for Zachary Self's room were met with a denial of any guest with that name.

Something wasn't right.

Undeterred, Sims ignored the rain and strolled around to the back of the building, where she found a covered, dimly lit alley that looked like a short tunnel connecting the two busy streets on either side of the hotel. Taking a quick look inside, she saw several metal dumpsters and a rear door. She also saw two police officers with automatic rifles.

As she watched from the shadows, the two officers suddenly stepped away from the door. They moved out into the middle of the alley, taking up positions that gave them a wide-angle view in both directions, as if looking for something, or someone, in particular. Sims froze, knowing that it was unlikely she could be seen, but not wanting to attract their attention.

Suddenly, Sims gasped as a sheet of water soaked her from head to foot. Concentrating on the guards and the back door, she hadn't noticed the black Range Rover SUV hurtling into the parking area with its lights off. As it turned into the tunnel, the vehicle struck an unfortunately-placed puddle of dirty rainwater, throwing it up and over Sims.

"Really?" Sims exclaimed as she turned to see what would happen next.

The big SUV slid to a stop between the police officers and its left rear door popped open.

A second later, a young man stepped out of the hotel's back door with a strikingly tall black woman. While he was in view for only a moment, there was no mistake. Zach!

Before Sims could react, the woman took Zach by the arm, seemingly forced him into the car, and ducked in after him. The SUV sped away, disappearing in the opposite direction and out into the night.

Sims didn't understand what she had just seen. *Why were the authorities moving Zach? And to where? Why would they keep him from communicating with his friends or even answering his phone? It didn't make any sense.*

Sims briefly considered confronting the two policemen, but she correctly decided it wouldn't be worth the trouble given the reaction she had received earlier. Plus, at the moment, she looked more like a drowned rat than an accomplished FBI agent.

Putting herself together as best she could, Sims walked back to the main road. She got lucky, catching one of London's black cabs just as its last passenger stepped out.

The cabby, noticing his fare's condition, handed her a clean towel from the front seat.

"Hell of a night to be out and about without a brolly, Miss," the cabby said, after Sims gave him the address of her London hotel.

Sims hesitated and then got it. "An umbrella, yeah, should have brought one along, I suppose."

"Too right," the cabby agreed. "Never can tell what might happen with the weather in London!"

"Too right," Sims repeated, gratefully wiping her face and arms.

As soon as she arrived back at her room, Sims reported her unsettling attempts to make personal contact with Zach to Agent Deal.

"I don't get it, Boss. We're supposed to be working with the British on this one, right?" Sims asked, irritated, and still wearing wet clothes.

"I've called Sir Nigel at MI5. He says the officer in charge, an Eva McWilkinson, called in a change of location less than an hour ago. She didn't communicate the secondary location citing security protocols," Deal responded, all business.

"Have the techs been looking for the location of his phone?" Sims asked, already knowing the answer.

"Of course. Its last location was inside the hotel."

"Do the rest of Zach's team know he's gone missing?" Sims asked, meaning Michael, Sarah and Bubba.

"No. I sent them to Bubba's flat for the night. I'm sure we'll hear something from the Brits soon. Let's keep this to ourselves for a few hours. If it doesn't resolve by then, we'll take matters into our own hands."

Sims hated waiting.

"Okay, Boss. But something smells fishy to me."

"I'll keep you informed. Get some sleep. You may need it."

But Deal should have known that Stella Sims wouldn't rest until she found some answers.

After ending her call, Sims changed clothes, donned her overcoat, and remembering to grab her umbrella, headed back out into the London night.

Sims grabbed a taxi back to the Lanesborough and took a few minutes to consider her next move. Without any contact from Zach or MI5, she had nothing to go on. Only her instinct as an FBI investigator led her back to the Lanesborough's parking lot. But her intuition had served her well in the past, so she pulled the collar of her overcoat up to shield her neck against the damp English weather and followed her gut.

Confirming that the police were gone, Sims walked casually into the covered alley, stopping at the back door where she had witnessed Zach emerge with the female agent. Using a small but powerful flashlight she always carried, Sims closely inspected the area end to end, including the locked back door and short staircase. The exhaustive search took almost an hour, producing absolutely nothing.

Sims sat down on one of the hotel steps to consider her options. Almost immediately, the back door flew open, banging against its stops and causing Sims to jump off the step and spin around. Just as she did, a wide backside, covered by black and white checkered pants, emerged through the doorway accompanied by grunts, assorted expletives, and the unmistakable scrape of something heavy being dragged outside.

It turned out to be one of the hotel's female restaurant staff tugging at what had to be a very heavy plastic garbage bin.

Relieved after her initial start, Sims decided it would be best to announce her presence.

"That looks heavy," Sims said to the other person's back.

Without turning around, the woman grunted, "Too bloody right!"

With a final heave, the big garbage can bumped over the door's threshold and onto the small landing outside. Only then did the woman turn to see who was behind her.

"What have we here? Just why is a skinny blonde American girl sniffing about my alley this time of night?" the plump older woman asked, pushing several strands of long greying hair behind one ear.

"Sorry if I startled you," Sims replied, trying to sound non-threatening. "I'm looking for a friend of mine who was at this hotel, but left abruptly."

"Well, you're not likely to find him out here," the woman snorted.

Sims took on a worried expression. "Yes, I know. But the last I saw, he was being hustled out this door and into a big black Range Rover. I haven't heard from him since."

"Might this be the young lad on the telly? The one what saved Lady Carol earlier today?" the large woman asked, obviously suspicious of Sims' story.

"Well, yes," Sims admitted. "They wouldn't let me in the hotel earlier. And when I walked around outside waiting, I think I saw him run out that door and, I don't know, kind of forced into the car. I've been waiting around all night, but I haven't seen him again. You didn't happen to see him leave or anything, did you?"

The older woman's stiff posture and accusatory tone relaxed as she listened to Sims' increasingly sympathetic story.

"No, dear. I've been in the kitchen. But Lance, one of the dishwashers, was down here all night. Let's ask him."

"Oh, that would be wonderful! Thank you so much!" Sims gushed, keeping up her needy act.

"Call me Bett. Step in out of the cold and I'll find him. He's a bit of a skiver, but he's not bad all in all."

"Thanks, Bett," Sims answered. "But, what's a skiver?"

"A lazy sod, that's what. That's why I was dragging out the rubbish bin by myself!" Bett said, chuckling at Sims' question.

Sims followed Bett down the same hallway Zach had taken just an hour or so earlier. They found Lance asleep in a corner, sitting on a large tub of detergent, his legs stretched out under the stainless steel dishwashing station.

Bett kicked the tub, causing the skinny older man to rouse enough to open one eye.

"Oh, blast! What you gone and knocked me about for?" Lance cried.

"Get your arse off that bucket! This lady here needs to ask you something important," Bett shouted, waking Lance enough to find his bearings.

Seeing Sims for the first time, Lance jumped to his feet and pulled off the dirty hat that had been covering his eyes during his nap, revealing a shock of mussed gray hair.

"Well, now. Why didn't you say a lovely little bird needed my attention?" he asked, smiling. "What is it I may do for you, my lovely?"

Sims didn't actually believe the elderly dishwasher could help, but she was quickly running out of options. She repeated her story about looking for Zach and asked whether Lance had seen him leaving earlier in the evening.

"Indeed, I did. Indeed, I did!" Lance replied excitedly. "I heard a bit of commotion an hour or two back. Nobody ever comes down here, so I stole a peak around the corner there. I seen the young hero come out of that stairway door with two ladies. And, you'll not believe this, but both them ladies had guns drawn like you see in the movies. Now, uh, not being one to stick my nose where it don't belong, I ducked back in, right quick like."

"What did the two women look like?" Sims asked.

"One was tall and black. Near as tall as Bett here. The other was shorter and had on sunglasses," Lance replied, obviously thrilled with being able to tell someone about the odd encounter. "And both were just as beautiful as magazine models, they were!"

Lance's comment about the women caused Bett to snort loudly.

"I don't suppose you saw the car they got in?" Sims asked hopefully.

"No. Sorry. But you might ask me mate Phillip. He works at the newsstand just down the block. He sees everyone that comes in and out of here. Those blokes at the stands see and know more than you might rightly expect. Right observant they are!"

Without ever identifying herself as an FBI agent, Sims left the hotel after thanking both Bett and Lance for their assistance

Sims quickly found the nearest newsstand. Sure enough, a balding man wearing a tweed jacket and smoking a cigarette sat nonchalantly waiting out the last hour before closing time. She knew following up on this particular lead had almost no chance of success but her dogged nature insisted that she pursue any clue, however insignificant.

"Good evening!" Sims said, walking right up to the counter.

Phillip stood. "How may I help a fair young lady with this evening?"

Sims smiled. "Are you Phillip? Lance over at the hotel said you might be able to help me."

"I am he," Phillip replied. "I don't suppose you are looking for reading material then?"

"Actually, I'm looking for a friend that left the hotel about an hour and a half ago. He's the young man that saved the Duchess on the train today. I don't know why, but he was suddenly moved out of the hotel and driven away..."

"Aye. In a black Range Rover. It came out from the hotel alley, turned right and flew right by here. A government vehicle no doubt. No tag. Blacked out windows. We don't see them often, but we take notice when they are about. There're only a few special vehicles like that. We call that one Jimmy because it has a small 'j' stenciled just under the bonnet."

"We?" Sims asked, impressed.

"Us newsagents. Being on the streets all day and night, we see quite a bit. Nobody ever thinks about us knowing things. But you've come to the right place, you have," Phillip explained. "But, you're not just a friend looking for your mate, are you? FBI?"

Astonished, Sims answered, "Yes, as a matter of fact. How did you know?"

"I saw you round and about the hotel this evening when the press and everyone was here. You flashed a badge trying to get inside, but were turned away. Plus, you're obviously from the states. I'm no Sherlock Holmes, but I can put two and two together," Phillip explained with a warm smile.

"Might other, uh, newsagents have seen this particular car tonight?" Sims asked, her excitement growing.

"No doubt about it. Let me make some calls. I watched your young Zach on the news, and he seems like a good boy. I don't see the harm in helping you find him. But best leave it between us, if you understand."

"You have my word," Sims agreed.

"You're what?" Deal snapped "I ordered you to stay at the hotel."

"Yes, sir. But something kept bothering me about how they moved Zach. Maybe it's nothing, but I didn't think it would do any harm to make some casual inquiries around the hotel," Sims explained, a bit breathless. "So, I take it we haven't heard anything from MI5?"

Twenty minutes earlier, Phillip, the newsstand operator, had placed several calls, asking about sightings of government Range Rovers. She barely understood Phillip's thick London accent as he chatted with other newsagents. On his third call, Phillip looked up and gave Sims a knowing wink. One of his friends had, indeed, seen the vehicle nicknamed Jimmy flash by his place a few hours before, heading onto King Street in the nearby neighborhood of Hammersmith.

Sims knew she was getting close.

After a hurried but short ride in yet another black cab, she found the corner Phillip had identified. The other newsagent, who had agreed to stay a few minutes after closing time, told her he had lost sight of the Range Rover after it made the turn down King Street.

Sims decided to proceed on foot. If she could find the Range Rover, she could find Zach.

"No, we haven't heard anything yet. But that doesn't mean you did the right thing tonight either," Deal answered, his voice losing some of its irritation. "We don't have jurisdiction over here, except to the extent our guests allow."

"I understand. I'm not out flashing my badge. Just asking around," Sims explained. "Boss, if this is all normal procedure, why are they keeping us in the dark? It doesn't make sense. In fact, I'm standing outside a cheap tourist hotel on King Street in Hammersmith right now. It's only a couple of miles from the Lanesborough where they had him before. I believe Zach is here."

"How the hell do you know that?" Deal demanded.

"I found the SUV they used to move Zach. Boss, I'll explain the whole thing, but I'm certain it's the same vehicle. If it's here, we have to assume Zach is too," Sims said calmly.

In fact, Sims had just walked away from a parking garage tucked behind the Sickle and Harrow pub. A big hotel chain corporation had apparently taken over the building, installed a slick new budget hotel, but left the old pub in front. The hotel's parking deck could only be accessed by a narrow cobblestone alleyway from King Street.

Knowing there would be security cameras inside, Sims had entered the parking deck, craning her neck around, mimicking a befuddled tourist looking for her car. She found the black SUV one level down, parked in a corner. Making one quick pass by the vehicle, Sims could see the "j" stenciled on one fender. Having found her target, Sims walked out of the deck, making a show of feigned frustration. She waited to call Deal until she was half a block away from the Sickle and Harrow.

"What's the move, Boss? Contact MI5 again?" Sims asked.

"Hell no. I've been sitting on my ass here long enough waiting on those clowns. Blue Team will be at your location in approximately seventy minutes. I'll have the Techs load them up with surveillance gear. Can you watch the entrance to the hotel from your position?"

Sims liked what she was hearing. "Yes, sir. I have a tracker on me. Should I plant it on the car in case they leave?"

"No. They're too good. They'd find it. Just stay put and report if the situation changes," Deal ordered.

"Will you tell Michael, Sarah and Bubba?"

"Not yet. They have work to do on campus tomorrow. Our mission here is to flush out terrorists. I want them to stay focused on that."

SIXTEEN

Oxford
The next morning.

"Bubba! Put some damn pants on!" Michael shouted from the pull-out couch.

"I got on my skivvies!" Bubba replied as he walked slowly through the small living area of their off-campus apartment, wearing only a pair of red and white checkered boxer shorts. "And they're my good ones, too!"

Sarah poked her head out from under the covers next to Michael. "Nice shorts!"

"I know! My mamma got 'em for me before we left," Bubba said, pausing a moment.

At over six feet tall and pushing three hundred pounds, Bubba's physique came from a steady diet of beer and carbs. His substantial belly fell over the front of his shorts even as he flexed both arms into a "muscle-man" pose.

Michael groaned. "That's *not* the first thing I want to see in the morning. Especially while sporting a blistering case of jet lag."

Sarah just smiled. "Well, *I* think you're cute. Now go take a shower and get dressed. We have to be at registration on campus in an hour."

"Yes, ma'am," Bubba replied, sheepishly rubbing one hand through the thick hair sticking up all over his head. "But we gotta get breakfast, too. I ain't going to no English college on an empty stomach."

Bubba disappeared into the bathroom.

"Unbelievable!" Michael said, falling backward into his pillow.

After eating what Bubba called 'more of that weird English food' at a local café, the three registered for classes. Afterward, they decided to explore the famous university.

A fact unknown to most, Oxford University has no founding date. Education at the site is said to have taken place in the city as early as 1096. And, unlike most universities, Oxford has no formal campus, only buildings scattered throughout the city. The university is organized into thirty-eight separate colleges and offers a full range of academic studies. Widely considered one of the great learning centers of the world, the university has produced the likes of Stephen Hawking, Edwin Hubble, T.S. Elliot, and J.R.R. Tolkien, to name just a few.

None of this was lost on the three friends strolling along the streets, taking in the cool morning atmosphere and marveling at the beautiful facades of the town's famous architecture.

When they reached the Science Area, Bubba launched into a near continuous lecture about the significant discoveries made in building after building. They finally paused for a brief rest on a bench in the beautiful Botanic Garden.

"Wow. I can't believe we're actually here!" Sarah commented.

"Yeah, I can't wait to get inside the new Engineering Research Laboratory. I bet they got some fun stuff in there!" Bubba exclaimed with almost childish delight.

"Yeah, it's all awesome," Michael agreed. "But I wish Zach was here instead of holed up in some fancy hotel."

They all missed Zach. Without his unique personality, the group just didn't seem complete. They had no idea about the intrigue surrounding his disappearance the night before.

"Michael, let's call Agent Deal to see when he's coming back," Sarah suggested.

Michael pulled his phone from his pocket and called Deal's private number.

After a few rings, the gruff FBI agent picked up. He immediately wanted to make sure all three had successfully registered and were ready to enter university society. When Michael asked about Zach, Deal became evasive. He didn't know exactly when Zach would get back from London. As the call ended, Deal said he wanted to meet them in an hour back at the consulate.

Not satisfied, Michael called Zach's cell phone. Receiving no answer, he looked at his friends.

"Deal isn't sure when he's coming back. I tried Zach directly, but still got no answer," Michael explained, sounding both disappointed and worried. "It's not like Zach to be out of touch."

"I'm sure he's fine," Sarah said, putting one hand on Michael's shoulder.

"Hey, buddy! Come on! Our skinny little friend will show up soon enough. In the meantime, this place is full of weird and fantastic stuff. We should enjoy it," Bubba added.

"Yeah, you're right, I guess," Michael replied, trying to sound a little brighter. "Let's go see if we can find…"

Before he could finish his sentence, something suddenly crashed through the tree above their heads. All three jumped to their feet and covered their heads as leaves and small branches rained down.

Scurrying away, they looked back in time to see a massive white drone smash into a low branch, stop for a moment, and then tumble to the ground.

Bubba was the first to approach the fallen craft. As an aerospace expert, he knew quite a bit about drone technology. But at almost six feet wide, the flying robot was far larger than the drones Bubba had studied.

Just five years ago, drones were nothing but an oddity. Most were toys, controlled by small hand-held radio transmitters that drew curious onlookers as they flitted about in public parks. Yet, drone technology had advanced quickly. High-definition cameras provided a perspective that could only be gained in the past by using a helicopter. The military, law enforcement, and first responders of all types quickly adopted drones to provide a safe means to gain intelligence on enemy positions, locate criminals and find victims.

The business world found innumerable uses for the technology. Package carriers were already experimenting with pre-programmed drones to make deliveries. In the transportation world, savvy entrepreneurs studied the possibility of developing a safe, stable platform to fulfill the promise of a flying car.

Curious, Bubba examined the craft from a few feet away. Eight legs sprouted from a circular central fuselage. Electric motors, mounted vertically at the end of each slim leg, powered twenty-four-inch propellers. Even in its damaged condition, it eerily resembled a gigantic white spider. It now rested on one side, two broken legs propped awkwardly up against the old tree's massive trunk.

Bubba motioned Michael and Sarah over and they all three stood staring at the strange object that had just fallen out of the sky. Michael stepped around to the side and bent down to peer underneath the central fuselage. Just as he did, one of the propellers sprang to life six inches from his face.

"Hey!" Michael exclaimed as he fell backward, crab-crawling away from the machine.

Bubba and Sarah burst out laughing at Michael's less than graceful escape.

"That wasn't funny!" Michael said, lying flat on the ground and breathing hard from the drone's surprise revival from the dead.

"Oh, man! Yeah! Yeah, it was buddy!" Bubba managed between breaths. "I've never seen nothing as funny as you. I bet you almost wet your pants!"

Sarah managed to stifle her laughter long enough to ask if her boyfriend was alright.

"That thing could have taken my head off!" Michael replied, starting to find humor in the incident.

"No, it couldn't," a voice said from behind the group.

Michael, Sarah, and Bubba turned around to see a man with Middle Eastern features in his mid-20s approaching quickly, an open laptop cradled in one arm.

"I am quite sorry for the start though," the young man apologized in an impeccable English accent. "I tried to reboot the onboard computer, and it seems at least one of the engine pods responded. Unexpectedly, of course."

The man walked directly over to Michael, and with his free hand, helped him to his feet.

"I am Ali Badran. I apologize once again for my intrusion on your afternoon."

"No harm, no foul," Michael replied. "I'm Michael King and these are my friends Sarah Marshall and Bubba Adcock."

"It is my pleasure to meet you all," Ali said, smiling warmly.

At five feet nine inches, Ali looked short compared to Michael and Bubba, who both stood over six feet. But his engaging smile, sparkling eyes, glossy black hair, and friendly manner made him instantly likable. And Sarah couldn't help but be impressed with Ali's exotic good looks. *Wow. This guy could be a movie star!*

"So, this is yours? It's impressive," Bubba said, shaking Ali's hand.

"Well, thank you. While I am the developer of this prototype, it actually belongs to the engineering college," Ali explained. "Although, it doesn't seem to be quite so impressive in its current state."

"Looks like an IMU failure," Bubba observed.

Ali looked up at Bubba, impressed.

"Yes, quite. An engineer, are you?" Ali asked.

"Aerospace. Here to do some work with the university," Bubba replied.

"I was testing a new gyroscope and magnetometer in the inertial measurement unit, or IMU, as you said. The results are as you see here, unfortunately," Ali explained, sounding disappointed.

"This is obviously an advanced prototype. I haven't seen an eight-rotor unit. At least not one this size. Were you using first person view control?" Bubba asked, now intensely interested in all aspects of the technologically advanced prototype.

"Yes, and I must say that flying into that tree was a bit terrifying in FPV. I have the video here if you want to watch," Ali offered with a grin.

Bubba, Sarah, and Michael gathered around Ali's laptop. The video showed a view from the middle of the aircraft looking forward. Two propellers could be seen at the edge of the screen, framing a breathtaking view of the town below.

The high-definition camera on board provided clear and stunning details of buildings, cars, and individuals. After circumnavigating the entire city, the screen showed the drone clearly descending under control. Data of all kinds streamed along the sides of the video clip on the computer screen showing speed, altitude, course and in-flight diagnostic data.

Then, one of the readouts turned red and began to blink. At the same time, the camera's view changed, suddenly pointing directly at the ground. As they watched, the top of a large tree grew quickly on the screen. For a split second, the three friends glimpsed themselves relaxing on the park bench. The next moment, the screen filled with leaves and branches and the view jumped violently around. The last second of the video showed a view from the ground looking back up at the tree before dissolving into static.

"That's cool!" Michael exclaimed when the show ended. "Uh, I mean, the part other than the crash."

"No worries," Ali replied, understanding Michael's comment for what it was. "I was gutted at first. But these things do happen. And yeah, that is quite cool."

"I'm glad I wasn't, you know, actually flying in that when it crashed!" Sarah remarked. "The viewpoint made it seem like I was."

"Sarah," Ali replied, "that's the beauty of drone technology. It can do amazing things. And if it crashes into something, nobody has to be on board when it happens."

"What's the plan now Ali? Back to the lab?" Bubba asked, not trying to hide his excitement. "How about letting me help lug your baby home?"

Ali paused for a moment looking quizzically at Bubba. "Ah, yes. I must apologize. Sometimes it takes me a moment to process American idioms. But, yes, your help would be welcome. Sarah, Michael, would you care to join us?"

"Thanks, but no," Michael answered. "Sarah and I have to meet a friend on the other side of town. Bubba's the man you want. Just watch him around your lab, he can get overly excited around stuff like yours."

"Indeed?" responded Ali. "I'm quite sure we'll get along famously then. But I am disappointed. Perhaps we can meet later so I can buy you a pint? It's the least I can do after giving you a fright."

"Sarah and I will have to take a rain check for today. But we'd love to meet up sometime soon. By the way, a 'pint' means a beer, Bubba," Michael kidded as he and Sarah turned and walked away.

"I knew that!" Bubba called to Michael's back.

SEVENTEEN

Bubba couldn't help himself. As soon as Ali took him inside the aerospace engineering lab, he began exploring every corner of the world-class facility. Back home, Bubba's university offered complete and up-to-date laboratories and equipment, but they couldn't compete with the offerings inside Oxford's newest science building.

Proud to show off the lab, Ali took time to demonstrate several computer-assisted design stations where engineers could reconfigure 3-D renderings of various aircraft with different wing designs, engine mounting points, and much more. The supercomputer installed in the basement allowed engineers to run their new designs through various aerodynamic tests without requiring a physical model or wind tunnel. While Bubba had worked with similar but less advanced programs in the United States, he couldn't wait to try out a few design ideas of his own on the more sophisticated software.

"Impressive," Bubba announced after sitting at a terminal for a few minutes, deftly using the system to view several cutting-edge ideas for an airliner fuselage.

"I see you have used this system before?" Ali asked, confused by Bubba's aptitude with a program that only existed at Oxford.

"No. Nothing this advanced. I've used CATIA several times at home. Dassault asked us to work on some ideas for their new corporate jet design about a year ago. This is similar but provides, I'd say, three times the data points per square meter of skin surface. That sound about right?" Bubba asked.

"Indeed. Bubba, I believe you haven't been forthright about your knowledge and experience. Very few of our best engineers could move from CATIA to this system without training," Ali responded, with true admiration in his voice.

"Aw, heck. I guess I just got lucky for once," Bubba said, dropping back into his country boy persona.

Ali just shook his head and chuckled. "Since you aren't properly bowled over with this, let me show you something you have not seen before."

Bubba jumped at the invitation, always keen to immerse himself in new technology. Ali led him down a long hallway and stopped at a locked door bearing a red and white sign which stated: NO ADMITTANCE WITHOUT PROPER AUTHORITY.

"You sure it's okay if I go in there? It looks like it's supposed to be top secret or something," Bubba asked warily as Ali swiped a magnetic card and entered a five-digit code into a keypad.

"I must say, Bubba, I applaud your sense of propriety. But I assure you, I have full authority to let anybody I like see this," Ali replied, opening the door.

"How's that? I thought you were just a graduate student," Bubba asked.

Ali grinned. "Yes, I am. But, you see, my grandfather donated this to the college."

"Rich guy, huh?" Bubba said without judgment and looking into the completely dark room.

"Well, I'd have to say yes. Although he's not quite as wealthy as some of the other members of the royal family," Ali responded, without a hint of sarcasm.

"Yeah, I hear you. My daddy ain't as rich as my uncle either. Wait! Did you say *royal* family?" Bubba exclaimed, turning back to his host.

"Oh dear, I didn't mean for that to sound arrogant," Ali said, sheepishly. "I forget Americans don't really do royalty and all that nonsense."

Ali explained how his family came from the United Arab Emirates, or UAE, one of the oil-rich countries that surround the Persian Gulf. His grandfather was a member of the royal family.

"No kidding? So does that make you a prince or something like that?" Bubba asked.

"Yes, well, something like that," Ali replied.

"Okay then, Your Highness or whatever, what have you brought me here to see?" Bubba asked, obviously needling Ali over his title.

Ali instantly decided he very much liked the big American. Sometimes fawned over by the more formal British students and professors, it was refreshing to be treated like a regular guy.

"Right, we'll get right to it then," Ali said, turning on the lights.

Bubba found himself standing in an empty room, one very dim overhead light providing just enough illumination to see inside. A perfect windowless square, the room's only distinguishing feature was a gray carpet-like material covering the walls, floor, and ceiling. Devoid of furniture of any kind, Bubba's eyes were drawn to eight tiny boxes, also covered in the gray material, mounted in the eight corners of the room where the walls met the floor and ceiling.

"Okay, either you and your granddaddy got scammed, or this room is much more than what it appears to be," Bubba said, confused.

Ali pulled a small remote control from his pocket and held it up for Bubba to see.

"Step further inside, my friend," Ali prompted, ushering Bubba into the middle of the space.

Intrigued, Bubba waited while Ali shut the door.

"Behold the newest innovation in design!" Ali announced, as he pushed one of the three buttons on the remote control.

Bubba watched a faint glow appear in the eight small boxes. Then, a second later, he found himself standing inside the cockpit of a modern jet airliner.

"Holy crap on a cracker!" Bubba cried.

Intellectually, Bubba knew he was not actually standing inside an airplane's cockpit. He had used virtual reality headsets with three-dimension generating computer programs many times while working on various engineering projects. But the goggles and headsets needed for a VR experience couldn't produce the feeling of physical presence that left the aeronautical genius stunned and disoriented.

After taking a few moments to let his brain adjust to his new surroundings, Bubba began examining the space in which he stood. Familiar with many current cockpit layouts, Bubba immediately recognized the interior of an Airbus A321XLR. The newest plane offered by the European manufacturer had updated pilots' positions, seating, and instruments. As compared to other airliners, pilots of the A321XLR enjoyed a much-simplified arrangement of controls and switches. Instead of a steering wheel style yoke, pilots controlled the plane with a simple joystick. The dizzying rows of knobs, switches and lights that covered most cockpit interior surfaces on more conventional aircraft had been replaced by two large monitors placed in front of each pilot. A laptop-like computer could be lifted from between the seats and unfolded to face either control position.

With his engineer's mind noting every detail of the advanced controls, Bubba suddenly realized he had nearly forgotten where he was, and more importantly, where he was not. Turning, he found Ali standing near the door to the passenger cabin.

"Ali, this is truly amazing! I had no idea holographic virtual reality had come this far!" Bubba exclaimed.

Ali walked up and stood beside Bubba. "Oh, my friend, this is much more than a simple holographic display. Let me show you."

With Bubba watching over his shoulder, Ali leaned over the pilot's seat, touched the virtual control stick and pushed it forward. Immediately, the view through the front windscreen changed. Fluffy clouds moving past the window smoothly transformed into a view of the ground rapidly growing larger before their eyes. A moment later, warning lights began to flash on the instrument panel and a voice began to urge: "Pull up. Pull up."

As Ali smiled back at Bubba, and with the earth coming ever closer through the window, alarms began to sound and another more urgent voice prompted: "Pull up! Terrain! Pull up! Terrain!" Meanwhile, the howl of near-supersonic air rose in the space to a deafening pitch.

Through the windscreen, a city appeared through the clouds. As Bubba watched, a cluster of skyscrapers appeared to grow closer and closer. Glancing at the instruments, Bubba saw the numbers on the altimeter spinning down. The effect was all too real. If Bubba's equilibrium had not been telling him he was safely and firmly planted on the ground, his eyes and ears would have fooled him into believing he was about to die in a fiery crash. He had to force himself not to shout for Ali to pull the plane out of the dive.

At the last moment, Ali pulled back on the stick, causing the virtual aircraft to veer away from the imaginary city.

In the next second, the cockpit disappeared entirely, replaced by the gray interior of the room they had first entered.

"Well?" Ali asked, expectantly. "Is that not incredible?"

Bubba swallowed hard, his senses trying to catch up with reality.

"Yeah, dude. Yeah. That's incredible all right. But you owe me a beer after nearly scaring the crap out of me," Bubba replied. "Plus, you have to explain how this thing works. It's at least two generations more advanced than any holographic imager I ever read about."

"I think a pint and an explanation are certainly in order," Ali said, smiling.

Fifteen minutes later, Bubba and Ali sat ensconced in a dark booth at a local pub. Ali pulled out a laptop and turned it so Bubba could see the screen. After a few keystrokes, Bubba watched a representation of the Airbus aircraft they had been "flying" back at Ali's lab. Ali played back the near crash for Bubba.

At first, the plane flew straight and level through a partly cloudy sky. Suddenly, its nose tilted down and a few seconds later, Bubba watched the plane nose dive toward the center of a generic-looking city.

"The graphics are amazing," Bubba observed. "But I don't recognize the city."

"That's because it doesn't exist," Ali answered. "As you might have guessed, the main purpose of our holographic imaging device is for design and testing of prototypes before undertaking the expense of actual construction. A byproduct, if you will, of all that computing power is the ability to model any building on earth. What you saw was a computer-generated cityscape made up of hundreds of buildings that actually exist — but are located in many different countries. We certainly could have recreated any city on earth, but we undertook to construct our own cityscape to test the system's abilities."

"Just incredible," Bubba stated, with true professional admiration.

"I am a guest in this country. Oxford has been good to me and my family. What we hope to achieve is the safest, most reliable, and most efficient airliner ever created. And with these new holographic tools and enough computing power, we can design that aircraft and test it in every situation imaginable before anyone assembles a single part," Ali explained.

"Well, count me impressed. I'd love a chance to work with y'all on this project while I'm here. You think there's a chance that could happen?" Bubba asked.

"I certainly do!" Ali responded enthusiastically. "A new set of eyes and another brain may be just the thing to get us to the next level."

"So, who do you need to talk to about me coming on board?" Bubba asked, assuming some dean or professor oversaw the project.

"Nobody. Nobody at all," Ali replied. "Right or wrong, money buys privilege. And it's my privilege to invite you onto our team."

EIGHTEEN

"We don't have anyone to meet," Sarah said, after she and Michael left Ali and Bubba.

"Yeah, we do. Deal said he wanted to see us when I called him about Zach. I didn't have a chance to tell you guys before the drone nearly killed us."

"What about Bubba?" Sarah asked.

"I don't know. But we came here to meet people and keep our ears open for anything suspicious. We can't do that sitting in Deal's conference room," Michael rationalized, having no real idea how Deal would react when they showed up without Bubba.

When they arrived at the consulate a few minutes later, they found Deal sitting with one of his techs in front of an open laptop. He waved them into the conference room without looking up.

Saying nothing, Michael and Sarah walked around the table and stood behind the FBI agent.

On the screen, they could see what looked like the tops of several buildings and a busy-looking street scene. They didn't know yet that they were looking at the roof of the hotel Sims had located earlier.

A moment later, a white van entered the screen and parked a half-block down the street from the hotel. As they watched, the back doors opened and four people emerged. Blue triangles bearing numbers one to four designated the location of each person. A fifth triangle remained superimposed over the driver's side of the van.

From prior experience, Michael and Sarah knew this was Deal's Blue Team.

Michael desperately wanted to ask what was going on, but knew better. Obviously preoccupied, Deal gave short but detailed orders to Blue Team. In response, the operators dispersed, casually taking up tactical positions around the hotel.

"What is White Two's location?" Deal asked the tech.

During field operations, Deal was always referred to as White One and Sims as White Two.

"Unknown at this time," the tech responded without emotion. "She left her locator and ear piece under a planter two blocks from the hotel."

"Too much chance of her signal being picked up by those inside?" Deal asked, already knowing the answer.

"Yes, sir. Smart move, too. There's enough electromagnetic energy emanating from the north side of that building to fry a chicken."

"Blue Team, hold at your observation points," Deal ordered over his comm unit. "Anyone have eyes on White Two?"

"White One, Blue Two. I have White Two. She is sitting in the hotel lobby reading a magazine."

"Blue Two, keep your eyes on her. Let me know if she changes position," Deal responded.

With his people in place, Deal finally turned to Michael and Sarah.

"Grab a chair you two."

"Something happening?" Michael asked.

Without preamble, Deal described how they had lost contact with Zach after he arrived at the Lanesborough Hotel the night before and how Sims had been able to track him down, despite being stonewalled by his MI5 contact.

"That's what this operation is about?" Sarah asked, worried. "You're going in there to get Zach?"

"No," Deal replied simply. "Blue Team will observe and report only. We don't have enough information yet, and we certainly don't know enough to risk a confrontation with the intelligence service of our closest ally. This might be nothing more than a communication breakdown."

"Maybe they're keeping him hidden for some reason. Like a threat on his life or something," Michael offered.

"Possibly," Deal replied, unwilling to fill in Michael and Sarah on the conversations he had with Sir Gregory.

"Well, there's no reason for MI5 to keep *you* in the dark!" Sarah observed.

"No, there's not. Something is going on and I'm not waiting for MI5 or anyone else to feed me more bullshit. We're going to figure this thing out on our own," Deal stated. "And where the hell is Bubba? He's supposed to be here."

"It's kind of a long story, but Bubba's helping a nice guy named Ali fix a drone that almost killed us this afternoon," Sarah explained.

"What!?"

"Yeah, we were just exploring when all of a sudden..." Michael began, before Deal shut him down.

"Okay. Okay. You can explain later. I have an operation to run," Deal barked. "Just get his butt back here as soon as possible."

Taking Deal's lack of interest as their cue to leave, Sarah and Michael stepped out of the room.

"I guess we better give the big guy a call," Michael said, his eyes reflecting what they both thought.

"Yeah. He seems pretty pissed off at the Brits. I just hope Zach is okay," Sarah responded.

"It sounds like Agent Sims has her eye on things. I'm sure he'll be fine," Michael said.

NINETEEN

London

Sims sat with her legs crossed, casually scanning one of London's famous tabloid newspapers. If she had been paying attention to the paper at all, she could have read a tawdry story about a female newscaster having an affair with her co-anchor's wife. But Sims' focus was elsewhere.

Across the lobby, she watched a man wearing a dark suit, seated on a bench near the elevators. From time to time he rose and walked up and down a short hallway looking at his watch. Most people would assume he was a bored husband waiting for his wife to come downstairs for breakfast. But Sims knew better. The slight bulge under the left side of his jacket told her he was armed — and with more than a handgun.

She needed to communicate with Deal, but to avoid detection of her electronic signals, she had left her cell phone and radio outside, well away from the hotel. She would have to improvise.

Sims put down the paper and made a show of looking through her purse, making sure the guard down the hall saw her search anxiously through her pockets. After throwing her paper down and uttering an expletive, she walked over to the front desk, explained how she had lost her cell, and asked to use the hotel's landline.

The gracious clerk directed her to a house phone resting on a small table at one end of the lobby. Just as she wanted, the guard in the hallway would be able to watch her every move.

Sims sat on the arm of a couch, picked up the phone and crossed her legs, trying to paint a picture of an exasperated businesswoman. She dialed Deal's cell phone. He picked up immediately.

"What the hell are you doing in there, Sims?" Deal demanded.

Sims had to stay in character. "Sorry. I lost my cell somewhere between the airport and here. I've been waiting for some time, but Jackson hasn't shown up."

"So, you haven't seen Zach?" Deal asked, realizing Sims was in a compromised position.

"Yep, that's right. What? He postponed it until tomorrow?" Sims asked with fake disbelief. "What the hell am I supposed to do now? Just sit here on my ass? That's just great!"

Deal followed where Sims was going. "Good thought agent. Get a room there. Get past the guards and see if you can locate Zach."

"Well, I'll ask, but I don't know if I can get a room here or not..." Sims replied looking over to the desk clerk who had obviously been listening in.

The clerk caught her eye and typed away at his computer for a moment before looking up at Sims and nodding his head.

Sims gave the young man a brilliant smile and quick wave. "Well, the good-looking guy at the front desk says they have a room.

I'll have to pick up a few things to stay the night, but I'll make it work. Yes, sir, no problem. I'll fly back tomorrow."

"Bad luck, that," the young clerk said, smiling as Sims registered.

"I wasn't expecting to stay in London overnight, but I guess it's not the worst place to get stuck, after all."

"Pub opens at eleven. They do serve a nice lunch," the clerk offered.

"Thanks. I'll do that. Probably after a nap," Sims responded with a cheerful, but tired smile.

Sims took the room key, picked up her purse, and marched into the hall. She knew it would look suspicious if she ignored the big guard or if she paid him too much attention. So, she did neither. She tripped and fell, landing on her hands and knees. The contents of her purse scattered over the floor.

"Oh, shit!" she exclaimed. Then, while still on her hands and knees, she used one of the skills she learned working undercover. She made herself cry.

Picking herself up slowly, she felt a hand on her elbow.

"Are you alright, lass?" the guard asked with a Scottish accent, genuine concern in his voice.

Sims stood, straightening her suit and hair. "Yes, thanks. Just par for the course on a crappy day." Sims said, stifling her sobs.

"Sorry about that. Here now, let me help you with your things," the man said, gathering Sims scattered belongings. "You flew in from the States this morning, did you?"

"Yes, red-eye out of New York. Supposed to fly out again tonight, but that's not going to happen. God, now I'm a mess," Sims replied. "Thank you so much by the way."

"No problem, my dear. But be careful and get some rest," the guard said as Sims turned toward the elevator.

"Thank you, again."

She got in the elevator and pushed the button for her floor. She made it! Now she needed to find Zach.

Back in the lobby, the man who had just picked Sims up off the floor pulled out his cell phone. "She just checked in. Yes, ma'am, the blonde FBI agent. Made a nice show of it too."

TWENTY

Zach sat on the cheap striped love seat while Eva McWilkinson talked quietly on her cell phone. He was tired, hungry, confused, and wore clothes that still smelled like sweat, tear gas, and old lady perfume. He didn't feel like a hero at the moment. In fact, despite McWilkinson's assurances that this was all for his own safety, he was beginning to feel more like a hostage.

"Hey, y'all, how about we order a pizza or something? Is there some reason we have to sit in this crappy hotel *and* starve?" Zach blurted.

McWilkinson just turned away, still on the phone. But he had gotten the Bear's attention. The huge man had been standing next to the window, watching the street four floors below through a slight part in the curtains. After taking one last glance, the Bear ambled over to Zach and looked down at him.

"Look mate, this isn't a joke," the Bear said softly.

"I didn't say it was," Zach replied, standing, no longer intimidated by the mere presence of the massive agent. "But I need to let my friends and family know where I am. This isn't cool anymore."

Irritation at the situation fueled Zach's bravado, and the Bear knew it. He didn't blame the kid. MI5 had no choice but to take Zach into custody after the attack on the train and they hadn't given him an adequate explanation about why. But that wasn't the Bear's job. His job was to keep Zach safe.

Zach stood his ground looking up and into the eyes of a man a foot taller and over a hundred pounds heavier than him. The Bear just looked down, trying to take the skinny college boy seriously.

The rather ridiculous looking standoff ended when McWilkinson closed her phone and walked over.

"Zach, someone I expect is looking for you is right outside," she said.

Stella Sims had no gun and felt exposed as she walked down one of the long halls of the hotel. After briefly entering her own room, she surveilled the rest of the third floor for any sign of Zach or other guards. Finding nothing, she used the stairwell, emerging on the fourth, and top, floor.

Each floor of the L-shaped hotel had one long corridor and a shorter hallway at the far end. The long side of the fourth floor was empty. She had seen no guests and heard nothing from any of the rooms. *No wonder I could get a room here without a reservation,* she thought.

She carefully, but as casually as possible, approached the end of the hallway where it turned to the right. Considering her options, Sims decided to take a quick peek around the corner. If she caught a glimpse of a guard at one door, she could assume Zach would be inside.

She stepped quietly to the corner.

"Well, hello again my dear!" the guard from downstairs said, almost in her face.

Startled, Sims jumped backward, only to find two other men standing behind her.

She was trapped.

"I'm glad to see you've recovered from your spill downstairs, Agent Sims," the big Scott said, amused. "Not a bad act, that. Come now. Let's go see the young lad, Mr. Self."

The three Brits escorted Sims down to one of the rooms at the end of the hall and knocked on the door. It opened immediately and Sims stepped inside.

"Do come in, Agent Sims," McWilkinson said, greeting Sims as she walked in.

Sims saw Zach sitting on a small couch, while a veritable colossus of a man stood nearby with his arms crossed. The striking woman who had greeted her approached holding a badge and credentials.

"I'm Officer Eva McWilkinson, MI5. That's Officer Fred Blair. Welcome."

Sims produced her own badge. "Agent Stella Sims, FBI. I'm impressed. But a bit confused."

"Right. I'm afraid I owe you all an explanation, to be sure," McWilkinson said. "Oh, I'm sorry. I'm sure you know Mr. Zach Self as well."

"Hi, Stella," Zach said wearily, without getting up. "I'm glad you're here. Maybe they'll tell *you* what's going on. They sure won't tell me."

"Yes, of course. Maybe we should step into the adjoining room," McWilkinson suggested.

"Oh, hell no! If this is about me, you can talk right here," Zach objected.

"He's right," Sims responded. "Zach is assisting the FBI on this investigation."

McWilkinson hesitated, hiding her surprise at the revelation that Zach was part of Agent Deal's team. Finally, she said, "All right, straight to it then. Two terrorists made an attempt on Zach's life back at the Lanesborough. The attack was clumsy and obviously rash. But we lost one of our men."

"I'm sorry for your officer. You had no choice but to move Zach," Sims concluded.

"Right. Zach became a target as soon as he rescued the Duchess. We have to assume that whoever planted the teargas also ordered the attack. But that's just what I said, an assumption. In any event, we couldn't lose our newest national hero, now could we?" McWilkinson explained, smiling at Zach.

Zach didn't return the smile.

"What's your plan from here?" Sims asked.

"Yes, well I've been thinking about that. I think we should bring in your Agent Deal. I'd like to run an op that will require your team's assistance. I'm convinced we can take down this cell, but we'll need to bring them out into the daylight," the MI5 officer responded, looking down at Zach.

Zach's face turned white. "You mean, you guys want to use me as bait. Right?"

"I think that's just what she's saying," Sims replied, not taking her eyes off McWilkinson.

"I think I'm gonna be sick," Zach muttered.

"Oh, no you don't!" Bear roared from across the room.

TWENTY-ONE

Deal arrived at the hotel more pissed off than usual. He had agreed to help the Brits, but so far, he had found their cooperation wanting at best. If it hadn't been for his long friendship with Sir Gregory, he would have already pulled the plug on the mission and gone home.

Still fuming, Deal marched past the front desk without so much as a glance at the clerk. He found one of McWilkinson's men stationed in the elevator lobby.

"Let's go," Deal barked, vaguely waving his FBI credentials in the guard's general direction.

The MI5 officer correctly sensed that an introduction wouldn't be warmly received and simply pressed the 'up' button.

Stepping off the elevator, another agent further annoyed Deal by carefully checking his ID card and leading him to McWilkinson's suite. As he passed through the door, the MI5 officer stepped confidently forward.

"I'm Officer in Charge Eva McWilkinson," she said, extending her hand.

Deal glared into McWilkinson's eyes before saying anything in return. He didn't fall under the spell of her beauty, and for a moment, the two engaged in a silent power struggle. Deal's blue eyes, short gray hair, and strong jaw line contrasted with the MI5 officer's long black hair and dark, piercing eyes. The only thing the two seemed to have in common was their tough, unflinching personalities that immediately generated an intense pressure-filled atmosphere. Finally, Deal broke the silence with a single word. "Explain."

McWilkinson cocked her head slightly. "Explain what?" she replied, simply.

Zach found Sims' eyes with his own and opened them wide. *What's happening here?*

Sims made a slight motion with one hand. *Stay cool. It's okay.*

Deal's brows knitted even further together, his eyes never leaving McWilkinson's.

The MI5 agent stood her ground.

"Why the *hell* you disappeared into the night with one of my people!" Deal answered, jabbing an accusatory finger at McWilkinson's face.

McWilkinson flashed a brilliant smile and at the same time slapped his hand away.

"Now let me explain something to you," she said, menacingly. "This is the UK, not the sodding United States. *I'm* in charge here."

Far from decreasing, the stress in the room seemed to crystalize.

At last, Deal broke the icy situation by walking past McWilkinson and sitting down at a small table pushed up against the room's only window.

"Okay, lady," he said, throwing up his hands. "It's your party. But if you want our help, and I can tell you Sir Gregory does, I want to know what happened with Zach. And right now."

"First, you may call me 'Officer' or 'McWilkinson,' not *lady*. Second, bringing you up to date was never going to be a problem, Agent. We had no way of knowing Mr. Self was part of your team. To his credit, he kept that fact strictly to himself. And, as I've already explained to Agent Sims, an immediate threat to Zach's life made it necessary to move him quickly and very, very quietly. For his safety, I decided that the fewer people with knowledge of his whereabouts the better. I did what was necessary," McWilkinson explained, still standing.

Deal remained skeptical. "Well, I don't know about that. Sims found you. What makes you believe whoever threatened Zach's life couldn't do the same?"

"Agent Sims is obviously uniquely skilled at her profession," McWilkinson responded.

Deal studied the MI5 officer for a moment. She wasn't evasive and her body language didn't betray any lack of confidence. He decided she knew what she was doing.

"Let's get down to it then," Deal suggested, moderating his tone and gesturing to the other chair at the table. "What do we know? More importantly, what *don't* we know?"

McWilkinson sent the two officers that had accompanied Deal back to their posts and sat down across from the FBI agent.

"Right. We know that someone attacked the train carrying Lady Carol and Zach using tear gas. We don't know why they used tear gas or how it was placed on the train. Also, we obviously don't know who did so. Nobody has yet claimed responsibility for the attack."

"Any reason Lady Carol, in particular, would be targeted?" Deal asked.

"Two, in fact. First, she's a member of the royal family and a favorite of the Queen. Second, Lady Carol stubbornly refuses security and often rides public transport, making her a soft target," McWilkinson responded. "To be clear, we don't even know if she was a target at all. Terrorists often aim their mischief at public transportation — trains, buses, the tube, what have you. It could have been a simple coincidence that Lady Carol was there."

"And Zach?" Sims asked.

"We have to assume Zach's heroics and the subsequent media attention piqued someone's interest," Deal responded.

"Agreed," McWilkinson said. "But what hasn't been released to the press is an actual attempt on Zach's life at the hotel. Two un-identified males dressed as hotel staff tried to shoot their way past our guards at the room we set up as a decoy. I've received reports that both tangos were killed. But we lost an officer in the exchange of gunfire. Fortunately, we had Zach on another floor."

"I had no idea and I'm awfully sorry for your loss. Thanks to you and your people," Zach said, sincerely. "But for the record. I'm done with this hero garbage!"

"Calm down, boyo," the Bear said, patting Zach's shoulder with a meaty hand. "Officer McWilkinson knows her stuff. They never had a chance."

TWENTY-TWO

A sharp rap at the door of their flat startled the three terrorists just as they completed their evening prayers. They never had visitors.

John pointed at Tony, indicating he should move to the door while he and Simon quickly rolled up their prayer rugs, picked up two compact submachine guns, and took positions on either side of the door.

"Yes?" Tony asked through the closed door.

The answer caught all three men by surprise. *"Aldhiyb yati,* the Wolf comes."

John nodded at Tony to respond with the prearranged code.

"May the sheep fear the wolf," Tony said in Arabic just before unlocking and opening the door.

Two Middle Eastern men dressed in jeans and leather jackets moved into the flat and silently eyed John and Simon's weapons. The larger and more muscular of the two men, sporting a short black beard and shoulder length hair, locked his piercing black eyes on John and held out his hand. The message was unmistakable — hand over your weapon.

With only the slightest hesitation, John removed the weapon's strap from his shoulder and handed the compact machine gun over. Simon quickly followed suit.

While the second man, clean-shaven and younger than his partner, checked the flat for others, the bearded body-guard frisked John, Simon and Tony. Once satisfied the apartment was secure, the bearded man turned to the door.

"The flat is safe, my sheik."

"On your knees. Avert your eyes," the younger bodyguard ordered.

The three terrorists dropped immediately to the ornate rug and stared with unblinking eyes at the floor.

Small pearls of sweat appeared on John's forehead. A personal visit from the Wolf was without precedent. Unbelievable! The fiery sword of Allah himself!

With a word from the Wolf, men and women strapped bombs to their bodies and gave their lives willingly and joyously in a suicidal fireball. On his orders, others took up weapons of every kind and mercilessly slaughtered men, women and children. Like the rest of the terrorist world, the three men now on their knees both feared and revered the mighty power of the Wolf.

Trying not to tremble, John, Simon, and Tony awaited whatever fate the Wolf carried with him through the door. And wait they did.

"Tea," a mild voice said in English.

The three terrorists could hear a pot filled with water and cups arranged on one of their silver trays. Minutes passed as the water boiled, finally culminating in a loud whistle when steam escaped from the spout. After the tea was poured, they heard the clinking of a spoon inside a cup. None of them moved or spoke. But they all felt the Wolf's intense gaze of judgment burning into their bodies.

After what seemed an eternity, the Wolf finally spoke.

"I am disturbed. You have disturbed me. Here I sit, in the city which is the beating heart of our enemy, drinking tea and looking at the men I personally chose to be my emissaries. Yet, I am disturbed. Your leader, John, I believe you call yourself here in this country, will now explain why my greatest operation has been jeopardized by an inept attempt on the American boy's life. Speak."

Sweat now poured down John's face and dripped from his nose, not from the exertion of kneeling and staring downward for fifteen minutes, but from the terror of the Wolf's words.

"My sheik, the death of the American student would have..."

The Wolf interrupted. "Would have? Would have? Those words have no meaning. You will now answer my question. Why have you jeopardized my operation? And since you decided to undertake an attack without my approval, why did you fail?"

John's mind raced. His life depended on what emerged from his mouth next. Then he knew. There was no answer.

"I...I...am sorry, my sheik. Allah forgive me."

"He might. But I do not," the Wolf said, pointing one finger at the top of John's head.

In less than a second the clean-shaven bodyguard produced a silenced .22 caliber pistol and pulled the trigger. The tiny bullet spat from the barrel with no more sound than a child's balloon popping.

A small spurt of blood marked the place where the round penetrated John's skull, its low velocity allowing it to stop in the center of John's brain, thus saving the fine carpet from an ugly stain.

The Wolf stood. "Tony and Simon, you will continue with my operation. Simon will lead you. I shall leave my trusted guard Asser here with you. You will find him useful. You will also find him vigilant. Do not disturb me further."

Before leaving, the Wolf motioned Asser to his side and spoke into his ear. "Finish the job they began. Do it quickly. We must avenge our martyred brothers."

Tony and Simon heard the Wolf leave and the door close before daring to raise their heads. When they did, they saw John's forehead still pressed against the floor as if praying.

They had not seen the face of the Wolf.

"Rise," Asser said in a convincing English accent. "We are ordered to finish the American and then continue preparations for the operation. You may call me Arthur."

TWENTY-THREE

Oxford

"An Arab prince digitally flying airliners at a city?" Deal asked, incredulous, when Bubba showed up at Deal's headquarters the next day. "And the Brits know about this?"

Bubba should have expected Deal's strong reaction to his report. But Ali's open explanation and demonstration of the hyper-advanced technology drove any thought that Ali might be a terrorist from his mind.

"Yeah, I guess they must. I mean, they got it right there in the middle of the university's aerospace engineering lab. It ain't no big secret as far as I could tell. He showed it to me, after all," Bubba replied.

Bubba understood his boss's attitude, but, if anything, he felt Ali was just showing off the capabilities of his invention to another engineer who he knew would be impressed.

"I get it, Boss. I do," Bubba continued. "But I was there in the room. I talked with Ali afterward for a long time. He's a solid guy with a brilliant mind and an incredible invention. I don't gush over another engineer's stuff very often, but the imaging I saw is getting close to the holodeck on Star Trek."

"What the hell are you talking about?" Deal demanded.

"Not a fan? Well, the holodeck is supposedly a holographically created environment where crewmembers can physically interact with computer-generated people, objects, and environments. Okay, it's on an old TV show, but what I'm trying to tell you is that with the flip of a switch, the entire room disappeared, replaced by an airliner cockpit. The projections were so dense, everything appeared absolutely solid. Bulkheads. Seats. Instruments. Everything! I felt like I was inside an actual plane," Bubba explained, hoping Deal would appreciate the technology.

"Alright. I get that part's a big deal. But you said Ali actually used the plane's controls? How could he do that when the controls are what? Made out of light?"

"Yeah, that's been the big problem with holograms. They produce, particularly in this case, a realistic three-dimensional picture, but that's it. Ali figured out how to physically interact with the hologram itself. Tiny blasts of plasma, projected alongside the light waves provide both tactile feedback to the user and act as an interface with the computer program," Bubba explained.

"So, when Ali pushed the control stick forward, causing the plane to dive at the fake city, he was physically interacting with the hologram?" Deal asked, unable to suppress his amazement.

"Exactly," Bubba said. "I'll spare you the details, but suffice it to say, it's beyond next generation and will revolutionize not only the aircraft industry but medicine, manufacturing, architecture, gaming, entertainment — you name it."

Despite Bubba's opinion about Ali, Deal couldn't ignore the basic facts.

"How close can you get to this guy?" Deal asked.

Bubba knew Deal wouldn't just take his impressions of Ali at face value. They had come to England to assist with a critical investigation into a possible terrorist cell at Oxford, and even Bubba had to admit the demonstration he saw could be seen as troubling.

"As close as you need, Boss. I've already asked to join his team and he agreed. So, if there's anything nefarious going on, I'll know about it," Bubba said with confidence.

"Stay on top of it," Deal ordered, and turned back to his laptop.

"Boss?" Bubba asked, ignoring the obvious clue from Deal that the meeting was over. "What's going on with Zach? We haven't seen the little guy in days. Is he okay?"

Deal looked back up at Bubba with a blank expression. "Zach is fine. He'll be back soon. Don't worry about him."

Somehow, Deal's assurance rang hollow.

TWENTY-FOUR

Zach stood uncomfortably on a small platform with his arms held awkwardly away from his sides. A three-sided standing mirror placed close to the platform displayed his discomfort from all sides while a tailor ran a hand up and down the inside of his pants leg.

"Hey! Watch it, dude!" Zach exclaimed.

"Sorry, sir. We're almost done here," the balding tailor replied, making a chalk mark at the exact point the striped pant leg would meet the top of Zach's patent leather shoes.

Across the room, Eva McWilkinson chuckled at Zach's discomfort.

"Very nice," Zach said. "Laugh at a guy while he's being fitted for a clown suit."

"Sorry," McWilkinson replied. "But you're not being tortured. You're being fitted with appropriate evening attire by one of the best tailors in all of London. Which means, in all the world."

Zach gave McWilkinson a withering look as he pulled on a jacket with long tails. The tailor fussed over every square inch, tugging and pulling at the shoulders and waist and slashing away with his little piece of chalk. When finally satisfied, the man carefully removed the coat.

"All done. Thank you, sir. I'll take the trousers and coat for final preparations and return them here."

Zach thanked the tailor, changed in the next room and returned, wearing his own jeans and a polo shirt. He immediately felt like himself again.

"You're going to look smashing tonight, Zach," McWilkinson commented, smiling.

"I'm going to look like a penguin."

"Now don't pout," McWilkinson teased. "Here we are in a very posh suite at the Savoy and you've just been professionally fitted for a bespoke evening suit. Your circumstances have changed quite a bit in the last twenty-four hours, if I'm not mistaken."

"Last time you told me how great my hotel was, a couple of terrorists tried to kill me, if I'm not mistaken," Zach replied, sardonically.

"Yes, quite," McWilkinson had to agree. "But that's in the past. And tonight, you've been invited to Buckingham Palace to dine with the royal family. You must look the part."

"As I understand it, we have both been invited. And also as I understand it, you are not at all sure there won't be another attempt on my skinny backside. So, forgive me if I'm not quite as thankful as I should be," Zach moaned, sitting down heavily on a huge white sofa and resting his head in both hands.

Zach had been through a lot. To cap off a truly nightmarish forty-eight hours, he had been less than enthusiastic to learn Agent Deal and Eva McWilkinson planned to flush out the terrorist cell by using him as bait. He found it difficult to look forward to dinner at Buckingham Palace when just driving there might get him killed.

McWilkinson sat down on the couch next to Zach. She wanted him to feel safe. She needed him to feel safe.

"Zach, nobody knows you're here. I have agents on every floor. We even have a man with the tailor at all times, just to be sure he doesn't mention your whereabouts to anyone. You can relax. I promise," she explained, trying to convey both confidence and compassion.

"I'm okay," Zach said, looking back at McWilkinson. "Anyway, how could a guy be in a bad mood when he's going to a palace with such a beautiful escort."

"Oh, god, Zach. You really must stop. It's *not* a date!"

"You think of it your way, I'll think of it mine," Zach replied, grinning widely.

"At least I know you are actually back to full fiddle," McWilkinson huffed, getting up from the couch. "We have a few hours until it's time to leave and I have to make myself presentable as well."

"I can't wait to see just how you make yourself more 'presentable' than you already are," Zach said, leaning back on the couch and flashing his best smile at the tall MI5 agent.

"You really are a wanker," McWilkinson declared. "In the meantime, you may call your friends. I think you know not to tell them where you are. Otherwise, you may tell them you're going to meet the Queen. It will be on the telly, anyway."

McWilkinson tossed Zach a cell phone.

"That phone has no geo-locator and can't receive calls. Otherwise, enjoy," McWilkinson said, as she moved toward the door.

As McWilkinson left, the Bear stepped through the door and stood just inside.

"Want to go get a burger or something?" Zach asked the Bear as a joke.

The Bear didn't move and no expression crossed his face.

"No."

In Oxford, Michael's phone rang. No incoming number appeared on the display, but he answered anyway.

As soon as Michael picked up, Zach exclaimed, "Hey, buddy! How's Oxford?"

"Hey! Hold on a second, I'll get Bubba and Sarah," Michael replied, obviously excited to finally hear from his best friend.

As soon as they gathered, Michael put Zach on speaker.

"Where have you been? Deal's been pretty vague," Michael asked.

"I'm still in London. A lot of stuff happening down here, I guess. You guys all doing okay?" Zach asked, relieved to be talking to his friends again.

"We hear they're treating you like a superhero or something. Maybe they'll even make you a knight," Bubba teased.

"Sir Zachary. Doesn't sound that bad actually," Zach responded, jokingly.

"When are you coming back? We miss you," Sarah asked.

"Probably after I go meet the Queen of England at Buckingham Palace. I got a new suit and a beautiful date."

"What? Really?" Sarah blurted.

All three of Zach's friends started asking questions at once. After a few moments, Bubba began laughing so hard he had to sit down.

"What's so funny?" Michael asked.

"Are you kiddin' me? Zach all dressed up in a new tuxedo or whatever, walking down a red carpet, bowin' and kissin' rings?" Bubba managed to say between gasps of air. "I guess I was just thinking about the look on your daddy's face when he sees an entire country fussing over you!"

"Hadn't given it a thought," Zach replied, coldly. "But now that you mention it, I wouldn't mind if the old man found out what crow tastes like."

"Oh boy! He's going to get a big old heaping helping!" Bubba managed to say.

"Okay, okay," Michael broke in. "When is this? Can we see you before?"

"The thing is tonight for sure," Zach replied. "But I don't know when or any other details. They told me that something about it will be on television later."

After catching up for a few more minutes, Zach said he had to go and promised he would call after his visit to the palace.

Michael, Sarah, and Bubba couldn't believe their friend was going to have dinner at Buckingham Palace. Chance placed them all on the train when the attack occurred. Now, some forty-eight hours later, one of them would be dining with the royal family. It didn't seem possible.

Finally, Sarah jumped out of her seat. "Let's go!"

"Let's go where?" Michael asked, a little confused.

"London, of course. We may or may not get to see Zach, but we should be there even if it's just standing outside the gate to wave at him going in. It's only four o'clock. We can be in London in less than an hour. Trains run all the time. Come on!" Sarah could barely restrain herself.

Michael and Bubba both knew this side of Sarah. She wouldn't take no for an answer. It's a good thing she didn't.

TWENTY-FIVE

A chilly London breeze blew through St. James Park just outside Buckingham Palace, causing Sarah to seek refuge under Michael's arm. Luckily, the rain predicted for the late afternoon held off, allowing Michael, Bubba, and Sarah to join the usual crowd of sightseers without needing umbrellas.

Having seen one vehicle enter the north gate of the palace, the trio chose a spot nearby hoping to catch a glimpse of Zach when he arrived. Unlike the red-uniformed guards standing motionless before the front entrance, three serious-looking soldiers dressed in black and green camouflage fatigues and holding automatic weapons strolled about casually just inside the massive iron fence.

"You think those guards mind us hanging around the gate?" Sarah asked, looking over her shoulder.

"Oh, I don't think they mind. They haven't given us a second look in the last half hour," Bubba answered.

"I doubt Royal Marines of the Special Boat Service care anything about three obviously American tourists," Michael commented.

"Who?" Sarah asked.

"They're like special forces. Like our Navy Seals. Badass to the bone!" Michael explained.

"I thought those dudes in red coats and bearskin hats guarded the Queen. And come to think of it, just where in all of England did they find those bears anyway?" Bubba asked.

"Those are the Queen's Guard. I would guess that after the recent attack on one of the royals, they called in the special forces to beef up security," Michael answered, not knowing he was actually correct.

"I'm sure they are super cool, but I wish Zach would come by. I'm getting cold out here," Sarah said with a shiver.

"And I need a beer and maybe some of that fried fish they got in the pubs," Bubba complained.

Just as Bubba finished speaking, the guards started to move toward the gate. While two took up positions on either side, the third pushed a button. As the gates parted, Michael, Bubba, and Sarah got a clear view into the palace courtyard. Interestingly, only few tourists took any notice that something unusual was happening. When the gate stopped moving, the guards continued their casual sauntering about, drawing no attention to the fact that someone important was obviously about to either enter or leave the palace.

In the distance, the group heard sirens approaching.

"Simon, do our people have them yet?" Arthur demanded.

Simon sat hunched over his laptop on the floor of the terrorists' flat, watching intently as a small target cursor moved over a map of central London. On the right side of the screen, an open dialogue box displayed the text of an ongoing chat he maintained with the person actually controlling a drone.

"Not yet," Simon responded, his voice betraying frayed nerves.

Even though the Wolf had left him nominally in charge, Simon knew Arthur would report any failure on his part. And failure meant death.

"What are they doing? It appears they are lost or incompetent!" Arthur snapped.

Tony, monitoring the operation from another screen, answered to deflect some pressure away from Simon. "The drone operator is maneuvering to find the perfect position to watch the target's movements. While he does so, I understand the computer program is building a virtual model of all possible routes from the hotel to the palace. Once done, Simon will confirm the exact place he wants the strike to occur and give the final order."

Arthur grunted in disapproval. "This looks like a child's game. I find no pleasure in killing infidels with a toy. I prefer the feel of my enemy's hot blood on my own hand."

"This toy, as you call it, will stab at the very heart of our enemy. We hold the knife, but we hold it like a ghost from afar. What could strike more fear into the enemy?" Tony explained, his eyes not leaving his screen.

Outside the palace grounds, Michael, Bubba, and Sarah listened as the sirens became louder.

"Do you think that's Zach?" Sarah asked.

"It seems weird they would be using sirens or a motorcade or something just to bring a guest to dinner. But who knows?" Michael answered.

They didn't have to wait long to find out.

Moments later, two police cars, lights flashing and sirens wailing, appeared from behind the Victoria Memorial and sped toward the open gate. A massive maroon Rolls Royce followed closely behind. As it passed within yards of where the three friends stood, they saw the smiling face of Queen Elizabeth II. Prince Phillip sat bolt upright next to his wife, dressed in a navy-blue military uniform.

Then, as quickly as they appeared, the royal couple's car passed through the open gate and disappeared behind the palace walls. The huge gates closed immediately.

"Well, I'll be damned," Bubba said under his breath, for once at a loss for words.

Londoners rarely catch a glimpse of the British monarch in a lifetime, yet, the three young Americans had been in town for less than two hours and found themselves waving back at the famous lady from just across the street.

"Oh, wow! I can't wait to tell my mom!" Sarah nearly squealed, pulling out her phone.

Michael looked back up the road. "Yeah, but where's Zach?"

TWENTY-SIX

"Don't you look smashing!" McWilkinson remarked when Zach appeared wearing his new evening attire.

"I feel like a trussed-up turkey," Zach grumbled, tugging nervously at his collar and tie while looking at himself in the suite's full-length mirror.

"If you'll stop fidgeting with the bits and pieces, we can leave. Mustn't keep Her Highness waiting," McWilkinson announced, moving toward the door.

Zach hesitated. "Are you sure about this? I mean, for real? I know you explained the plan and all, but…"

McWilkinson had gotten to know Zach in the past couple of days. The brash young American, confident in front of TV cameras, and unafraid to flirt with a model turned MI5 agent, was opening up to her.

"You're frightened," McWilkinson said, finishing his sentence. "No shame in it. But I'm confident. It's vitally important we take down the terrorist cell before they hurt someone else. And we have a solid plan in place to do just that."

After listening to McWilkinson and Deal's scheme to spring a trap on the terrorist, Zach had agreed to participate. But as the time to leave approached, he became understandably wary. Everything had to go perfectly. If it did, and the terrorists made an attempt on his life, Deal's Red and Blue teams would be ready.

"Tell me again how this will work," Zach said, summoning as much courage as possible.

"We are going to walk right out the front door of the hotel. The press will be everywhere. Just smile, wave, and you know, be Zach. We'll be outside for less than thirty seconds and under an awning until we enter the vehicle. You know what to do?"

"Yeah, I know. I know. Don't dawdle," Zach replied, knowing he and McWilkinson would be exposed as soon as they walked out the door.

Then, trying to change the subject, Zach asked about the royal family. Despite his near unfailing confidence around people, Zach had to admit he was more than a little intimidated by the prospect of dining at Buckingham Palace.

McWilkinson walked up to Zach and straightened his tie. "Well, you may be surprised, but I've done this before. The Queen is delightful and will put you at ease immediately. Prince Phillip, her husband, looks intimidating on the telly but is one of the kindest men I've ever met."

"It sounds like you know the family personally," Zach observed.

"Yes. Well, I once dated Prince Harry for a period of time. So..."

"So, you really do know the family!" Zach exclaimed, smiling for the first time.

"Yes. Quite. But I wouldn't have made a very good princess anyway," McWilkinson responded, only half-joking.

"I believe you would have made a stunning princess, my lady," Zach said, gallantly bowing just as he had practiced all afternoon.

"Enough. The car is waiting. We'll be at the palace in five minutes," McWilkinson said, once again all business.

Hundreds of cameras flashed as McWilkinson and Zach walked out the front doors of the Savoy. Just thirty minutes earlier, Deal and McWilkinson had intentionally leaked Zach's presence at the hotel. The resulting press coverage and social media posts would tempt the terrorist cell to make another move. But this time, Deal's team and a wide range of British law enforcement would be ready.

Zach paused momentarily to smile and give a quick wave before ducking into a gleaming black Range Rover with blacked-out windows. The camera flashes continued, even as the big SUV pulled away.

"Hey, Bear," Zach said, greeting the huge MI5 officer he found himself sitting next to after jumping in the car.

The Bear remained silent.

"You don't have to worry about your shoes tonight," Zach joked nervously.

At the street, two police motorcycles with flashing blue lights pulled in front of their vehicle, while two blue and yellow police cars took up positions on either side. The police escorts led Zach's vehicle around the block before increasing speed along Victoria's Embankment. Sirens wailed as they blasted along the west bank of the Thames. Then, as they passed under the bridge at Charring Cross station, Zach's vehicle braked hard. An identical black Range Rover appeared out of the darkness, taking up station with the police escorts. Without slowing, the escorts emerged from under the bridge and turned right again toward St. James Park and the palace.

"Damn! That was smooth!" Zach commented.

"Now that's done and dusted, we'll just pop around the other side of Westminster Abbey and on to the palace," McWilkinson said, opening her cell phone. "Agent Deal, the decoy vehicle will be appearing on The Mall momentarily."

It had been nearly an hour since Michael, Sarah, and Bubba had seen the Queen enter Buckingham Palace. Twilight was falling over St. James Park and street lights were coming to life. The palace itself glowed in a mixture of golden light from the setting sun and bright spotlights pointed up at the mighty structure.

"Hey, we've been out here for hours. When are we going to find something to eat?" Bubba griped.

"Not until we see Zach," Sarah replied stubbornly. "We're not moving from here yet and that's final."

Michael and Bubba gave each other a look. *I guess we're not going anywhere yet.*

Michael put his arm around Sarah, who had crossed her arms and taken up a rather defiant stance. "Okay. Okay, we'll stop complaining. Anyway, it's kinda romantic out here right now, huh?"

Then, Michael noticed Sarah scowling.

"What's the matter?"

Sarah pointed over the tops of the trees lining the wide street leading up to the front of the palace called The Mall.

"Do you see that?" Sarah asked, squinting at something. "Is that a drone? Or am I seeing things?"

Michael looked at where Sarah pointed. It took a minute, but then he saw it — a large black drone hovering just over the treetops.

"Hey, Bubba. You see that drone over there?" Michael asked, tapping Bubba on the shoulder.

"What?" Bubba said, looking for himself. "Yeah! I see it. That's a big one. Let me take a closer look."

Bubba pulled his cell phone from his pocket and aimed the camera at the drone.

"That won't work," Michael commented, before remembering who he was talking to.

"Your phone won't get a decent picture of it from here, but mine will. I made a little tweak or two of my own design. I also installed an infrared filter and enhanced the programming for better night vision," Bubba explained, aiming his camera into the darkening sky.

After snapping a few shots, Bubba spent a moment studying the images. Suddenly, he looked back up at the drone. "Oh shit!"

"What?" Michael asked, trying to get a look at the photo on Bubba's phone. "What's the matter?"

"I can't be absolutely sure, but I think that thing is carrying a bomb."

TWENTY-SEVEN

With the light of the evening sky fading quickly into night, the friends' ability to see the menacing drone faded along with it. The flying robot's black paint and near-silent operation made it almost impossible to detect without Bubba's high-tech phone camera.

"I have a really, really bad feeling it might be after Zach," Sarah pronounced suddenly. "He's been all over the news for saving the Duchess of Cambridge from a terrorist attack. Maybe somebody is looking for revenge!"

"Now wait a second, that's kind of a wild theory," Bubba objected.

"No, it's not," Sarah insisted, looking up into Bubba's face. "The Queen of England just passed right by here a little while ago. Wouldn't she make a much better target? So, the only other person we know is going into the palace tonight is Zach. What's that tell you?"

"Yeah, I see..." Bubba began. "Wait! Where's Michael?"

Bubba and Sarah looked up in time to see Michael sprinting across the broad avenue, hurdle a low fence surrounding St. James Park and disappear into the trees.

"Michael!" Sarah shouted, despite knowing he was too far away to hear.

Turning to Bubba with near-panic on her face, she asked, "What is he doing?"

"Just being Michael. If I had to guess, he's going to try and climb a tree and bring it down all by himself," Bubba responded, not at all surprised by Michael's actions.

Sarah's phone rang. It was Michael.

"What are you doing?" Sarah demanded.

"Can...you...still...see...it?" Michael said, still running.

Sarah didn't waste time trying to stop her boyfriend.

"Not really, it's too dark. If Bubba's camera didn't have night vision or whatever, we wouldn't have any idea it was even there. What do you want us to do?" Sarah asked, with Bubba listening carefully.

"I'll ... think of something."

Just as he stopped talking, sirens could be heard in the distance. Bubba and Sarah looked simultaneously back at the north gate. Once again, they started to slowly part. Someone else was about to arrive.

Zach!

"Michael, do you hear the sirens? It must be Zach. We think the bomb might be meant for him," Sarah said, trying to remain calm.

Michael didn't hesitate. "Get to one of the guards and convince them to shoot it down!"

Bubba and Sarah looked at each other and then ran across the street toward the opening gate. Their actions immediately drew the attention of the guards. As they got closer a giant sergeant stepped forward holding out one hand.

"Stop right there!" the soldier ordered, while expertly swinging his assault rifle off his back.

"Please, sir, there's a drone above those trees. We think it may be a bomb!" Sarah pleaded, as she pulled up well short of the gate.

"What? Step back young lady!" the huge sergeant ordered again, this time more sternly.

Bubba caught up with Sarah a moment later. Unaccustomed to running of any kind, Bubba had to lean over with both hands on his knees while he caught his breath. A second later, he handed Sarah his phone.

"Show him," Bubba managed between gasps of air.

"Sir, please. Our friend Zach Self, the student who rescued the duchess from the train two days ago, is about to arrive. We saw a drone over those trees. My friend here saw a bomb attached to it. Please, just take a look," Sarah urged, holding out Bubba's phone showing a picture of the drone he took just moments before.

"If this is a joke, you both will be placed under arrest," the sergeant growled, while holding out his hand for the phone.

After looking at the photo, Sarah pointed to the spot on the other side of the statue where they saw the drone. The sergeant spoke into his shoulder-mounted radio, then stepped forward and peered in the direction Sarah was pointing.

"I don't see a thing, young lady."

Bubba finally recovered enough to join the conversation. Taking the phone back, he made a few adjustments, found the still-hovering drone on the screen, and handed the phone back to the guard.

Holding the camera up and then looking into the night sky, the sergeant's eyes grew wide.

But even as Sarah and Bubba did their best to convince the palace guard they were telling the truth, the sirens grew louder and closer. They had a minute, at best.

"What on earth is happening here Sergeant Major?" an officer demanded, walking up behind the group gathered at the gate.

The sergeant explained the situation in the clipped and efficient language of the military while displaying the live image on Bubba's phone.

The young-ish lieutenant recognized the threat immediately. Though theoretical, the palace guard had been warned over the past few years about the possibility of an attack utilizing various drone technologies.

Britain's Special Boat Service trained its officers to make decisions and the lieutenant didn't hesitate to do so. "Sergeant Major, please be so kind as to shoot that thing out of the air."

The sergeant raised his weapon and tried to find a target in the night sky. Sweeping his sight back and forth across the tops of the trees, he simply couldn't see the black drone. Bubba and Sarah could make out flashing lights coming at them slowly down The Mall — directly into the target zone of the drone.

"Sir, I can't identify the target without night vision gear," the sergeant reported.

Then, inexplicably, a beam of light flashed up out of the forest, falling directly on the underside of the hovering drone.

With his target now clearly illuminated, the sergeant fired three shots in quick succession, startling the crowd of tourists, who began running in all directions.

Sparks flew from the fuselage of the drone from the first shot. The second tore off one of its long arms. They didn't know if the third shot found its target or not.

Now barely able to remain stable, the drone lurched backward and plummeted momentarily toward the tree tops. For a second, it looked like the craft would plow into the park's old forest and tear itself to pieces. But it didn't.

Bubba and Sarah could barely follow the drone's path as it limped away from the park and disappeared from sight. They completely missed seeing a black Range Rover as it passed safely through the palace gates.

"Nice shot, dude!" Bubba declared, sticking out his hand to the sergeant.

"Yes, well, we didn't bring it down, did we?" the sergeant replied coolly. "I say, I wouldn't have had a shot at all if someone hadn't put a light on it like that."

Sarah's phone rang, startling her back into the moment.

After answering, and listening a moment, Sarah looked back at Bubba and the military men.

"We need to get going," Sarah said, touching Bubba's arm and giving him an urgent look.

"Well, thanks so much for your assistance. If you hadn't insisted we look at your phone..." the officer in charge began.

"Hey! No problem!" Bubba answered. "But we really need to go."

"Come on!" Sarah urged, walking quickly away toward where Michael had disappeared into park.

Several other officers appeared at the gate, distracting the sergeant and lieutenant long enough for Bubba and Sarah to blend into the crowd of onlookers gathering nearby.

Sarah quickly outpaced Bubba in her rush to find Michael.

A minute later, Bubba found Sarah and Michael sitting on a park bench entwined in each other's arms.

"Oh, come on!" Bubba exclaimed. "Get a room!"

Sarah and Michael, hearing their friend's voice, stopped kissing and carefully looked around before responding.

"Sorry, bro. There's a pissed-off park ranger or whatever around here somewhere looking for whoever snatched his flashlight and ran into the trees. I needed to look innocent," Michael explained with a guilty smirk.

TWENTY-EIGHT

Randall Snow unwound the black and white Arab headscarf called a shemagh from over his face and around his head. He hated wearing the hot and uncomfortable thing, but it provided the proper look and hid his face when he transformed himself into the Wolf. Snow left the long robes that completed his disguise in the dimly lit small basement room where he recorded long rant-like messages for his followers in front of worn, scarred walls and an assortment of jihadist flags. With his latest online performance for his devotees finished and uploaded to social media, Snow could relax for the rest of the evening.

Tossing the piece of cloth over a nearby couch, Snow loosened his Savile Row tie and sat down in his favorite soft leather armchair. Next to the chair, he found a crystal snifter of Louis XIII Rare Cask brandy already warmed to the perfect temperature by his personal butler, Nigel. The richly furnished townhouse in the exclusive London neighborhood of Chelsea where he now relaxed was one of the most expensive and luxurious addresses in London. Snow liked to think of it as the Wolf's Den, but he kept that name to himself. To everyone else, it was simply one of the many homes owned by a little-known and reclusive hedge fund manager.

There was nothing remotely Arabic, Middle Eastern, or Muslim about the furniture, the townhouse, or Randall Snow. At fifty years old, the ex-Texas Ranger's heavily muscled five-foot-eleven-inch frame and thick gray hair, now dyed a deep brown, gave him a formidable presence. Blue eyes peered out from under heavy eyebrows – a trait that would have been a problem except for the well-known myth that the original Wolf also had blue eyes. Snow had developed perfect Arabic while working as an intelligence analyst in the United States Army. During multiple tours in Afghanistan and Iraq, he had interrogated hundreds of extremists and insurgents, giving him an intimate understanding of their mindset and motivations. It had been his idea to find and kill the real Wolf in order to take over his persona. Now, posing as the famed terrorist leader, Snow could manipulate extremists all over the world.

Snow rolled the expensive brandy around the bottom of the sifter before deeply inhaling its rich aroma. He downed the entire contents of the glass, enjoying the warmth of the liquor. With soft jazz music playing in the background, he sat back, closed his eyes, and savored the moment of peace.

Snow felt more than heard Nigel walking softly across the white and gold antique Persian rug.

"Yes, Nigel?" Snow asked, without opening his eyes.

"Sorry to disturb, sir, but Santiago is on the secure line."

Snow had been expecting the call. Nigel placed a telephone in Snow's hand before discreetly stepping away.

"Snow, 3737," he said into the phone without further greeting.

"Report on your progress," a coarse female voice said without identifying herself.

Snow knew the voice well.

"Good evening, Madam Director. I can report our operation in the UK is underway. Our initial efforts with the drones have been a complete success."

"The attack on the train carrying the old royal successfully caught the attention of the media. The story went worldwide," Margie Franks agreed.

"It certainly did, Madam Director."

"And your mock attack on the American student this evening? Did MI5 and Agent Deal's team take the bait?" Franks asked.

"Oh, yes. They had officers all over St. James Park hoping to snare the terrorist cell that made the attempt on Zachary Self at the Lanesborough. Just as we hoped, the appearance of the drone overhead carrying a bomb has made them paranoid and focused on the possibility of more such attacks," Snow responded.

"Good. Keep up the pressure. I want Special Agent Frank Deal running around England like a chicken with its head cut off."

"He will. Our main operation here in the UK is set to proceed in less than a week," Snow reported.

"Excellent. Are your operators and followers still under control?"

Snow had to smile at the question.

"Absolutely. My people here will have the attack drones ready on time. And, we now command an army of true believers through our social media arm – all willing to lay down their lives with nothing more than a word from, well, me. Once we found and removed the real Wolf, taking his place was simple. It's truly amazing what people will do when they become blinded by effective propaganda," Snow replied, holding his snifter up for Nigel to refill.

"Don't get cocky, Snow. The Directors expect results."

"And you'll have them. When the time comes, the eyes of every law enforcement agency in the world will be laser-focused on London."

143

"And you'll have them. When the time comes, the eyes of every law enforcement agency in the world will be laser-focused on London."

TWENTY-NINE

MI5 Headquarters
London

Sir Gregory Fender poured two cups of Earl Grey tea and handed one to Eva McWilkinson. Like Sir Gregory's attire, the overly-decorated antique china clashed with the director's ultra-modern office.

"Pity the terrorists didn't show up in person last night," Sir Gregory remarked, talking about McWilkinson and Deal's operation.

"Yes. But the military successfully foiled a suspected drone attack. I'm now considering whether drones may have been used in the attack on the Duchess's train," McWilkinson said.

Sir Gregory sipped at his tea, considering McWilkinson's statement. "Troubling. We've been studying the possibility of our enemies using drones in many different scenarios. Keep me apprised of anything you find about that in regard to the train attack."

"Yes, sir," McWilkinson replied. She was used to Sir Gregory's almost bland manner. But she also thought he dismissed the topic too quickly.

"So, I understand our friend Frank Deal is utilizing some unusual assets in his investigation?" Sir Gregory asked, while adding a bit of lemon peel to his tea.

"Yes, quite unusual," McWilkinson replied, taking a sip and setting the cup and saucer down on Sir Gregory's desk. "I admit to being surprised when the FBI appeared to claim Zachary Self as a member of their team."

Gregory chuckled. "Yes, Frank certainly uses unconventional methods, but it's those same methods that are the key to his success. What else did you learn when he came to collect Mr. Self?"

"Other than the fact he is pig-headed, arrogant, and rude? Quite a bit, actually," McWilkinson replied.

"No doubt Frank can be abrasive," Sir Gregory agreed. "Go on."

"Along with Zachary Self, he has at least one other agent in the country, Stella Sims. I must say, she is quite good at her job. After leaving the Lanesborough, it took her only a matter of hours to track us down."

"Yes. I met Agent Sims when Frank got into town. I would expect Frank's second in command to be incredibly skilled. What else?" Sir Gregory asked, looking over the top of his teacup.

"Once Sims found us, Deal's operatives effectively surrounded our location. If our surveillance wasn't up to snuff, we would never have known they were in the area," McWilkinson responded with admiration.

"But our techniques were better?"

"Yes. But just," McWilkinson replied. "We had the 'home field advantage' as Agent Deal so eloquently pointed out. I believe he was right. In any event, we know that Zach Self is working with the FBI at Oxford. Zach mentioned several times he had friends at the university waiting on him. We don't know who they are, and neither he nor the FBI agents would confirm whether those friends are also working with Deal. I presume that is the case."

Sir Gregory just nodded. "I'm not surprised. Operational security."

"Sir Gregory, may I ask why the FBI is here in the first place? I've been assigned to investigate the attack on the train and subsequent attempts on Zach Self's life. I'm not aware of any intelligence that would require assistance from the Americans. Is there something I need to know?"

Sir Gregory sat back in his office chair and considered McWilkinson's question. Without a doubt, Eva McWilkinson had one of the sharpest minds at MI5. But the FBI agent had demanded autonomy and McWilkinson and Deal had already knocked heads once. Plus, Zach Self's unexpected heroics had drawn the entire nation's attention, possibly compromising Deal's investigation, and nearly causing him to pull his team out of the country.

And Sir Gregory needed Agent Deal's team to stay in the UK.

"No, Ms. McWilkinson. That will be all."

"Yes, sir."

McWilkinson knew Sir Gregory wasn't telling her everything. She would have preferred to know more about the operation the head of MI5 was keeping to himself and that apparently required the assistance of the Americans. But she said nothing.

"Excellent. I'll look forward to your report on the train incident."

Despite his long relationship with Frank Deal, Sir Gregory needed to know what Deal's team of college students were doing at Oxford without raising the FBI's suspicions. Sending Eva McWilkinson wasn't an option. He needed someone else.

THIRTY

Simon entered the apartment he shared with Tony and Arthur and immediately changed into long white robes. He found operations in the West challenging in many respects, but he considered picking out different sets of clothing to wear every day both irritating and sinful. As it is written in the Quran: "Allah loves not the proud and arrogant."

Tony, who was on the computer monitoring social media for any mention of the drone incident near the palace, noticed Simon grab the hookah pipe and begin angrily filling the room with sweet-smelling smoke.

"Brother?" Tony asked gently. "Is everything alright?"

Simon's eyes shifted to look at Tony without moving his head. "No."

Tony had feared this moment. Since the failed drone attack on the American, Zach Self, he had been awaiting the Wolf's harsh judgment. Now, it appeared Simon may have news.

"You have received some communication from the Wolf?" he asked, trying not to sound frightened, but failing.

Simon glared back at the younger man. "Yes. From his people. I am told our sheik is not concerned with the outcome of the attack on the American. He is now only interested in the progress of his main operation. I informed them that while the attack itself was foiled at the last second, the drone otherwise performed flawlessly."

Relieved beyond words, Tony asked, "Shall I have Arthur join us?"

"Do so."

A moment later, Arthur sat down on the floor with Simon and Tony. After passing the pipe and informing Arthur of the Wolf's response to the attack, Simon changed the subject.

"I have another matter to discuss. Ali Badran has foolishly brought an American into the drone lab."

"A student?" Tony asked.

"Yes," Simon replied. "I'm not sure of the significance of this development yet but it bears attention. I have not met this American in person, but I understand his name is 'Bubba' – some sort of American nickname. Bubba Adcock. Ali assured me he is an accomplished aeronautical engineer."

"Shall I research this Bubba Adcock?" Tony asked.

"Yes. Do. We need to know more about this interloper," Simon responded.

Tony got up, opened his laptop, and began expertly running searches focused on social media and aeronautical engineering sites.

"Does he pose a threat to the Wolf's plan?" Arthur asked. "If so, I can rid us of him with ease."

Simon waved Arthur's suggestion away.

"Not yet," Simon said, sucking on the end of the hookah. "First, I don't want to attract any unnecessary attention. Killing him would raise too many questions. Second, if he is as talented as Ali claims, he might be invaluable in increasing the payload capacity of the drones that we need for the Wolf's operation to succeed."

After a few minutes, Tony sat down to report his preliminary findings.

"Adcock is a student in his second year at Southern University. He has won several awards and is the subject of one article in "Aerospace Today" magazine naming him as one of the country's most talented young engineers. He has already published four academic papers and is heavily credited in eight others. I have downloaded them for your review, but they all seem to address complex aerospace engineering technologies that only you will understand. His family owns several food stores that provide the Adcock family with a comfortable existence. I found nothing that ties him to any law enforcement agency."

"Thank you, Tony. I shall review the papers and article," Simon responded.

Arthur, who had been sitting quietly suddenly blurted, "How close are you to bringing the drones' lifting ability up to our requirements? The Wolf has ordered the attack for one week's time. Will they be ready? If you fail, we all fail."

Simon looked at Arthur, irritated at his rash outburst.

"I am well aware of the Wolf's requirements. Do not forget that he left me in charge of this operation. But to answer your question, we are very close to the 68-kilogram weight capacity the Wolf demanded. I foresee no problem in achieving our final goal in the allotted time. I have personally kept our manufacturing facility in Kensington apprised of every development. When the time comes, and with the blessings of Allah, we shall have no less than eight drones ready to strike at the heart of our enemy."

"And *you* should not forget how the Wolf responds to failure," Arthur growled in return.

"Only Allah decides the fate of men," Simon retorted. "If Allah guides the Wolf's hand to take my life, it shall be gladly given. I pray only to be useful and earn the honor of martyrdom should Allah so choose."

THIRTY-ONE

Zach's visit to Buckingham Palace caused an intense but brief media sensation. Only twenty-four hours later, however, the nation's focus shifted to a member of Parliament who got caught cheating on his wife.

The next day, Zach found himself sitting alone at a table in one of Oxford's pubs in the middle of the afternoon with his brand-new evening suit draped over a chair and his still-packed suitcase at his feet. Nobody seemed to recognize him. He was yesterday's news.

Zach sipped at his pint of lager in the mostly empty pub, feeling a bit sorry for himself. Almost from the minute he landed in England, his life had been turned upside down. He had been gassed on a train, attacked by terrorists, hounded by media, used as bait, and shipped off to meet the Queen. He wanted nothing more than to see his friends. But Deal told him to lay low for a couple of days to save their cover and keep them away from any news coverage. Sure, the visit to the palace had been exciting, especially accompanied by the gorgeous MI5 officer, but now, he felt deflated and more than a little lonely.

When the bell above the door tinkled, Zach didn't even look up. Then he heard a familiar voice coming from the bar.

"I'd like me a pint of Guinness if you can spare one!"

Bubba!

Zach spun around to see Bubba, Michael, and Sarah standing at the bar. It took a lot of self-control to keep from immediately jumping out of his seat. They obviously knew he was there, but instead of coming over, they chatted among themselves while the bartender poured three pints of the dark brown Irish stout.

Finally, he couldn't stand it any longer. Zach walked casually over to his three best friends and introduced himself as if meeting them for the first time. After some made up banter about where they were from in the U.S. and where they went to school, Zach offered to buy the next round and invited them to join him at a table.

When they were safely out of earshot from the bartender and the few other customers, Zach had to hold himself back from gushing about everything that had occurred.

"God, it's good to see you guys!" Zach said quietly.

"Deal said we should wait a day or two before we 'met' you, but that wasn't going to fly," Bubba responded. "It's good to see you, too."

"Yeah, Sarah convinced Agent Sims to tell us where you were as long as we were careful. How are you holding up, buddy?" Michael asked with genuine concern.

"I'm fine now. The last couple of days were a wild ride, though," Zach answered.

"Deal wouldn't tell us much," Michael said.

"Yeah, I'll tell you about everything later. Meeting the Queen was awesome until they told me somebody might have tried to kill me with a drone!" Zach replied. "I'm starting to think I pissed somebody off."

Michael, Sarah, and Bubba had decided not to tell Zach about their involvement with the attempted attack outside the palace. They had barely managed to walk away before the palace guards could take an official statement and they didn't need Deal getting on their case for blowing their cover.

"So, at least tell us about the Queen and Prince Phillip!" Sarah urged, barely able to control her excitement.

"Down-to-earth. Normal kinda people. We ate burgers the prince cooked on a grill…"

"Zach! Really!" Sarah scolded.

"Okay, okay," Zach replied. "I got this fancy tuxedo or whatever, and I had a gorgeous date. They fed us some kind of bird called 'squab.' Tasted like chicken. The Queen is actually extremely nice and thanked me over and over for saving her cousin. Way overly-fancy but all and all pretty cool. I had to bow and stuff, but I didn't mind."

"Oh, for God's sake, Zach!" Sarah huffed, irritated at Zach's lack of detail.

"So, what's been happening here?" Zach wanted to know.

"A lot. Buy us another round, and we'll fill you in," Bubba said, pushing his empty glass across the table. "You wouldn't believe the advanced technology they're working on at the university."

"Like what?" Zach asked.

"Massive drones with incredible first-person flight control. I already met the guy who practically owns the project, and he invited me onto his team! And, you aren't the only one who's been hobnobbing with royalty," Bubba gloated with a jovial, satisfied smirk.

"What royalty?" Michael asked skeptically.

"Remember that guy we met in the botanical gardens? Ali? Turns out he's some kind of prince from an oil-rich middle-eastern country," Bubba bragged. "And, Zach, you wouldn't believe the holographic imager he showed me. We went into this room, he turned it on, and all of a sudden, we were in the cockpit of a new jet airliner. I swear, it looked as real as this bar does to me right now."

"Sounds cool!" Zach exclaimed.

"Yeah, and he controlled the plane by actually touching the holographic image. We dove right at a make-believe city. He pulled up just in time. Incredible!"

Zach didn't respond.

"What?" Bubba asked, noticing his friend's shock.

"Did you tell Deal about this?" Zach asked.

"Yeah. And he gave me the same look you're giving me now. But I'll tell you what I told him. Ali is a good guy. I'm sure of it. You'll see when you meet him."

"Damn. I hope you're right, dude. Because that sounds like a perfect tool for training people to, you know, crash airliners into cities," Zach said.

THIRTY-TWO

Frank Deal hated complications. Yet, after arriving in the UK less than a week before, he had encountered almost nothing else.

Meeting with Sims in his makeshift office at the U.S. consulate in Oxford, Deal knew he needed to make some progress investigating the terrorist threat Sir Gregory and MI5 faced. Bubba's friendship with Ali Badran, and Badran's demonstration of interactive holography, had caught his attention. But then again, no serious terrorist would openly display the plan for a real attack scenario to someone he barely knew. Badran's drone technology, though, could have been the platform used for the attack on Zach near the palace.

Deal had Sims check on Badran's movements during the palace attack. She reported that he had been speaking at a symposium on plasma physics during the failed attack and could not have been in control of the drone spotted by Sarah and Bubba. But the FBI agent wasn't satisfied. Delivery of a bomb by drone required sophisticated technology – far beyond the capability of your average terror cell.

Badran would remain on Deal's radar.

Stella Sims sat quietly as Deal's mind churned through possibilities. Over the past two years as his second in command, she had seen Deal display an uncanny ability to find leads where nobody else thought to look. Sometimes, the man just needed time to think.

"Has Zach integrated back into his team?" Deal asked, meaning with Bubba, Michael, and Sarah.

"Yes, sir," Sims replied, confidently. "I was at the pub where they reconnected last night. Their meeting looked clean and natural. Excellent work on their part."

"Good," Deal responded. "A little faster than I would have preferred, but we don't have any time to waste. I want Bubba to get as close as possible to this Ali Badran. There's a link to the drone attack there somewhere. I want him to check it out."

"He's already on Badran's team working on the holographic projector and drone tech. Michael and Sarah are meeting Bubba and Badran later today. Even though they don't believe Badran has ties to terrorists, they realize the need to gather all available information about him, including known associates," Sims explained.

"Alright. Let's see what they can find," Deal agreed.

In Ali Badran's lab, Bubba sat hunched over a brightly lit table wearing a pair of magnifying goggles. With intense concentration, he deftly manipulated a tiny soldering iron, making nearly microscopic electronic connections inside the power control unit of Badran's latest drone. Engrossed in his work, he didn't notice Ali enter the lab with another man and stand right next to his workstation.

Bubba stopped soldering and carefully inspected his work. Satisfied, he sat up, stretched his back, and lifted the heavy goggles onto this forehead.

"Do you think you have that circuitry sorted, my friend?" Ali asked, looking over Bubba's shoulder.

Bubba looked up, surprised to find Ali and another man standing next to him. "Oh! Hey. Well, if 'sorted' means fixed, then yes. She's good as new. But try not to smack the poor thing into any more trees."

"Yes, well, I'll try," Ali answered with a smile. "I'd like you to meet my right-hand man here in the lab, Simon Stockwell."

Bubba stood and stuck out his hand. "Bubba Adcock. Pleased to meet you."

Simon's heavy black eyebrows didn't lift from their semi-scowling position as he met Bubba's eye and shook his hand. Bubba got the distinct impression Simon didn't approve of him.

"Yes. Likewise. Ali told me we had an American working in the lab," Simon replied coolly.

"Simon is running our simulations on the drone's payload capacity. I must say he has been invaluable."

Bubba held Simon's gaze a moment longer to see if the other man's demeanor would warm a bit. It didn't.

"Excellent. I hope we get a chance to work together," Bubba said, smiling broadly.

"Yes. Well. I have work. If you'll excuse me?" Simon said, turning and hurrying off toward the other end of the laboratory.

As Simon walked away, Bubba didn't know whether to be suspicious, offended, or both.

"Friendly," Bubba said to Ali.

"Oh, don't mind Simon," Ali replied. "He's not the most personable sort, but I couldn't do without him."

"Is he a friend of yours?" Bubba asked.

Ali chuckled. "He's something of an odd bloke. Comes to work, does an excellent job, and goes home. He came to us from the Politecnico di Milano, one of the best engineering universities in Europe. I believe he's Egyptian by birth but has lived here in the UK his entire life."

"Well, if he has the chops to work here with you, he's got to be good at what he does," Bubba said. "If you're still up for joining me and my friends for a beer later, invite him along. Maybe we can thaw some of that ice out of his veins with a few pints."

"I'll do that," Ali answered. "But I'm quite sure he'll decline. I'm not entirely sure he has any friends. If he does, I wouldn't be surprised if they were as surly as him."

Bubba had a funny feeling about Simon. He liked and trusted Ali, but Simon Stockwell's attitude toward him wasn't just surly. Bubba got the distinct impression Simon didn't want him in the lab at all. No, he thought, it's more than that. His appearance in the lab had scared Simon.

The rest of the day passed quickly with Bubba and Ali making substantial progress on expanding the carrying capacity and range of Ali's drone. At around 6:00, the other lab assistants prepared to go home for the night. Still engrossed in their work, Bubba almost didn't notice Simon slipping out of the lab without a word.

Excusing himself for a moment, Bubba called Michael.

"Where are you right now?" Bubba asked.

"Sarah and I are just around the corner, actually," Michael replied, noticing the stress in Bubba's voice.

"Can you see the front of my building?" Bubba asked quickly.

"Just a second," Michael replied.

After a moment, Michael reported he could see the entrance.

"Watch for a Middle Eastern looking guy in jeans and a black leather jacket. I think he's carrying a backpack."

A minute later, Michael saw Simon appear in the lobby, pause to check his phone, and walk outside.

"Yeah, we see him. Short hair, close cut beard and a bad attitude?" Michael asked.

"That's him. I don't have time to explain. I just have a hunch. Can you see where he goes?" Bubba asked.

"No problem. Who is this guy?" Michael asked.

"Maybe a problem."

THIRTY-THREE

"What's going on?" Sarah wanted to know.

Michael took her hand and turned Sarah to face him.

"Don't look. There's a guy on the phone near the entrance Bubba wants us to follow."

"Really? Did he say why?"

"No. But he wasn't joking around. You up for this?" Michael asked, already knowing the answer.

Though more cautious than Michael, Sarah loved a challenge.

"Sure! But shouldn't we call Agent Deal or Agent Sims?" Sarah suggested.

"Let's just casually see where this guy goes. I'm sure Bubba will tell us more as soon as he can. If things get dicey, we'll call Sims. Okay?"

Sarah gave Michael one of her skeptical looks. "Okay for now. But we aren't supposed to be playing secret agent."

They didn't have time for further discussion. Simon walked away, heading in the direction of the train station.

Keeping Sarah's hand in his, the couple followed Simon at a discreet distance. They didn't want him to notice them following, but it soon became apparent they didn't need to worry. Simon was in a hurry.

"You think he's trying to catch a train?" Sarah asked.

Michael looked at his watch. "Probably. Trains to London leave every thirty minutes. The next one should be at 6:30 or so. That's in ten minutes. If he's going to London at all."

Sarah pulled out her phone. "I'm calling Agent Sims. If he's getting on a train, we're going to need help."

Just as they expected, Simon walked directly to the train station, bought a ticket, and waited on the Oxford to London platform.

"I don't see Agent Sims yet. Let's get tickets just in case," Michael suggested.

"Fine. But I'm not exactly dressed for a night out in London."

As the train arrived, Michael and Sarah found a spot on the platform where they could see Simon. When he boarded, they did the same, but in a separate car. The evening train was full and the young couple felt safe from discovery.

"You think we'll be able to find him when we get to London?" Sarah asked. "Things get crazy in the train stations."

Without warning, someone dropped into the seat opposite Michael.

"Why don't you leave that to me?" Agent Sims asked quietly. "You two aren't supposed to be following people."

"Yeah. Sorry," Michael responded a bit sheepishly.

"You're fine. But call me first next time."

"What can we do to help?" Sarah asked.

"Agent Deal said for you to get on the next train back to Oxford. We'll have all the help we need."

Sims told Michael and Sarah how Bubba had called Deal and explained his suspicions about Simon.

"Do you think that's enough to mount a full-scale operation?" Michael asked. "I mean, Bubba only just met the guy."

"Usually, no. But we're in a tight spot. All signs point to something big happening. And soon. We might be grasping at straws here but it's all we have right now. Believe it or not, Deal listens to you guys. So, if this Simon Stockwell makes Bubba twitchy, he's at least worth looking into."

"What's the plan?" Michael asked.

Sims leaned forward so others on the train couldn't hear.

"Don't worry about it."

When the train pulled into famous Paddington Station forty minutes later, Sims told Michael and Sarah to point out Simon, then casually hang around the platform until all the passengers departed. Once they did, they were to buy tickets and return to Oxford.

It took only minutes for the train passengers to disembark and start toward the exit. One car ahead, Simon stepped out and melted into the throng of commuters. When Sims had him in sight, she inserted a tiny earpiece and touched her ear to activate its voice activation feature.

"White Two to White One. Subject in sight. Male, five foot-ten, short black hair and short beard. Jeans and black jacket. Dark blue backpack. I'm on him."

Without another word, Sims joined the crowd, disappearing into the massive train station.

Michael and Sarah sat down on a nearby bench, their surveillance mission over.

"Well, crap! I feel like we're going back to Oxford with our tails between our legs," Michael pouted.

Sarah put her hand on her boyfriend's shoulder.

"Yeah. I know. But Sims didn't say *when* we had to go home. We're in London. Let's do something fun!" Sarah suggested, trying to perk up her boyfriend.

Michael shrugged. "We're supposed to meet Bubba later. Remember?"

When Sarah didn't answer, Michael looked up. Something had caught her eye.

"What are you looking at?"

"I could swear I saw someone at the back of the crowd trying to catch up to Agent Sims," Sarah explained, standing. "Let's go!"

"What?"

"Just come on!" Sarah urged, grabbing Michael's hand and pulling him to his feet without further explanation.

Before he could object, Sarah raced away down the platform.

"Aw, damn," Michael said, breaking into a sprint.

Suddenly, Sarah stopped running. Michael caught up to her a second later.

"That guy. The muscleman with the blue shirt. He's following Sims, I know it!" Sarah said, pointing ahead.

Michael could see who she meant. Sure enough, when Sims made a turn into a staircase, the man Sarah pointed out jogged ahead to the same corner and looked around it before taking the staircase down himself.

"Yeah. I think you're right. Let's go!" Michael agreed, hurrying ahead.

Now Sarah had to catch up to Michael. While she did, she somehow managed to find Sims' number on her phone. No answer.

"I tried to call her," Sarah said, when she caught up to Michael.

"Try Deal," Michael suggested. "Muscleman is at the bottom of the stairs. We better keep him in sight until we reach someone."

"Deal doesn't answer either. Probably some kind of operational security," Sarah reported, panting.

Now close enough to keep the man in the blue shirt in sight, Sarah and Michael slowed to a walk. Up ahead, they could just make out Sims' short blond hair. There wasn't any doubt about it now. Sims was being stalked.

Sarah kept trying Sims and Deal as they walked along trying to look nonchalant.

Finally, someone picked up Deal's phone.

"You were told to return to Oxford," the voice said.

"I know," Sarah responded, getting Michael's attention and pointing to the phone. "Tell Agent Deal someone is following Agent Sims. Six feet, muscular, light blue long sleeve shirt, dark, maybe black, shoulder length hair. He walks with an odd gait. Like he has an old football injury."

"Hold one."

"Damn. Nice description girl!" Michael said. "I didn't notice a limp."

"It's not really a limp. He just slightly favors his right leg."

Sarah heard a beep in her ear. Deal picked up.

"Can you stay with this guy until I get a member of Blue Team to you? Sims is aware, but she needs to stay on Simon."

"Yes, sir," Sarah replied confidently. "There's a lot of people around and we'll keep our distance."

"Blue Three is two minutes out. We'll track your phone. Don't take any chances."

"Copy that," Sarah agreed, hanging up.

"*Copy that*?" Michael commented.

"We have to keep him in sight until help gets here. Can you still see him?" Sarah asked her much taller boyfriend.

"Yeah, his shirt almost glows in the dark. Wait! He's moving faster! He might be trying to catch up to Sims!"

Michael and Sarah picked up their pace, then began jogging along the sidewalk, weaving and dodging around startled pedestrians. As they gained some ground on their target, he suddenly burst into a sprint.

Fearing an attack on Sims, Michael charged ahead of Sarah. The man in the blue shirt was fast, but Michael was faster. In the few seconds before he reached the other man, Michael saw him draw a short knife from behind his back.

Suddenly, the muscleman veered to the right into a small park, intending to catch Sims on the far side of the wooded area.

But now, Michael saw his chance. He had an angle.

The next instant, Michael crashed into the other man, hitting him low and hard at the knees. The impact felt like he had just tackled two oak trees.

The two men rolled apart and jumped to their feet facing one another. Michael couldn't miss the murderous look in his opponent's eyes or the flash of steel from the wicked-looking knife.

Then, a shrill whistle sounded to Michael's right and he saw two policemen running in their direction. In an instant, the man in the blue shirt sprinted away through the trees.

"What is going on here?" one of the officers demanded, shining a flashlight in Michael's face.

Michael had to think fast. He couldn't get involved with the police.

"I'm sorry, officer. That gentleman and I had a little disagreement. He thought I might not object if he made a play for my girlfriend," Michael explained as Sarah walked up. "He was wrong."

The officer looked at Sarah. "Was there a bloke bothering you, miss?" the officer asked, not fully buying Michael's explanation.

Sarah saw Michael's eyes grow wide.

"Absolutely. He was being rude. I asked him to leave me alone but…"

The officer looked back at Michael and Sarah as Sarah brushed leaves and debris off Michael's sweater.

"Are you alright?" she asked.

"Sure. Absolutely. Again, I'm sorry officer. I just can't let someone treat my girlfriend like that."

The officer glared at Michael for a moment before saying, "Alright then. Let's not have any more of that sort of thing."

As the officers walked off Michael heard one of them scoff, "Americans."

After the police left, Blue Three appeared from nowhere.

"Nice tackle, kid. Are you okay?"

"Uh, thanks. Yeah. You're Blue Three I take it?" Michael asked. "I could have used you a minute ago. That guy had a knife."

"Three and a half inch skinning knife with a fixed blade. I watched from behind that tree back there," Blue Three said, throwing a thumb back over his shoulder. "I got here in time for you to square off on him. If the police hadn't shown up, I would have gotten involved. Wasn't necessary."

Michael just shook his head. "Okay, I guess."

"Shouldn't we go after Agent Sims?" Sarah asked. "There could be more people following her."

"There's not. Blue Team is fully deployed now. Again, you guys did great. Now, *obey orders* and go back to Oxford before Deal gets really pissed off."

THIRTY-FOUR

A mile away, Sims stood a block down from an abandoned warehouse that looked like it had been around since the 1940s. Most of its white paint had peeled away and a long row of broken windows three stories above the street gave the place a ghostly feel. She couldn't guess what it might have been in the past, but a few minutes ago, she watched Simon unlock a side door and disappear inside.

"White Two to Blue Team. He's inside. What do we have on the thermal?"

"Blue One to White Two. One individual near northwest stairwell, second floor. Looks like he's sitting down for a smoke."

Sims didn't like it. After being followed from the train station, this felt like a trap.

"White Two to Blue Team. Hold! Hold! Back away from the building. Deploy the Black Hornet. Let's see what our suspect is up to."

On the other side of the street, Blue One reached into the canvas bag slung over his shoulder and pulled out a tiny drone. The six-inch long nano-surveillance unit looked like a toy helicopter. A single rotor sat above a roughly square body that housed a high-definition video camera. Another small rotor sat at the end of a delicate-looking tail. Holding the miniature drone between his thumb and forefinger, Blue One flipped a switch. With hardly a sound, the Hornet leapt into the air.

Controlling the drone with a cell-phone size device that produced a high-quality first-person view, Blue One flew the drone up the outside wall and through one of the broken windows. With infrared mode engaged, Blue One piloted the Hornet around the top floor. Except for trash and assorted refuse from vagrants, he found nothing.

Sims watched the video feed on her own cell phone.

"Drop her down one floor," Sims ordered.

Blue One quickly found a metal stairway near the center of the building and piloted the drone down to the next floor.

Almost immediately, the drone's camera picked up a bright orange and red silhouette sitting on a box. Every few seconds, the figure raised a cigarette that momentarily glowed white on the infrared video display.

"Get closer," Sims ordered. "Let's make sure that's our guy."

The Hornet slowly advanced toward the indistinct figure.

Then, the man stood and appeared to look directly into the drone's camera.

"Back off," Sims ordered. "Don't spook him."

But it was too late. Sims watched the man toss his smoke away and walk quickly toward the hovering drone. But when he reached the center of the building he suddenly dropped to his knees.

Slowly, as if wanting to be sure they saw what he was doing, Simon reached into his pocket and removed what looked like a small box. Placing the device in one hand, he reached both hands far over his head and looked up toward heaven.

Allah Akbar!!!

"Cover!" Sims yelled into her mic.

One second later a series of deep explosions rolled through building from front to back. Huge plumes of fire, smoke and dust shot sideways through every window. The walls briefly expanded outward, as if taking a deep breath, before collapsing inward on themselves. In mere moments, the entire warehouse disappeared, replaced by a pile of fiercely burning rubble.

Arthur watched the warehouse explosion from the roof of a nearby cheap hotel. After easily evading the police in the park, he had called Simon, informing him he was being followed. There was only one explanation. MI5 or some other law enforcement service considered him a suspect. Arthur remembered Simon's last words.

"I must not be captured. I know my duty."

The terrorist felt no remorse, even though he had sent Simon to his death. Earlier in the evening, Arthur told Simon that some evidence might have been left behind at their manufacturing facility after technicians removed their completed attack drones. Simon had become angry and insisted he personally recheck the warehouse — just as Arthur knew he would.

Arthur drew a detonating device from his pocket and stomped it to pieces under his foot. It had just been dumb luck that Simon picked up a tail after leaving the lab in Oxford. If his late cell leader hadn't been forced to kill himself, Arthur would have done it for him.

At least this way, Simon died a martyr.

Arthur stuffed his long hair under a hat, pulled a grey hoody over his light blue shirt, and turned toward the stairs.

The success of the Wolf's operation now rested in his hands, and he happily accepted the chance to prove himself. In just days, the hated English would howl in despair and cower in terror. And he would find favor with the Wolf and become a legend to the faithful.

After arriving back at the East End flat, Arthur called Tony into the living area. Donning an expression of grief, he described how Simon had bravely martyred himself by standing proudly inside the old warehouse as he detonated the charges.

Tony just nodded somberly. "Then he is in paradise as we speak."

"Yes. He did what he must. Now, we have more work to do. Please inform the Wolf of this development through the usual channels and assure him I will carry his plan forward on schedule," Arthur ordered.

Tony could hear the pride in Arthur's voice and found it disturbing. He was growing tired of the hubris appearing in the souls of those who should be leading their war against the infidels. Unlike Arthur, Tony fervently believed they fought for a righteous god and not for personal glory.

THIRTY-FIVE

Late that evening, a threat of rain hung in the air as Michael, Sarah, and Zach walked across town to The Eagle and Child pub. The narrow yellow building on St Giles' Street was built in the 1600s. Three hundred years later, its owners served drinks to famed writers such as C.S. Lewis and J.R.R. Tolkien. Oxford had many famous old pubs, but Sarah usually insisted on this one because it made her feel close to some of her favorite authors.

"You're kidding!" Zach exclaimed as they neared the pub. "You actually tackled a guy with a knife?"

"I told you, I didn't know he had one when I did it," Michael fibbed.

He hadn't told Sarah he had seen the other man draw a knife before tackling him to the ground.

"And, I didn't have any choice. He was obviously going after Agent Sims," Michael explained.

Zach had known Michael since the 6th grade and he could tell when his best friend was hiding something. But he didn't say anything.

Sarah put her arm through Michael's.

"A member of Deal's Blue Team told Michael he did good," Sarah added with pride.

"Yeah, maybe I should ask Deal if I can be on one of his tactical teams!" Michael joked.

"Oh sure. He'd be glad to have you. You know, after you finish college, enlist in the Navy, become a Seal, and join the FBI," Zach mocked. "But I'm sure he'd let you fill out an application now if you asked."

They all laughed. But Michael turned Zach's god-natured ribbing around in his mind. Maybe the idea wasn't so far-fetched.

The door to the pub creaked loudly as they ducked inside.

"Oh, wow!" Zach said quietly, as soon as they got through the door. "You guys get a table. I'll be along in a second."

Michael and Sarah immediately recognized what, or more precisely who, had grabbed Zach's attention. A lovely dark-haired girl sat crossed-legged at the bar sipping a pint of beer. Alone.

"Okay, buddy. We'll be in the back," Michael replied, slapping Zach on the back.

"Good luck!" Sarah whispered.

Zach took off his jacket and placed it over the back of a bar stool one seat away from the girl. Through the corner of his eye, he could see she was olive-skinned with wide-set coal-black eyes and long, silky black hair. Delicate hands played with her glass, and she looked into the distance as if in deep thought. A bright red rain jacket hung over the back of her barstool.

After a minute, she looked over and caught his eye. He smiled and nodded.

"Hi," Zach said.

"Hello," she replied in a silky British accent. "Having a nice evening?"

Zach couldn't believe his luck when she smiled back.

"I am. At least now. Thanks. I'm Zach. Zach Self," he blurted.

His introduction sounded awkward, even to him.

"I know who you are," the girl replied. "You're the bloke who saved the Duchess and met the Queen. I saw you on the telly. You're quite the hero."

Zach didn't really expect to be recognized so easily.

"More lucky than anything, really," Zach replied, a little sheepishly. He wasn't comfortable being thought of as a hero. "Anyone would have done the same thing."

"Don't be daft," the girl responded. "Most people would have just legged it off the train without a second thought."

Zach gave the girl a confused look. The British slang caught him off-guard.

Seeing his confusion, she gave a little laugh that almost hurt Zach's feelings.

"No! No! All I meant was, don't be silly. Most people would have just run away. Sorry," she said, quickly. "I'm Amina. Amina Kent."

Amina stuck out her hand and Zach took it warmly.

"May I buy you another beer, Amina?" Zach asked, hopefully.

"Perhaps I should buy you one. The whole country owes you a debt of gratitude," Amina countered.

"If a British girl as lovely as you bought me a beer, I'd consider that debt paid in full!" Zach replied.

"Then come join me and let's get the country evened up," Amina suggested, patting the seat next to her.

Zach had never met anyone like Amina. She was charming, confident, and easily the most captivating girl he ever met. Conversation came naturally to her and he found himself enthralled.

After about fifteen minutes, Zach asked if she would have dinner with him.

"Zach, I'm sorry. I can't tonight," Amina answered, sounding just a bit disappointed.

"Oh. Sure," Zach replied, trying not to get discouraged. "Maybe some other time."

Amina held Zach's gaze for a moment as if judging his reaction. "No. Not *maybe*. Give me your phone."

Zach couldn't get his cell phone out of his pocket quickly enough.

Amina took his phone and placed it directly over her own while she entered her number.

"There. You'll call soon, won't you?"

"Absolutely!" Zach answered. "Soon."

Amina rose from her seat, donned her raincoat, and headed toward the door. Just as she was about to walk outside, she turned and looked back at Zach.

The young man's heart nearly jumped out of his chest. Somehow, in just a few minutes, Amina had cast a spell on him.

While Zach chatted up Amina, Michael and Sarah found a cozy seat near a window in another room. Night fell early that time of year and the streetlights added a warm glow to the street scene outside. A light rain fell through the yellowish light, causing the road and sidewalks to glisten as if coated with glass.

"This is awesome!" Michael declared after they got settled. "An English pub and a gorgeous girl. I still have a hard time believing we're here."

"I know!" Sarah agreed. "And I'm sitting in the same room where some of the most famous writers in history read each other's manuscripts!"

"And, of course, the handsome lad you're with makes it perfect?" Michael asked, looking at his girlfriend.

"That's the best part," Sarah said, snuggling up to Michael.

"You think Zach will actually join us?" Michael asked.

"Maybe. We'll see how he does," Sarah replied. "I give him a fifty-fifty shot."

"Well, maybe Bubba and Ali will make it, even if Zach doesn't," Michael said, looking back out the window.

Outside, Eva McWilkinson sat watching the pub from inside her Mini Cooper. She knew she was supposed to keep away from Deal's investigation, but she had grown protective of Zach, especially after his close calls in London. She justified the surveillance to herself as part of her investigation into the train attack and to ensure a national hero didn't attract more attention from terrorists.

Watching through the pub's windows, Zach's encounter with the dark-haired girl looked innocent enough. But McWilkinson's training wouldn't allow her to take anything at face value. She considered the possibility the terrorists had switched tactics. She also entertained the idea that Sir Gregory might have assigned another agent to get close to Zach. The girl with the red raincoat looked too young to even qualify for MI5 service, but the intelligence world didn't operate strictly within the rules. Agent Deal's team being the perfect example.

McWilkinson decided not to take any chances.

When Amina got up to leave, the MI5 officer grabbed her surveillance camera and snapped a series of photos. She got lucky, catching several clear images of Amina's face in just a few seconds. After uploading the images into her tablet, she ran the pictures through the MI5's ultra-sophisticated facial recognition software. The program automatically compared Amina's picture to criminal records, passport photos, driver's license pictures, surveillance camera footage, and social media files.

After three minutes, the program displayed its results: "NO MATCH FOUND"

McWilkinson stared at the screen a moment. In the years she had used the facial recognition software it had never once failed to identify a subject. Until today.

Who are you?

THIRTY-SIX

Bubba and Ali arrived in time to see Zach and Amina exchanging telephone numbers. Bubba led Ali toward Michael and Sarah's table without acknowledging Zach. But when he chuckled as they rounded the corner, Ali became puzzled.

"What's so funny, my friend?"

"Just our friend Zach. The little guy making moves on the girl back at the bar," Bubba replied.

Ali snuck a peek backward.

"Ah, yes. Quite a lovely girl indeed. Will he be joining us?"

"Maybe. Depends on the results of his experiment," Bubba replied.

"I don't understand. Experiment?"

"Yeah. In scientific terms, Zach theorized he could get a date with that girl. Now, he's running an experiment to see if his theory is correct. If it fails, he'll join us in a few minutes. We'll see, but I really want you to meet him," Bubba explained.

"I see," Ali replied. "You really are a unique bloke, Bubba."

"I know! And I'm lovable too!" Bubba exclaimed. "Come on, there's Michael and Sarah."

As it had been several days since the drone crash in the Botanic Garden, Michael and Sarah reintroduced themselves.

"Thank you for inviting me. I hope I am not being presumptuous, but it's not often I get the chance to have a simple pint with friends," Ali said.

Bubba slapped Ali lightly on the back and raised his glass. "Not at all! Here's to friends and a simple pint of beer!"

At that moment, Zach appeared carrying five pints of cold lager. Bubba jumped up and rescued two glasses that looked close to slipping from his hands.

"This round is on me!" Zach announced, setting the cold drinks down on the table. Turning to Ali, Zach stuck out his hand and introduced himself.

"My word!" Ali exclaimed, jumping to his feet. "I had no idea I would be meeting a national hero tonight. Bubba! You failed to warn me! May I present myself. Ali Badran at your service."

"My pleasure!" Zach responded a little awkwardly, as Ali pumped his hand enthusiastically.

Everyone settled back in their seats, and Zach was glad that Ali did not make any further fuss over him. Zach knew about Ali's royal background, but found him unpretentious and genuinely friendly.

Sarah couldn't help being intrigued by Ali. And her curiosity got the better of her.

"Ali, Bubba tells us you are actually a prince. Maybe it's inappropriate of me to ask, but can you tell us about that?"

"Of course," Ali said, sitting his glass back on the table. "What would you like to know?"

"Like, where's your home? Are you close to your family? Stuff like that," Sarah responded.

Ali could see Sarah's sincere interest. She wasn't fawning or attracted to his position. She just wanted to get to know him better.

"Yes, well, my family is part of the UAE or the United Arab Emirates. As you may know, about fifty years ago, seven emirates, like small countries, came together to form the UAE. Each emirate is led by a sheik, sort of a king or leader of the clan. My grandfather is the sheik of one of those families. The smallest one, in fact, the RAK. But that's why I'm called a prince. One day, it shall fall to me to be sheik."

"You don't sound all that happy about it," Michael observed.

Ali looked into his beer and nervously turned the glass in circles. "I cannot say that I am."

Somehow, asking Ali about his future had darkened the mood at the table.

"I'm sorry, Ali," Sarah said softly, reaching across to touch Ali's arm. "I'm afraid I pried into business I shouldn't have."

"Oh, no!" Ali objected. "The image I have to maintain most of the time can be exhausting. I am thankful to be with people I feel comfortable talking with."

Michael had been observing Ali carefully. Sure, the pressures of his position had to be immense, but they lay in the future. Something else was wrong. Something imminent. Michael asked if he was right.

"You must have a third eye, Michael," Ali responded. "Yes, there is a crisis brewing for my country."

Ali explained how his family originally came from the rocky highlands in the far eastern region of the UAE. Using a map on his phone, Ali showed them a point of land on the Saudi Peninsula that jutted out like a horn into the Arabian sea.

"This is my ancestral home, Khasab. But as you can see, it is not in the UAE, but now belongs to Oman. My family owns rights to oil they just discovered near Khasab, but Oman is disputing our claim. The Iranians are now saying that they too have a right to the land's resources — under false pretenses, of course. But as you can see, Khasab sits less than forty miles from Iran at the narrowest part of the Persian Gulf called the Strait of Hormuz."

Sarah asked, "And this is putting pressure on your family?"

Ali nodded. "Indeed. The other emirates desperately want my family to defend our claim to the oil field. My grandfather is doing the best he can, but he is in failing health. My father died when I was an infant…"

"So, you are the next in line," Michael concluded, finishing Ali's sentence.

Ali looked more disheartened than ever. "Yes. I am a scientist, not a politician. I am unprepared for such a responsibility. Yet, I could be called home at any moment."

"Wow. That just sucks!" Sarah blurted.

Sarah's unexpected reaction caused Ali to laugh. "Yes. Yes, it does! But worrying will not change what is to come. I should just enjoy the night and the fine company I find myself in."

"Agreed! And we should all enjoy another round of beer! And maybe some of those fish and chips while we're at it!" Bubba pronounced.

"Yes. And I am buying this evening," Ali announced.

The others objected, but Ali insisted.

"Despite my boorish story earlier, I have two reasons to celebrate tonight. First, meeting new friends is one of life's greatest joys. Second, and Bubba doesn't even know this yet, but thanks to his help, we have achieved 150 pounds or nearly 68 kilograms of payload capability on our drones with a flight time of over two hours! We are about to revolutionize not only package delivery, but perhaps the entire transportation industry."

"You've run the initial test protocols?" Bubba asked, excitedly.

"Yes. Not just simulations. I took the vehicle out late last evening and ran an initial real-world flight evaluation. There is little we cannot now lift, carry and deliver anywhere within the extended range of the drone's new power cell."

THIRTY-SEVEN

Randall Snow, aka the Wolf, picked up one of his three cell phones and entered a series of numbers that both unlocked the device and engaged complex scrambling software. The program not only hid his identity and scrambled the signal beyond all possible recognition; it also implanted a code that made it appear the call originated in Geneva, Switzerland.

With this phone, he communicated only as the Wolf. And very few people had his number. As the day for the main operation was approaching, Snow decided the Wolf should speak directly with the team responsible for launching the attack.

"We are secure. Speak," Snow ordered in his perfect Arabic.

"My sheik, this is Tony. May I report?"

"You may report," Snow responded.

"Thank you, my sheik. Your drones are ready in all respects. On your command, we will upload the final data sets and transport them to the initiation points you identified," Tony said. "Also, as you ordered, the warehouse housing our manufacturing facility was destroyed. I must also report that someone followed Simon to the facility and he died in the blast."

"I understand. Simon died a martyr. He shall find his reward in heaven. Your team may proceed with final preparations and transport to the launch points. The instruments of death to be carried by the drones shall be provided at a time Allah shall choose. Do nothing else until I so order. Do you understand these things?"

"Perfectly, my sheik."

Snow hung up without another word. *Cattle don't require thanks.*

"Nigel!" Snow called out to his butler. "Please get Santiago on the phone. And bring me a brandy. I want to celebrate a little."

"Of course, sir."

A moment later, Nigel reported he had Santiago holding.

"Madam Director," Snow said, picking up the phone. "I have good news."

"Then spill it, Snow. I don't have time for small talk," Margie Franks replied in her usual brusque tone.

"The drones are nearly ready. We are beginning final preparations tomorrow."

"Good. You're on time. What kind of range do you have?"

"Enough so that we can hit any target within a hundred miles of our launch sites. Once we begin, we can attack with single drones or swarm a target from multiple directions," Snow reported. "I've transmitted a map of our launch points. Targets and timing will be at your discretion."

"Excellent. Keep your johnson in your pants until we get back to you," Franks said.

"Of course, Madam Director," Snow replied.

He didn't notice that Margie Franks had abruptly hung up on him.

Snow picked up his large tablet computer and opened the map of drone launch locations. Six red dots roughly surrounded the city of London. A red circle around each dot delineated the maximum range of the drone assigned to the individual launch sites. One red dot appeared just outside Edenborough, Scotland. The final drone would be transported across the Irish Sea to the Isle of Man.

The interlocking circles brought most of the British Isles within range of one or more attack drones.

THIRTY-EIGHT

The Pacifico Hotel
El Quisco, Chile

The famously luxurious Pacifico Hotel caters to only the most privileged clientele. Perched on some of the most expensive real estate in South America, the forty-story glass and steel hotel offers stunning views of the Pacific Ocean and Chilean coastal range. Guests choose the Pacifico not for its vistas, beaches, or exemplary service, but for the privacy and discretion guaranteed by the hotel's professional staff and remote location.

Fifty miles from the county's capital of Santiago, guests arrive by private helicopter. Inside, they enjoy unique suites, each designed by world-class decorators. Once ensconced in the Pacifico, visitors lack for nothing. Several gourmet chefs provide five-star meals delivered by white-gloved butlers around the clock. Anyone rich enough can experience the singular experience of the Pacifico. But only twelve people on earth may stay on the top floor.

Since the hotel opened more than twenty years ago, the entire top floor has been reserved for the twelve Directors of an organization dubbed The Cause.

Just before midnight, a black Airbus Dauphin 2 executive helicopter settled gently onto the Pacifico's rooftop helipad. In seconds, hotel staff unrolled a dark blue carpet leading from the highly polished elevator to the helicopter's already-open door.

Stairs lowered to the carpet with a soft hum as a couple emerged from inside, chatting amiably and sipping from crystal champagne flutes. Without acknowledging any of the staff, they descended the stairs, crossed the carpet and disappeared into the elevator. After dropping one level, they headed straight into the top floor's expansive conference room.

"Before the others arrive, how about filling me in on the UK operation?" Alexander Monroe asked ex-governor Margie Franks.

Margie looked up at the striking seventy-six-year-old real estate tycoon. Monroe's full silver-gray hair, square jaw, and muscled physique made him look at least twenty-five years younger than his actual age. Margie, a fit sixty-two, couldn't deny her attraction to her fellow Director. And she didn't hide it.

Placing a hand on the lapel of his Armani sport coat, Margie looked into Monroe's bright blue eyes.

"You know that's against the rules, Alexander," Margie replied, edging her body closer to his.

"Why don't we wait for everyone else to arrive, uh, in my suite," Monroe offered suggestively.

"Now that's a not a bad idea. Unfortunately, we don't have time," Margie said, turning to pluck a bottle of Dom Perignon from an ice bucket. "But I suppose a quick preview of our meeting wouldn't make any difference."

"Fantastic! We'll revisit the other issue after the meeting," Monroe responded, taking a seat in a dark grey leather club chair.

Margie sat on a matching couch, allowing her knee to touch Monroe's.

"Killing the real Wolf terrorist asshole and replacing him with Snow was inspired, Alexander. Through him, we now have complete control of the Wolf's followers all over the world. And Snow operates the entire network with nothing more than a costume and an internet connection," Margie began.

Monroe laughed. "And the masses wonder how people like us make so much money. They just believe whatever they see on a screen. Amazing! But, go ahead."

Margie refilled their glasses before continuing. "The next phase begins within the next twenty-four to forty-eight hours."

"That's nearly two weeks ahead of schedule, Margie. I congratulate you on the efficiency of the operation. It must have been quite a task to get all the assets in place," Monroe said, saluting Margie with his glass.

Margie returned the compliment. "Thank you, Alexander. Your idea about how to use the lost nuclear weapon was nothing less than inspired."

"Has it been put in place?" Monroe asked, already knowing the answer.

"It will be by this time tomorrow night. Once it is, we have to move quickly. We cannot risk it being discovered."

"Agreed. Then let the countdown begin!" Monroe exclaimed, a smile of self-satisfaction on his face.

Port of Khasab
Oman

The old coastal freighter, the Queen of the Sea, made its usual turn into the Port of Khasab on the northwest tip of the Arabian Peninsula. If the ship's name ever fit, it long ago became a joke. The old freighter now bore the scars of neglect. Streaks of rust ran down its sides, obscuring the black and white color scheme. Bullet holes from an attack by Somali pirates almost a decade before still pockmarked the bow. Onboard, two dozen shipping containers sat side by side on the open deck, carrying two weeks of supplies for the local tourism and cruise industry. Every two weeks, like clockwork, the Queen of the Sea delivered food, linens, beverages, replacement parts and maintenance supplies that kept the port's small fleet of cruise ships afloat.

That morning, the cargo included something much less conventional.

Even as the ship slowly pulled up against its usual berth, cranes swung over the ship, ready to snatch the shipping containers off the deck.

Ashore, Dr. Dave Knox carefully observed the unloading process while holding a single piece of paper in his hand – authorization for the dock workers to place one special shipping container on a tractor-trailer idling nearby. A well-placed bribe insured the dock workers unloaded the container he needed first. Next to Dave, a huge black man wearing desert fatigues and dark sunglasses waited with thickly-muscled arms folded across his chest.

To Dave's relief, the overhead crane moved directly to a marred and dented blue container situated on the far side of the ship. Once the crew attached appropriate straps, the container lifted high into the air and swung quickly across the dock. Dave had a moment of panic when it shifted slightly just before it lowered slowly onto the bed of the transport trailer.

Dave's driver, a bad-tempered Omani who called himself Ajmal, walked around the trailer securing the twist-locks that held the container in place. As he worked, the driver sweated profusely, adding to the already greasy appearance of his skin. Dark shifty eyes under a heavy brow glanced from side to side as if he expected trouble at any moment.

Dave followed the driver, enduring a fog of cigarette smoke and double-checking every lock. Meanwhile, Dave's bodyguard paced back and forth behind the rig appearing to be bored. But Dave knew this was an act. If the man's imposing appearance wasn't enough to discourage anyone from approaching, the skills he learned as a commando with the Kenya Defense Forces would.

With the cargo properly loaded, Ajmal climbed into the truck's cab.

"We go! We go now!" Ajmal shouted in broken English, waving Dave inside.

With Dave's bodyguard standing next to the container on the trailer, Dave climbed into the cab. He didn't expect luxury, but the interior of the truck didn't even look functional. An incomprehensible tangle of multi-colored wires fell like strange jungle vines below the remnants of a dashboard that had been covered by corrugated tin roofing material. Dave's seat looked like it had been attacked by a mountain lion and smelled like urine.

"We go!" Ajmal announced again, grinding the gearbox into first and releasing the clutch. The truck bucked and jerked until it gained forward momentum. Dave could appreciate the need to fly under the radar, but this much local flavor didn't seem necessary.

Dave couldn't believe where he was or what he was doing. Two days before, Margie Franks had insisted he meet the cargo container in Oman, dismissing Dave's arguments that his expertise wasn't needed. Nonetheless, within 36 hours he found himself in Muscat, Oman, waiting on a flight to the hot, dusty town of Khasab.

Finally rolling smoothly down one of the few paved roads in the area, Dave produced a map and showed Ajmal their destination.

Ajmal looked at the map, shrugged and stuck another cigarette in his mouth.

"Okay. Tibat. Okay. Two hour," Ajmal proclaimed, turning onto the Khasab Coastal Road.

"Okay, good," was the only thing Dave could think to say.

"Tibat *no* good," Ajmal said, looking at Dave and smiling through stained, crooked teeth.

Dave didn't know what the Omani meant. But it didn't improve his mood.

THIRTY-NINE

"What was Simon working on?" Deal demanded, standing inside Ali's lab at Oxford.

Bubba and Ali stood beside one of the lab stations while Deal walked around picking up various pieces of electronics and drone parts. Simon's suicide, combined with the attempted drone attack, led to only one conclusion. Simon had used Ali's advanced drone technology for terrorist activity.

"Agent Deal," Ali responded, calmly. "All of our research is open for your inspection. Simon was working with me on improving the capacity and range of our drones. I have kept the university fully informed of our progress. Several of the world's most esteemed aeronautical engineering professors here have both followed and supervised our progress."

"Yeah, Boss. I have been here working closely with Ali. Not to brag, but I helped his team make advances that leapfrog everything else available on the market today," Bubba added.

Deal slammed a hand down on a stainless-steel lab table hard enough to make the instruments and parts resting on it jump. He had missed the clues, and they were running out of time. If it hadn't been for Bubba's hunch about Simon, they might not have the few hours, days at most, to stop whatever plan Simon had been a part of.

"Alright. What can these things do? What's their maximum range and payload? What are we dealing with here?" Deal asked, getting back to the business of catching terrorists.

"We have not run a maximum range test. But the maximum payload is 150 pounds. Our calculations show that with a max load and with a fully charged power cell, the range will be approximately 100 miles," Ali replied.

"Was there any security in place to keep this technology safe?" Deal asked.

"We were working on drones for commercial use. This was not a classified project," Ali responded.

"Then, no," Deal concluded. "Great. How many of these things are there?"

"One," Bubba answered. "And it's sitting on that table at the back of the lab."

"Could this Simon have produced more? Copied what was happening here?" Deal wanted to know.

"Parts would not have been difficult to acquire. But Simon would have had to duplicate our software and power cell upgrades," Ali replied. "He was a gifted engineer, so..."

"Yes," Deal said, finishing Ali's sentence.

"Yes," Ali agreed.

"Then he could build more than one," Deal said.

"Shit," Bubba said, suddenly realizing the scope of possible terrorist activity using drones had just increased exponentially.

"Necessary parts are available, but not plentiful," Ali observed. "If he marshalled all the available parts in the UK and even America, he could build six, maybe ten, with identical capability to ours."

"Alright then, geniuses, let's look at worst case scenarios. Can you put together some possibilities? Assume targets are all in the U.K. Also assume they have ten drones with the same capabilities as the one here in the lab. We don't know what they plan to use as a weapon, but gas or high explosives of some kind make the most sense to me. Since we don't have that information, let's concentrate on range and targets," Deal suggested.

"I agree, but concerning the payload, there's another possibility, Boss," Bubba said, his face uncharacteristically serious.

"I know," Deal replied. "A dirty bomb."

"Or a small nuke. It doesn't take much fissile nuclear material to make a bomb that can take out five or six square blocks and irradiate a city for decades. Plus, putting together a rudimentary but working nuclear weapon isn't as hard as most people think," Bubba added.

"Is it possible extremists could obtain such material?" Ali asked, stunned by the possibility.

"Unfortunately, yes," Deal answered. "The Russians' nuclear security has been a joke for almost thirty years. We know of at least two instances where plutonium has been sold to unknown parties by corrupt Russian officials. We Americans have lost seven nuclear weapons over the years. Four of those are still missing."

"That is disturbing," Ali commented.

Deal had studied such nightmares many times. "Yeah. Drones dropping nerve gas or delivering high explosives could kill a lot of people. Detonating nuclear weapons can start a war that could kill *everyone*."

Bubba and Ali worked for the next hour running scenarios through a program meant to schedule drone-delivered packages. By entering delivery addresses, the weight of packages, and type of drone used, the program provided the most efficient schedule, flight routes, and recharging times.

Deal provided a list of targets he felt would attract terrorists, including Big Ben, Parliament, Buckingham Palace, the London Eye, Westminster Chapel and the British Museum. The events of September 11, 2001, proved that destroying a treasured national landmark did an excellent job of terrifying the people and provoking changes throughout an entire society. But even as he assembled his list, the FBI agent knew the terrorists always had the upper hand in one crucial way – without unequivocal intelligence, nobody could perfectly anticipate where or when they might strike.

In military terms, the terrorists had the element of surprise.

"Okay, Boss. Come take a look," Bubba said when they finished. "We'll put it up on the big monitor."

Using a remote control, Ali cast a map of southern England centered on London onto a monstrous screen mounted on the wall. Red dots identified Deal's targets.

"We began by simply drawing a circle one hundred miles out from each target. This represents the drone's maximum range carrying maximum payload. They can launch from the edge of the circle, but they could not recover the drones because they would consume all their available energy just getting to the target," Ali explained. "As you can see, the potential launch area encompasses all of what we consider southeast England from Norwich in the northeast to Bournemouth in the southwest. They could even launch from a boat in the English Channel."

"That doesn't do us any good. The area is just too big," Deal growled.

"Certainly. So, we speculated that the terrorists would indeed want to recover their drones, if possible. Each would be incredibly valuable to their cause and supremely expensive to replace. Plus, if the drones returned, they wouldn't risk leaving evidence behind. So, we narrowed the circle to fifty miles," Ali explained as the circles on the screen tightened.

"All this is doing is telling us what we already know. Drones are easily transportable, can be flown from anywhere without an airstrip, and that we have no chance of finding them in time," Deal said.

"We have to define a problem before it can be solved, Boss," Bubba explained.

Ali added, "Your observation is correct Agent, except these drones are extremely complex and require an exceptional amount of support. They aren't like drones you can pull out of a box and take pictures of your house from the air. In fact, they will need a facility comparable to this one to fully utilize their capabilities. They will need high-capacity computing capability and a dedicated charging station – like Tesla uses for its home car charging systems."

"And have you narrowed down where they might find facilities that match those criteria?" Deal asked.

"There are only two in the entire country. Our lab here in Oxford and the aerospace labs in Cambridge," Ali pointed out.

"Good work," Deal said.

At that moment, Ali's phone rang. Looking at the screen, his face went pale.

Deal noticed Ali's expression. "You better answer it."

Ali pressed the phone to his ear. "Yes?"

After listening a moment, Ali sat down heavily in a lab chair and placed his forehead into his hand. His entire body seemed to drain of life and a tear rolled down his cheek.

"I understand. I shall return immediately."

Bubba knew right away what the call was about. He put a hand on Ali's shoulder and asked, "Your grandfather?"

Ali just nodded.

"I'm sorry, buddy," Bubba said, as gently as possible.

Deal remained silent. He knew all about the precarious situation in the UAE and Ali's potential responsibilities from Sims' in-depth research on the Arab prince.

Ali took a few deep breaths and stood.

"Agent Deal. I'm afraid I must leave. Bubba knows everything you need to assist with your investigation. I pray you are successful stopping whatever is happening here. I consider England my second home."

"I understand Your Highness," Deal replied, intentionally using Ali's new title. "Can we assist you in any way?"

"If I had my wish, I would ask Bubba to accompany me to my country. I have come to consider him a trusted friend," Ali replied. "But he must stay here. His expertise will be needed."

"I agree," Deal said.

Bubba thought a minute.

"I wish I could go along, too. But I have an idea," Bubba pronounced. "How about getting Michael and Sarah to go with you?"

"I would welcome them with open arms. I will need someone I can rely on who will not try to influence me when I get home," Ali said, his mood brightening a bit.

"I can't spare them either," Deal said flatly.

"Hold on, Boss," Bubba said. "Consider this. You brought us here to figure out whether there is a terrorist threat with some connection to Oxford. With the drone attack on Zach, Simon's intimate involvement with this new drone tech, and his suicide, I think we have the answer to that question. Plus, isn't it a bit convenient that a terrorist threat here in the UK raises its ugly head just as the situation between the UAE, Oman, and Iran heats up? What if they are somehow related? Eyes on the ground there wouldn't hurt. In fact, maybe consider sending Agent Sims, as well."

Deal rubbed his chin, a sure sign he was considering Bubba's suggestion. Not for the first time, he found himself profoundly impressed by his young team's insight. And, even if it turned out that there was no connection between the threats in the UK and the simmering crisis in the Middle East, having an agent on the ground with access to one of the UAE's sheiks could provide valuable intelligence to the United States.

"Your Highness?" Deal asked. "Would you allow an FBI agent to accompany you to your country? Agent Stella Sims is one of our best."

Ali looked at Bubba for his advice.

"She really is the best. I'd trust her with my life and have done so in the past. You can, too."

"Then by all means, yes!" Ali responded, thankfully. "But I must ask that she not reveal herself as an American law enforcement officer when we arrive. Officials in my country will write off the appearance of three young friends at my side as a simple whim of youth. An FBI agent would be more difficult for me to explain. We must leave immediately. Please have Michael, Sarah, and Agent Sims meet us at Oxford Airport near Kidlington in one hour — if they agree, of course. Bubba. Agent. Best of luck here."

After they all shook hands and Ali left, Deal and Bubba stayed behind a moment.

"Do you really think there could be a connection between what's going on here and the situation in Ali's country?" Deal asked.

"Yep. Wasn't it you that said never to believe in coincidences?"

"Yes. But the connection is tenuous at best."

Bubba nodded. "Agreed. But what does your gut tell you, Boss?"

"That something bad, real bad, is about to happen in both places."

"So, what's our next move?" Bubba asked.

"I'm going to call Sir Gregory about the lead you and Ali suggested about the lab in Cambridge. Then, I'm going to send Red Team up there."

FORTY

"I understand," Amina said, standing alone in the ladies' room of a quaint Italian restaurant near the center of Oxford. "I'm with him now. How do you want to proceed?"

After listening to her orders, Amina ran a brush through her hair and freshened her makeup in the mirror over the sink. Satisfied, she returned to her table.

Zach stood and gallantly held out Amina's seat as she sat down.

"I have horrible news," she said, sounding a bit stressed. "I have to run up to Cambridge tonight. My boss needs me to pick up a packet of documents that must be filed in court tomorrow. Quite a bother."

"Really!?" Zach responded, disappointed. It had been almost a week since he met the beautiful girl at the Eagle & Child and he had been looking forward to their date for days. "We haven't even ordered yet."

"I wish it could wait, Zach. He's a high-powered barrister who doesn't take no for an answer, I'm afraid. One of his solicitors has located original source documents at the university's law library that are crucial in a massive international law case. By the time I return, it will be quite late," Amina replied, gathering her things.

"Oh?" Zach said, beginning to feel like Amina was intentionally cutting their first date short.

Amina reached across the table and put her hand on Zach's arm.

"Yes. I do have an idea, though. Why not come along? The drive is bloody boring. But if you come along, we can at least spend the time getting to know each other," Amina suggested, looking at Zach with deep, searching eyes.

Zach jumped at the offer. "Absolutely! I'll pay and meet you outside in two minutes!"

Amina took her coat and walked quickly outside. Once alone, she pulled her cell phone out of her pocket. "Tell them I will have the American in Cambridge within the hour. We will be in the back lot of the Faculty of Law Building."

University of Cambridge
Aerospace and Aerothermal Engineering Laboratory

"How many more drones still need to be calibrated?" Arthur demanded. "The Americans know we are here."

"We have completely programed five and sent them on to their launch points. We have these three, which still require the proper uploads. We need another three hours," Tony responded, not looking up from his computer screen.

"You have one."

"Is it worth risking our lives and the operation to complete these as well?" Tony asked, instantly regretting his well-intentioned question.

Arthur bent down and hissed into Tony's ear. "Your life is not your own. It belongs to God and his instrument on earth, the Wolf. Do not question his decisions or mine again. All drones will be at their launch points tomorrow morning as the Wolf has ordered. *All.* If you fail in this task, you will die by my hand."

Tony nodded. "Then I will not fail."

Sweat ran down Tony's neck despite the lab's 60-degree temperature, maintained to cool the school's Cray supercomputer. Simon's death had forced Tony to take over the final drone preparations. He knew he could finish the job, but it stretched his abilities to the maximum. Tony prayed he would complete his responsibilities on time. But he also prayed for the patience to persevere against Arthur's personal ambition and constant threats.

"I must leave now," Arthur announced. "It may cost my own life, but I have a plan to buy the time we need."

Tony wanted to scoff at Arthur's feigned offer of personal sacrifice. Instead, he kept his eyes pointed at his computer screen.

"Then may Allah protect you."

Or choose you be martyred, as the prophet sees fit, Tony thought ruefully.

Near midnight, Amina drove her aging Volvo into the parking lot behind the Faculty of Law Building at the University of Cambridge. The law school's ultra-modern wave-like curving glass exterior stood out among the other traditional, classic buildings on campus. Metal sculptures placed on the manicured lawn added to the school's unexpectedly contemporary feel.

Zach knew that lawyers around the world considered Cambridge's law school to be one of the best. He stared up at the structure for a moment, thinking about what it would be like to actually attend such a prestigious institution.

"Impressive, isn't it?" Amina asked, noticing Zach's interest.

"Absolutely. I'm actually considering going to law school someday. I bet this place is tough to get into," Zach responded, a little wistfully.

"I don't know. You have royal connections now. Maybe the queen could ring them up for you," Amina suggested, needling Zach.

"Ha! I'm old news," Zach replied. "Where is this guy you're meeting?"

"Probably just finishing up. It looks like we have a minute. Want to get out and have a look around? I could use a walk after our drive," Amina offered.

Amina and Zach got out of the car and strolled around the building.

"I know of a cozy bench we could wait if you're not too cold," Amina suggested, putting her arm through Zach's and leading him across the parking lot to a small stand of trees.

Zach couldn't have been happier. He was with a beautiful girl on a lovely evening and things looked promising!

Amina sat on a bench where the lights from the parking lot couldn't penetrate. Zach sat down close to her, enjoying her warmth and the exotic scent of her perfume. When she turned her face to him, he couldn't help but lean in for a kiss.

The barrel of a gun pressed against the back of Zach's head terminated the romantic mood.

"Do not move," a voice said.

Zach slowly raised his hands and looked at Amina. The fact that she had led him into a trap dawned on him all at once.

"Why?" he asked.

Amina stood and looked the young man in the face. "I doubt you will live long enough to worry about *why.*"

"My men will take him to the safehouse. This worthless American's telephone will draw the FBI to our position," Arthur said, still pressing his gun against Zach's head.

"My source says the FBI team is to arrive in less than thirty minutes," Amina replied.

"My men will hold off the Americans as long as possible. We need all the time we can get in the lab," Arthur explained. "While the fools chase after this one puny infidel, we will finally have completed all preparations. I complement your handling of this diversion."

"I don't give a shit about your compliments. Only your money," Amina scoffed.

Zach stood motionless. Though terrified, he worked to keep his wits about him. With few options, he resolved to risk bolting into the trees at the first sign of an opening. Hoping Amina and the other man would argue further, he glanced around, trying to find the best path to quick cover.

Then something caught his eye.

From across the parking lot, someone was trying to get his attention. He could barely see a person crouched behind a large metal sculpture placed near the building. When he finally realized who it was, he was nearly overcome with relief.

Eva McWilkinson held out a hand. She wanted him to stay put.

Zach looked at McWilkinson and gave an almost imperceptible nod of his head.

"Take him now. Time is running out," Amina ordered, turning back to her car.

Arthur lowered his pistol to Zach's back. "Move."

Zach heard Amina's car start and drive away. At the edge of the lot, a white van waited with its side door open. Zach saw that they would have to walk right by McWilkinson's hiding place to get there. He needed to distract the man with a gun in his back until they passed by her position.

"Hey, man. You don't have to do this!" Zach whined, trying to sound as pitiful as possible. "I don't know what this is about and it's none of my business…"

"Shut up, or I'll shoot you right here. It is better if you live until we reach the safehouse, but it is not necessary," Arthur snarled.

Zach walked slowly with his head down, and he did his best to sniffle and wipe non-existent tears from his eyes – anything to keep the much larger man's attention on him for a few more seconds.

"You are a coward," Arthur declared with disgust as they passed the sculpture.

"Stop!" McWilkinson shouted, stepping forward with her weapon aimed squarely at Arthur's back.

She had the drop on the big Arab, but with the reaction time of a cobra, Arthur spun to his left and fired three quick shots at the MI5 officer. His first two shots went wide, smacking into the glass walls of the law school. The third ricocheted off the iron sculpture slicing a furrow across McWilkinson's scalp.

The MI5 officer fell backward, a river of blood instantly blinding her right eye.

In the brief confusion, Zach stepped forward, spun around and landed a vicious kick to the side of Arthur's knee.

Arthur grunted in pain, but the kick didn't do the damage Zach hoped. Instead, it just served to refocus the terrorist's attention back on him.

Zach saw hate and rage burning in Arthur's eyes as the terrorist's gun swung toward him. Once again out of options, Zach faked a move to the right and then sprinted away in the other direction.

Arthur gave a quick laugh. The young American was a sitting duck.

Even as Zach turned toward the trees, Arthur took his time, aiming to send the godless young infidel to hell with a single shot to the head.

His finger tightened on the trigger.

Then, the terrorist's head slammed forward, blood and bone erupting from the center of his forehead. Dead before he ever hit the ground, Arthur never felt the cold dark asphalt smash into his face.

Zach heard the shot and instinctively ducked. But nothing happened. At first, he thought the terrorist must have missed him. But then he heard McWilkinson call out. *Zach*!

Turning, Zach saw Arthur face down, his pistol still clutched in his dead hand. Beyond him, McWilkinson stood holding a scarf over a bleeding head wound.

Zach stood for a moment, catching his breath, and trying to come to terms with the fact that he wasn't dead. Then, seeing McWilkinson kneeling on the ground, he ran back to her.

"You're shot!" he exclaimed.

"Don't be a wanker!" McWilkinson snapped. "I know that. It looks worse than it is. Go to my car. There's a first aid kit in the boot."

Zach retrieved the kit and pressed a clean pad of gauze onto the three-inch gash on McWilkinson's scalp.

"You saved my life! Thank you," Zach said.

"You saved mine. We're even," McWilkinson replied.

"Bullcrap. I ran like a chickenshit."

"Oh my," McWilkinson said, laughing. "That's a quite lot of barnyard excrement."

"Huh?"

McWilkinson looked at Zach seriously. "You did exactly right. If you hadn't smashed his knee and run, he would have killed us both. You bought enough time for me to recover my senses. Well done. Now perhaps you should call Agent Deal."

Zach fished in his pocket for his cell phone. "Why not your boss at MI5?"

"I have my reasons."

FORTY-ONE

Tony's phone rang inside the aerospace lab. One of Arthur's men reported the events at the law school. The American had escaped, destroying their plan to use him as a decoy. Now, the FBI team could be at their location at any moment.

"Take the drones and go! Now!" Tony ordered several surprised technicians.

"But only one of the three is ready. That will give Wolf's operation only six weapons with which to attack our enemy. Arthur ordered they all be completed," a slight, wide-eyed, young tech objected.

Tony walked up to the man and slapped him hard across the face. "Arthur is dead. You will obey me now!"

Tony's team hurriedly packed up and carried the heavy aircraft out to a tall white van waiting outside.

Tony climbed in beside the drones. As soon as he closed the doors, the driver pulled slowly onto the streets of Cambridge. When the city lay a few miles behind, they turned west onto a busy two-lane highway. Tony kept a close watch out the back windows of the van, expecting to see the blue lights of a police car or a helicopter flying overhead. His fear of immediate capture began to ebb as they turned south in the direction of London on the A1 – Britain's version of an interstate highway.

Merging into the heavy traffic, they blended into the unending river of headlights moving south toward the nation's capital.

After just a few miles, the van exited the highway at a sleepy town with the quaint name of Biggleswade. Houses and apartments in town quickly gave way to lush English countryside. At that time of year, the fields lay quiet, the farmers not yet beginning the process of preparing the soil for the next growing season.

As the black night sky began to give way to the gray of dawn, they drove through a set of broken-down wooden gates hanging loosely on their hinges. The van bumped over a neglected field, slowly plowing through a light fog that hung over the ground. A minute later, they stopped in front of a metal building that once held pens for sheep and assorted farming equipment.

"Get the drone ready," Tony ordered, pulling his cell phone from his pocket.

The terrorist walked outside and drew in a long, deep breath of the clean country air. The first rays of dawn radiated though a grove of trees at the edge of the field, scattering golden light through the mist on the ground and making the dew on the field glimmer as if coated with diamond dust. He stood a moment longer basking in the feeling of being alive.

Perhaps heaven will be like this.

Gathering his courage, Tony swiped open his phone and made the call he knew could lead directly to his own death.

"Speak," the Wolf said.

"This is Tony. May I report?"

"Why is it not Arthur making this report?" the Wolf asked.

"Arthur is dead."

"Proceed."

"Six of eight drones are prepared. The Americans threatened the operation and we were forced to abort final preparations. All available drones are at their launch points, armed as instructed, and ready for operations. The drones intended for Scotland and the Isle of Man did not receive adequate programming," Tony stated, sounding as confident as possible.

"Who is responsible for this failure?" the Wolf asked, his voice low and controlled.

Tony knew that blaming Arthur would sound empty, even though it was the dead man's responsibility to delay the Americans. If he shouldered the blame himself, he would forfeit his own life. Either way, he stood in a dangerously precarious situation.

"Arthur undertook the mission to distract the enemy. He failed," Tony answered truthfully.

A long silence finally ended when the Wolf said, "You will ensure the other drones are ready to carry out their missions. Your life will be forfeited if even one drone fails. Do you understand this?"

"Yes, my sheik," Tony answered.

"You will deploy the drones today at 5:00 p.m. Attacks will occur as each drone arrives on target," the Wolf ordered.

"It shall be done, my sheik."

FORTY-TWO

Sir Gregory paced back and forth over the antique Persian rug in his office while Frank Deal briefed him on the events that took place in Cambridge.

"We think the attempt to kidnap Zach Self was a diversion to lead us away from where the terrorists were making upgrades or doing some kind of work on several advanced drones that we now know are in the hands of terrorists. If it hadn't been for Officer McWilkinson, Zachary Self would be dead," Deal explained.

"She is a remarkable officer," Sir Gregory responded. "And I'm glad our young hero was unharmed. McWilkinson suffered only a minor flesh wound during the encounter."

"Sir Gregory, I must ask, did you task McWilkinson with monitoring my team? Our agreement specified complete independence," Deal asked.

"Ah. No. However, I did order her to keep an eye on Mr. Self. Only for his safety, of course. Something must have caught her attention to have caused her to follow him and the unidentified girl from Oxford all the way to Cambridge."

"That's not really important now," Deal said, dismissing the issue. "Between six and ten extremely capable drones are already deployed somewhere in England. We don't know how they are armed or their intended targets. My team is working on possible ways to track the drones once airborne as well as any available defenses."

"Our best people are working on that, as well. Although, I'm informed low-flying drones are extremely hard to detect. I'm afraid we're in for quite a bad row," Sir Gregory replied. "By the way, I expected Agent Sims to accompany you today. But I'm sure you have her busily engaged in the investigation."

"Yes, of course. She's in Oxford working with our best technical expert, Mr. Adcock, on defensive measures. I'll give her your regards."

"Yes. Please do. I must admit my mind is raking me over the coals when I consider worst-case scenarios. If these drones are as capable as we think, they could attack anywhere, at any time. The public could become unhinged."

"We'll do our best to get these guys before that happens," Deal said, standing. "I'll be in touch."

Deal left MI5 headquarters and walked down the sidewalk next to the Thames River. In the distance, Big Ben stood keeping watch over the city. Across the river, the London Eye turned slowly, carrying tourists high into the air. Everywhere he looked, he saw possible targets. As much as that concerned him, something else bothered him more.

After two more blocks, Deal turned into a small restaurant. Sitting in a booth near the back, Eva McWilkinson was pretending to read the menu. The FBI agent slipped into the booth across from her and ordered coffee.

"Did you ask him?" McWilkinson asked.

"I did. He said he ordered you to keep an eye on Zach," Deal replied.

"He ordered me to stay completely away from your investigation. He lied."

"I could tell. But why?" Deal wanted to know.

"Amina Kent, almost assuredly not her real name, is the same girl I photographed outside the pub in Oxford. As I said, facial recognition came up with nothing. At the time, I thought Sir Gregory might have assigned her to get close to Zach – and your investigation. Did the FBI have any more luck?"

"We still don't know her true identity, and she is not with MI5. But she is certainly connected to Sir Gregory."

"What?" McWilkinson blurted almost too loudly. "How do you know that?"

Deal looked around to be sure nobody was paying attention and leaned forward.

"The day before she met Zach at the pub, this so-called Amina Kent entered Sir Gregory's private apartment at 11:00 in the evening. She left at 5:47 the next morning," Deal said.

McWilkinson's eyes grew wide and she had to work hard to control her reactions. Her worst fears had just been realized. Amina Kent tried to kidnap and kill Zach. And Sir Gregory knew about it.

"Explain," McWilkinson said.

"It's perhaps not my country's finest moment, but we maintain standard surveillance on Sir Gregory at all times. They recorded Amina Kent's overnight visit," Deal admitted. "After checking our logs, it seems Sir Gregory often, uh, entertained various women at his place. Female companions don't raise red flags – until we know the female is working directly with known terrorists. There's no doubt about it. The Director of MI5, the highest-ranking intelligence officer in the UK, is ..."

McWilkinson finished his sentence.

"A traitor."

After Deal left his office, Sir Gregory pulled an ultra-secure satellite phone out of his pocket and dialed.

After one ring, a voice on the other end said, "Santiago."

"London 7707. Please inform Director Margie Franks that I have confirmed Agent Deal's team is still in the UK. Our operation elsewhere is secure."

FORTY-THREE

"Please make yourselves comfortable," Ali said as he led Michael, Sarah, and Agent Sims into the luxurious interior of his private aircraft, a Dassault Falcon 7X. "I must excuse myself for a bit."

"Of course, Your Highness," Sims replied.

Ali stopped and turned toward the others. "I guess it's best if you call me that when others are around, but when we're alone, please call me Ali. We're friends. Agreed?"

"Sure, Ali," Sims said, returning Ali's somewhat forced smile.

"Good. I can't tell you how glad I am for you all to be here with me. If you need anything, just press one of these little blue service buttons," Ali said, pointing out a small switch on the armrest of a seat. "I'll join you again when I can. For now, just enjoy the ride. We'll be in my country in about seven hours."

After Ali disappeared, Michael and Sarah took a moment to look around the incredible jet. At the front of the cabin, four buttery soft cream leather captain's chairs faced each other. Underfoot, their shoes seemed to sink into deep wool carpet. In the next section, a full-sized sofa sat against the windows facing two sumptuous armchairs. Beyond, a highly polished bulkhead with a frosted-glass door provided privacy for the owner whenever he desired.

"Wow. Just wow," Michael commented, almost in a whisper.

"Yeah. How did we end up in the private jet of an Arabian prince?" Sarah asked, almost to herself.

"I have no idea," Michael replied, slowly. "I know one thing, though."

Sarah looked up at her boyfriend. "And what might that be?"

"I think we should make out on that couch!"

Sarah playfully hit Michael's arm. "Behave yourself!"

"Too bad!" Michael responded. "It may be a while before we can afford one of these babies for ourselves."

Sarah and Michael didn't discuss their future very often. They were both happy in their relationship and had been for a long time, but Michael's comment made Sarah smile. Without a word, she pulled his face down to hers and surprised him with an overtly passionate kiss.

"I thought you didn't want to make out!" Michael whispered, when Sarah let him go.

"No time for that!" Sims called from the front of the cabin. "We need to go over some things."

Michael and Sarah took seats across from Sims. As if she had been in private planes many times before, the FBI agent reached down and lifted a table hiding in the wall so that it sat between the seats. She placed her laptop on the table and turned it so Michael and Sarah could see the screen.

"Alright. In seven hours, we will land here, in Ras Al Khaimah, the capital of the Ali's emirate, the RAK," Sims said, pointing to a map of the UAE on her computer screen. "Ali will be met by members of the other six royal families that form the UAE. As the new sheik, or leader, of the emirate, he will be under extreme pressure. He must first deal with his grandfather's death and funeral. At the same time, he will have to make crucial decisions about the crisis over his family's oil rights just to the west in Oman."

"Damn. That's a lot," Michael commented. "He's only two years older than me. I can't even imagine taking on a load like that."

"And that's not all. As he told you, the Iranians are making claims to the same oil. It's like a three-way tug-of-war right now over what are believed to be substantial reserves. Tensions are about as high as they can get, and it wouldn't take much to start a war," Sims explained, seriously.

"And the Strait of Hormuz is directly in the crosshairs of all the claimants," Sarah added. "A war could shut down the entire Persian Gulf."

Sims agreed. "Absolutely. The entire world depends, in one way or another, on the continued flow of oil through the Strait of Hormuz. A war would create an immediate and profound oil shortage."

"And gas prices would skyrocket," Michael concluded.

"Precisely. And our friend, Ali, is stepping into the eye of the storm," Sims said, looking at Michael and Sarah in turn. "An oil crisis of that magnitude would be a disaster for the United States and our allies. Our job is to support Ali. At the same time, we have to identify any threat that could set off a shooting war."

"What do you want Michael and me to do?" Sarah asked.

"Stay as close as possible to the prince. Be his friend. Keep your eyes and ears open. Let me know anything, and I mean anything, you think is important. And remember. We're guests here. So, don't interfere. Let me say that again. *Don't* get involved."

For the next three hours, Michael and Sarah had little to do other than enjoy the rare experience of traveling in grand style. While Sims stayed in constant communication with Agent Deal back in the UK, Michael and Sarah settled on the couch to watch a movie that wouldn't be in the theaters for months. When it ended, the couple peered through the windows looking at the lights of Milan and Rome as Italy passed by thirty-five thousand feet below.

Finally, Ali reappeared from the back of the plane looking stressed and exhausted. The last few hours had obviously taken a heavy toll on the new sheik.

Michael and Sarah jumped up from the couch and led the nearly distraught young man to a chair.

"Hey, buddy. You okay?" Michael asked, as Sarah went to fetch Sims.

"Things are worse than I thought, I'm afraid," Ali said, trying to produce some kind of smile – and failing.

Sims appeared with a glass of cold water.

"Drink this. You look dehydrated."

Ali drank the entire glass of water.

"Thanks," Ali said, gathering himself. "I just spent three hours arguing with six old men – all of whom had just one thing in common. They all think I'm utterly useless. I'm afraid I may have bent some noses out of shape."

"How so?" Sarah asked.

"I told most of them to bugger off."

Ali went on to explain how the oil claims near Khasab had belonged to his family for generations. Per the agreements between the UAE royal families, control of oil reserves falls to the sheik who owns the claims. While all royal oil reserves are to be used to benefit the entire country, only the sheik can authorize release of the reserves within his control. The other sheiks wanted him to step aside and let them handle the negotiations with Oman and respond to the claims made by the Iranians. When Ali refused to relinquish control, he had come under punishing pressure from many directions.

"I can't do as they ask," Ali explained. "To do so would be a betrayal of my family and my people. No sheik has ever allowed such action, and neither shall I."

"What happens when we land?" Michael asked. "Are you in danger?"

Ali shook his head. "No. But my reception will be, shall we say, frigid."

After flying over empty desert for several hours, Michael and Sarah were surprised to see lush farmland in the distance as the plane descended toward the UAE. When the jet landed at Ras Al Khaimah International Airport, it did not taxi to the rather spartan terminal building. Instead, it continued on the single runway to a wide turnaround point, where an impressive crowd waited to greet the new sheik.

As soon as the plane came to a halt, Ali reappeared from the back of the plane wearing the traditional robes of his country.

"I haven't dressed like this in quite some time," he said, looking down. "I don't think it suits me."

"To the contrary. You look quite dashing," Sims commented.

"Thank you, Stella" Ali said, trying to remain strong. "I have several customs and ceremonies to attend to. Will you mind remaining on board for a bit longer? I've arranged to have you all collected and taken to my home straight away. I can meet you there in a few hours."

"We'll be fine, thank you, Ali," Sims answered for the group. "We are all sorry for your loss."

"You are too kind," Ali replied, gallantly bowing over her hand and bringing it gently to his lips.

With a nod to the crew, the door opened and a set of stairs lowered to an ornate red carpet. From inside, Michael, Sarah, and Sims watched Ali deplane and make his way past rows of flags held aloft by uniformed soldiers. At the end of the carpet, an elaborate ceremony began. Several men, dressed in colored robes, embraced Ali one by one.

They didn't see what happened next as the plane moved slowly away.

"Dashing?" Sarah asked, giving Sims a knowing look.

"I was being polite," Sims answered, a slight blush on her cheeks giving away her thoughts.

"Uh-huh," Sarah chided. "That kiss looked a little more than just *polite* to me."

FORTY-FOUR

Ali's arrangements for Sims, Michael, and Sarah went well beyond simply having them delivered to his home. Even as they walked down the stairs into the hot desert air, a man dressed in a starched white uniform welcomed them warmly in perfect English.

"I am Ahmed. His Highness wishes you a warm welcome to his country and profusely apologizes for not accompanying you to his home. He has asked me to see to your every comfort. As you can see, a car awaits."

While two other men in identical uniforms gathered their few pieces of luggage, the trio walked toward a massive gleaming black SUV. At the back of the vehicle, two unsmiling men stood guard in black suits and sunglasses.

After just a short walk through the Arabian sun, they welcomed the car's cool interior. Once seated, their substitute host climbed in the front. Sims noticed that as they passed the terminal building, two other identical SUVs pulled in line behind their vehicle.

"Looks like we have company," Sims commented.

"Our security escort," Ahmed responded.

"Is there some reason we need so much protection?" Sims asked.

Michael and Sarah looked at each other but remained silent.

"Please allow me to assure you of your safety. You are esteemed guests of the sheik, and it is the custom of our country that a host is responsible for his guests' comfort and protection. It is only twenty kilometers or so to the city center where His Highness resides. So please make yourself at ease," Ahmed explained, with a confident smile.

Sims gave Michael and Sarah a reassuring nod. But the couple couldn't help but notice how Sims' eyes continuously scanned to the front and sides of the car as they drove along a newly-paved four lane highway.

Michael didn't know what to expect, but the area didn't feel dangerous. Except for signs in Arabic and slightly different architecture, they could be driving through any suburban area in the United States.

Soon, they found themselves speeding down a modern interstate-like four lane highway. Huge palm trees planted at regular intervals in the middle of the road flashed by at an incredible pace. After just a few minutes, the cars pulled under the covered entrance to a set of ultra-modern twin glass towers standing on a man-made peninsula in the middle of RAK Harbor.

Michael and Sarah emerged from the car looking around in awe. While they knew many Arab countries had vast wealth from their oil reserves, they marveled at the incredible ingenuity necessary to transform the desert into this stunning, magically beautiful, avant-garde city.

Sims saw them looking around. "And this is a very small, out of the way, city. You should see Dubai or Bahrain."

Ahmed ushered them inside the east tower, past massive marble columns and across highly polished granite tile to a gilded elevator door bearing a royal crest. At their approach, two huge soldiers dressed in ornate white uniforms with red stripes down the pant legs came to attention. The visitors couldn't miss the guards' menacing-looking assault rifles.

The ride to the fiftieth story took under a minute. When the doors opened, Sims, Michael, and Sarah stepped into a vast open room, lushly furnished in gray and white tones. But the defining features of the space were the two-story-high glass walls framing a spectacular view of the Persian Gulf.

"His Highness bids you welcome to his home," Ahmed said, formally. "A variety of local delicacies, plus your favorite American foods, await your enjoyment. There are also several varieties of beverages. I believe Mr. King prefers a lager, while Ms. Sarah prefers a white varietal wine. My apologies, Ms. Sims, but your preferences were harder to determine. If you do not find what you like, please simply pick up one of the phones and I shall be at your service."

"I'll manage, Ahmed. Thank you," Sims replied.

"His Highness shall arrive in two hours. Until then, please relax here and recover from your journey. Once again, it is my pleasure to be at your service."

Ahmed bowed and stepped back into the elevator.

"I could get used to this!" Michael declared, looking over the ornate buffet set against one wall.

"Don't," Sims said with an edge in her voice. "I read U.S. intelligence briefing documents on the plane. We just landed in the middle of a crisis that could blow up at any time. If it does, where we stand now is ground zero. Plus, and of course all this is classified, those reports suggest that the Iranians may have already infiltrated this part of the UAE and that the Omanis are already moving military assets north toward the area where Ali's family holds oil claims."

Sarah and Michael looked at each other. Under normal circumstances, Sims would never have told them anything classified. The fact that she had shocked them both.

Sims put a finger to her lips and made a circular motion around the room with her other hand. The message was clear. The room was almost certainly bugged.

"So, keep your eyes and ears open but your mouths shut," Sims admonished a bit more forcefully than necessary, but added a wink at Sarah and Michael.

Diplomatically, America couldn't look like it was interfering in the brewing crisis. But if an inadvertent slip tipped off UAE security – Ali's people could choose to use that information or not.

FORTY-FIVE

Tibat, Oman

The ancient truck passed through the dusty coastal town of Tibat a hour before sunrise. Bare bulbs hanging loosely over mud and brick houses provided almost as much light as the truck's headlights. Dave could just see the waters of the Gulf lapping up against a rocky shoreline to his right. After another mile, all signs of human habitation disappeared, replaced by rocky hills on one side and a deserted coastline on the other.

Suddenly, the truck decelerated, throwing Dave forward. Catching himself against the metal dashboard, he saw the driver wheeling the truck off the road and onto a rock-covered beach. Ahead, an abandoned concrete wharf protruded into the black water.

Ajmal said nothing as he passed by the wharf. Then, showing considerable skill, he backed the trailer onto the long concrete platform. When the container bumped loudly against its locks, Dave jumped in his seat.

"Ha!" Ajmal laughed, enjoying Dave's nerves.

Dave remained silent as the entire tractor-trailer rig bounced onto the old dock. Finally, Ajmal stopped the truck and jumped to the ground.

Dave gratefully climbed out of the disgusting cab and found his bodyguard, who had already taken up his position at the rear of the trailer.

"Anything yet?" Dave asked.

The huge soldier lifted binoculars to his eyes and scanned the ocean.

"No."

"Okay. Keep your eyes open."

Back at the truck, Dave found Ajmal disconnecting air hoses and electrical connections preparing to leave.

And Dave couldn't let that happen.

While the driver's back was turned, Dave reached into his shoulder holster to retrieve his 9mm automatic pistol. He simply couldn't take the chance the Omani might tell his buddies about his nervous American passenger and the strange delivery point he demanded. His presence in Oman had to stay a secret.

As Dave slowly drew his pistol, Ajmal spun around, an ornately decorated silver revolver pointed at Dave's head. The man was no fool.

Dave could do nothing but drop his gun to the ground and raise his hands.

Ajmal peered around Dave. The bodyguard's attention was still focused out to sea, just as Dave ordered. For a moment, the preeminent aeronautical engineer thought he was about to die. Then, to his relief, the Omani driver backed slowly toward the cab of his truck keeping Dave's head centered in his sights.

"Goodbye, stupid American man!" Ajmal shouted as he scrambled inside.

Dave retrieved his weapon, but it was too late. A moment later, the truck shot down the wharf and accelerated back toward Tibat, leaving the trailer and container behind.

When the truck disappeared around a curve, silence and darkness fell over the dock. Dave knew that the driver's escape might jeopardize the mission. But even if Ajmal went so far as to report what occurred to the local police, which Dave calculated to be unlikely, he and his special cargo would be long gone.

Then, out of nowhere, a gun fired. Dave ran to the end of the wharf, joining his bodyguard, who was already jacking a round into the chamber of his small but powerful Uzi assault rifle.

"Return the signal," Dave ordered.

The bodyguard raised the muzzle of his weapon into the air and fired two rounds.

A minute later, Dave heard a boat approaching and pressed a button on a small satellite phone he kept in his pocket.

"About to embark on last leg of delivery. Approximately ten hours, twenty minutes. Operational security maintained. Are Agent Deal and his team still in England?"

"Affirmative," said the rough female voice on the other end of the call. "They are busy and will become more so very quickly. Our MI5 associate reports no information from any source suggesting your operation has been detected."

"It is critical to keep the FBI and Deal in England. They came too close to us the last time," Dave said.

"You do your job. I'll do mine!" Margie Franks responded.

FORTY-SIX

Oxford University

Deal marched into the aerospace lab in a foul mood. The Director of MI5, Britain's elite security service, had ordered Zach's kidnapping to divert attention away from terrorists preparing for an attack on his own country. Deal had no way to determine if Sir Gregory was working alone or if he had associates working within MI5. Other than Eva McWilkinson, he couldn't trust anyone at MI5. He had a theory about why Sir Gregory would betray his country, but that would have to wait. For now, Deal knew that his team would have to stop the drone attack by themselves.

"Where are we?" Deal barked.

After working on the problem for over 24 hours without a break, Bubba's eyes were bloodshot and his hair had become a mussed tangle. He completely ignored Agent Deal's gruff manner.

"Hi, Boss. This is going to be a tough nut to crack. Each of the drones uses a different proprietary encrypted signal to receive flight instructions and navigation. Without those codes, we can't control or even locate their positions," Bubba explained, standing and stretching his cramped back and legs.

"I don't understand," Deal said, frustration creeping into his voice. "This lab programmed the drones, didn't it?"

"To be precise, it developed the *process* for creating the codes. The codes themselves have to all be different. You can't have two drones flying around delivering packages with exactly the same programming."

"And?" Deal prompted.

"And that's what the bad guys were doing in Cambridge. This is cutting edge software that requires a massive amount of computing power. They couldn't bring the drones here to be programmed, so they took them up to Cambridge and used their super-computer to upload the necessary software and install the proper codes for controlling the drones remotely."

"Have you contacted Ali? Maybe he left a backdoor in the code we can exploit," Deal suggested.

"I talked to him hours ago. No such luck. That asshole Simon did most of the work creating the code. If there was a back door, it died with him in that warehouse. Maybe someone else has access to the codes, but I don't know who. Someone higher up the terrorist chain, or whatever?"

"Yes. Yes!" Deal agreed, showing an unusual bit of excitement. "And I know who might have them. But getting to him will be next to impossible."

Bubba looked back at Deal. "Who are you talking about?"

Deal sat down and brought Bubba up to speed about Zach's near-kidnapping and their failure to apprehend the terrorist cell in Cambridge. Then, as he explained Eva McWilkinson's revelation about Sir Gregory's treachery, Bubba's eyes grew wide.

"And, Bubba, I don't have to tell you that information has to stay strictly confidential. Sir Gregory wields a lot of power. If he suspects we know about him, he won't hesitate to send MI5 wet assets after us." Bubba knew what that meant – assassins.

"So, there's something I still don't understand," Bubba began. "Let's say Sir Gregory is behind this threat. Even so, why would he need the codes? Wouldn't he just give out the targets and walk away?"

Deal knew Bubba would ask that very question, and he had an answer.

"Sir Gregory knows everything that's happening in the country. He would want to maintain control in case something changes that would make him want to hit a more desirable target or bypass a target for some reason. The most successful terrorist attacks are flexible, able to adapt to situations as they arise."

After thinking for a moment, Bubba said, "Okay. Here's the bottom line as I see it now. The chances of us either reconstructing the codes or discovering a backdoor into the drones' software stands at near zero. Detecting drones flying at treetop level by radar also stands at near zero. We have no way to know where the drones are hidden. We can't predict their intended targets or when they will strike. Boss, we don't have a choice. Somehow, we have to get Sir Gregory to give up those codes. Otherwise, this thing is going to happen."

"Agreed. Get a cup of coffee and use that genius brain of yours to figure out how to get information out of one of the highest-ranking intelligence officers in the world. And work fast."

Pressure didn't usually bother Bubba. His lighthearted nature combined with a brilliant intellect provided him with powerful tools to solve problems with calm efficiency. But the challenge Agent Deal threw in his lap had no easy answer.

Soon after Deal left, Zach appeared, finding Bubba still in the lab agonizing over a solution to Deal's challenge.

"Hey, you look like someone stole your last beer and the store closed," Zach commented, seeing his friend in a rare funk.

"Hey," Bubba answered. "You okay?"

"Sure. I rescued a gorgeous secret agent from the clutches of the bad guys," Zach replied. "That's at least what she said. I'm for sure getting a date with Eva McWilkinson now!"

Bubba had to laugh. "You almost get killed and you spin it into a romantic opportunity?"

"Persistence is the key to getting the girl!" Zach crowed. "Anyway, why are you so screwed up?"

Bubba told Zach about his conversation with Deal.

"And you think Sir Gregory might have the codes or whatever to control the drones?" Zach asked. "Geez. Someone that high in the government working for terrorists? The question I have is: why? What could the head of MI5 have to gain by doing such a thing?"

"I literally have no idea," Bubba said. "I don't get it."

Zach thought for a few seconds before the answer came to him.

"Money and power, Bubba," Zach pronounced. "The world's two greatest motivators."

"Oooo," Bubba responded, sarcastically. "Not exactly a new idea."

"Well, listen a second," Zach urged. "Think back to last year. The conspiracy back at home that almost caused a second civil war? Why do you think The Cause really wanted to start its own country? It wasn't to preserve some treasured way of life or because of political differences. Not at all. The Directors, the people controlling their conspiracy, wanted two things – money and power. If they had succeeded, they would have complete control of an extremely rich and powerful country. Luckily, they didn't succeed with that. But the Directors disappeared. Three governors, one member of the Joint Chiefs of Staff and assorted billionaires – including the queen of bitches, Margie Franks."

"Yeah. So, what are you getting at?" Bubba replied, sitting up in his chair and paying attention.

"I'm getting to the fact the Directors never got caught. I'm getting to the idea that maybe Sir Gregory is a member of The Cause. Maybe even a Director."

Bubba had to roll Zach's idea around in his head a second. He had been focusing on the mechanics of how to get information from Sir Gregory. Zach approached the problem from another direction entirely – Sir Gregory's motivation.

"Seems like a stretch. But the pieces fit. The Directors tried to gain ultimate power through breaking up the United States. What if Sir Gregory is trying to sow the same seeds here? Maybe even with or for The Cause?" Bubba said. "And if that's really the case, I may have an idea. Call the boss."

Thirty minutes later, Deal found Bubba and Zach discussing Bubba's idea. When they filled in the FBI agent, Deal's reaction came immediately.

"Wow. I'd like to say that a connection to The Cause is insane, but I can't. The same idea occurred to me earlier today. What I don't understand is this – how is The Cause going exploit a major terrorist attack in the UK? Like 9-11 in the US, they could expect profound societal changes. Security upgrades. Rolling back personal freedom. Expanded surveillance of their own citizens. But those things take time. The Cause and its Directors want immediate results. Your theory is sound, but how do you guys think this can be used to get information out of Sir Gregory?"

"I'll need two things," Bubba said with confidence. "First, I'll need a laser scan of Sir Gregory's office or interior of his home. Second, a voice recording of Margie Franks."

"Oh! Is that all? I can get a recording of Franks, but the other one will be much harder," Deal commented. "Security around Sir Gregory is tighter than the Queen's. I can't even get my cell phone into MI5 headquarters."

"I have an idea about how to get the scan," Zach said, suddenly. "We'll need Eva's help."

"The *what*?" McWilkinson exclaimed.

"They call themselves 'The Cause'," Agent Deal repeated when McWilkinson appeared in the lab thirty minutes later.

"And this group is who you believe was behind the attempted takeover of several of your states last year?" McWilkinson asked.

"Yes. The Cause is made up of hyper-rich business people, successful politicians, and military generals. They infiltrated the highest levels of state and federal governments, manipulated the media, and successfully stole black-project technology. Their stated goal of creating a new nation out of several southern states failed. But our analysis indicates their real goal was to destabilize the U.S. In that, they succeeded. President Mallory is still trying to heal the wounds they inflicted on our society. Their leaders call themselves 'Directors.' They all fled the country and we've been trying to run them down ever since. They have unlimited funds and, so far, they have eluded all of our efforts to track them down," Deal explained.

"And you think Sir Gregory is part of this conspiracy?" McWilkinson asked.

"That's our working theory. It only makes sense they have branched out internationally. The truth is, though, we can't be absolutely sure," Deal admitted.

McWilkinson thought a moment. "There's something else," she said. "I didn't want to believe this could be true. After meeting Zach following the train attack and our encounter in the tourist hotel, I wanted to know more about this terrorist threat you were asked to investigate. Sir Gregory wouldn't allow me to follow up on it. I wasn't satisfied and made some discreet inquiries with friends in the anti-terrorist units. They said everything was basically business as usual. I let it drop, thinking Sir Gregory must have other assets assigned – along with your team, of course."

Zach said, "Well, that fits. I'm convinced. If anyone has the codes to the drones, he does."

"I agree that a massive terrorist attack would be horrible for the UK. But it wouldn't destabilize the entire country. And there's no reward for Sir Gregory other than a payment of some kind. Sir Gregory served this country with honor for decades. And, he is already wealthy. His family is one of the founders of England's biggest oil company. I'm having difficulty finding his motivation," McWilkinson said.

"For a terrorist attack alone, yes. I agree. The motivation isn't there. But I don't think he is looking for a massive payday. It's more. It's power. Power only The Cause could offer," Deal responded.

"Alright. The Cause aside, if there is actually a possibility he has the codes, we have to try and get them," McWilkinson acquiesced. "What do you need me to do?"

FORTY-SEVEN

MI5 Headquarters
London

Sir Gregory's phone buzzed.

"Yes?"

"Sir, Officer McWilkinson asks for a moment of your time. She says it's quite urgent."

Sir Gregory sighed. The drone attack would take place in less than eight hours, and he needed time to prepare. But ignoring an urgent request from one of his top officers would look suspicious.

"Yes. Send her in, please."

McWilkinson walked into the office wearing a skin-tight red dress that perfectly complimented her glowing skin and stunning figure. She chose the outfit on purpose.

"My goodness, Eva. May I say you look stunning this morning. What is the occasion?" Sir Gregory asked.

"Do you think so?" McWilkinson said, flirtatiously turning around in a slow circle holding her cell phone innocently in one hand. "I'm meeting a contact who finds me fetching and says he has information about the attack on the train and the Duchess."

"Yes. Well, that outfit will certainly put him off his game," Sir Gregory said approvingly. "I really should have invited you to join me and the PM this afternoon. We're having tea at Number 10. I'm sure he would have loved to hear about your investigation."

"Pity. The Prime Minister is always entertaining."

"So, what is this urgent matter?"

"Sir," McWilkinson began. "The incident with Zach Self in Cambridge... I must ask, is that related to whatever Agent Deal's team is here to help prevent? If so, I'd like to request assignment to that matter."

Sir Gregory sat down behind his desk.

"We have been over this already, Eva," Sir Gregory replied. "We have that situation well in hand. In fact, I doubt the FBI will be in the UK much longer. But should that situation change, I'll reconsider your request. Now, off you go to meet your contact."

Sir Gregory put on a pair of reading glasses, picked up a file, and turned his chair toward the windows behind his desk. The meeting was over.

Once outside the building, McWilkinson took a cab to one of London's upscale hotels. Inside the large, busy lobby, she made a show of looking for her nonexistent contact before finding a seat on a comfortable couch. Her surveillance wasn't entirely false, though. She wanted to be certain she wasn't followed.

McWilkinson toyed with her cell phone, casually scrolling through social media pages. After a minute, she opened the app Bubba installed back at the lab. With the press of a button, she sent the file containing the digital scan she just made of Sir Gregory's office directly to Bubba's computer in the Oxford lab. A text confirmed its receipt.

McWilkinson looked at her phone, amazed at how Bubba had created and installed a miniature laser scanner in the completely standard-looking device.

FORTY-EIGHT

Just a couple of hours after McWilkinson's meeting with Sir Gregory, Agent Frank Deal stood looking at a 17th century oil painting of the Thames River. He didn't like the painting. But the fact that it hung over the fireplace in the White Room at Number 10 Downing Street meant it had some sort of significance.

Deal's musings ended when the Prime Minister of Great Britain strode into the room.

"I also have no idea why that painting is so prominently displayed, Agent Deal," the Prime Minister commented, noticing Deal's scowl.

Deal spun around. "Prime Minister, thank you for seeing me on such short notice."

The Prime Minister smiled wanly and ran a hand through the unkempt crop of blond hair that had become his trademark.

"Yes, well, a call from Her Majesty asking for a few minutes of my time can't be simply ignored, now, can it? How on earth did you arrange such a thing?" the Prime Minister asked, offering Deal a seat in one of the room's gleaming white armchairs.

"I have an associate who recently saved a member of the royal family. He asked the queen for a favor," Deal admitted.

"Ah, young Zachary Self. I must confess to being surprised he is working with the FBI," the Prime Minister remarked.

"Yes, well, most people are."

"Alright, Agent, you have your meeting. I have five minutes, so its best we not muck about. What can I do for you?"

Deal succinctly laid out the terrorist plot to use drones for a mass attack.

"My God!" the Prime Minister exclaimed. "I get daily reports from MI5 on threats to the UK. This is the first I'm hearing of an attack. I need to get Sir Gregory on the phone immediately!"

"Sir," Deal said. "Please wait. There's more. Sir Gregory knows all about this. In fact, he brought my entire team here to aid MI5 in its investigation."

"Then why am I just hearing of this now?"

The Prime Minister stood and paced to the windows.

"Because he doesn't want anyone to stop the attacks," Deal answered bluntly. "MI5 has no open investigation into this threat. One of their best officers, Eva McWilkinson, checked with the anti-terrorist action teams at MI5 this morning. The tear gas explosions on the train that injured the Duchess is still their top priority."

"I know of McWilkinson. She dated one of the queen's grandsons at one time. Still, I find this incredible, Agent Deal," the PM responded, dismissively.

"Sir, we believe that Sir Gregory is working with a group called The Cause. President Mallory is on hold right now to confirm everything I've said. We don't have much time. The terrorists have between six and ten fully capable attack drones positioned here in

England. They could launch these attacks at any time. Please, sir, take the call from the President."

The PM walked to the door and shouted for his personal butler. "Henry! Is President Mallory on the line?"

"Yes, Prime Minister. Shall I bring you the phone?"

"Yes, you twit! Bring me the damn phone!"

The prime minister listened to the president for several minutes. Finally, he said, "Agent Deal will have my full cooperation, Madam President. Thank you for your assistance."

Turning to Deal, the PM said, "Alright Agent, what do you need me to do? Sir Gregory is due here in an hour for tea."

FORTY-NINE

At 3:30 that afternoon, Tony called the Wolf.

"You may speak," Randall Snow said as the Wolf from his Chelsea townhouse.

"This is Tony. Our six drones are armed as you ordered. Targets are uploaded. Myself and five other remote pilots are on standby. We await your order to launch, my sheik."

"Excellent. You have met my expectations thus far. I shall issue the order in an hour and a half. Are you prepared for any last second target changes?" Snow asked.

"Yes, my sheik," Tony answered. "Are targeting changes expected?"

"Do not become insolent now!" Snow growled. "You will be informed if that is to take place."

The call ended abruptly.

With preparations complete, the full weight of the wide-ranging attacks fell heavily on Tony's shoulders. Successfully bringing god's wrath on his sworn enemies would vault him into the upper echelon of holy warriors. Even knowing this, he had to steel himself to his task. People, perhaps even children, would die at his hand. Innocents who had done nothing wrong other than to be born and raised in a rich and corrupt society. He had to remind himself of the hardships inflicted on the innocent people of his home, who also had done nothing wrong, other than to be born in a poor country that could not defend against the greed and power of the West.

Setting aside his doubts, Tony swore a silent oath to stand fast in his duty and fear neither the retribution of the infidels or the torments of his own conscious.

Walking up to the black drone that sat on a metal stand, Tony admired the fearsome weapon. Eight legs, ending in vertically mounted propellers, emerged from a central glossy oval fuselage. Two red diodes on the 'face' of the drone imparted the weapon with an evil, animalistic, appearance. Mounted below the fuselage, six black gun barrels, arranged in a circle, looked like the horrifying mouth of some science-fiction alien.

Initially, Tony had wondered why the Wolf chose the M134 minigun. But after learning more about the weapon, Tony realized the choice was inspired. Weighing only 80 pounds, the minigun fired a standard 7.62x51 mm standard NATO round at well over 2000 rounds per minute. That kind of firepower couldn't stop a tank but would shred soft targets such as cars, trucks, and people in seconds. The minigun could move from target-to-target mowing down everything in its path until it ran out of ammunition. If all went well, the drone would then return to base, rearm, and continue to its next target.

Tony stood and took a step back to admire his handiwork. His enemies would only see the beast when it began spitting fire. Nobody would be safe. No one would feel safe. Anywhere.

Terror would soon hold Great Britain in an iron grip.

FIFTY

The Head Butler of Number 10 Downing Street ushered Sir Gregory into the Prime Minister's private study. The PM already sat in a comfortable leather club chair with a pair of reading glasses perched on his nose. He waved Sir Gregory to a seat next to him while he finished reading.

"Sir Gregory! A pleasure as always," the Prime Minister said in his normal, effusive manner.

"Prime Minister. It's good to see you," Sir Gregory responded.

"I must say, it has been a busy day. I welcome this break, however brief, and your company. I hope you have no crisis for me today."

"Thank you, sir. Thankfully, I don't have any important matters to discuss. So, we have this time to ourselves – unless you have any questions, of course," Sir Gregory replied.

Sir Gregory glanced at his watch. The attacks would begin in less than ninety minutes. He had actually suggested to Margie Franks that they begin during his weekly visit to Number 10.

"Good. Good. Nobody will disturb us. Would you care for tea or something stronger this evening?" the PM offered.

"While I would prefer a martini, tea with lemon will have to do. Thank you, sir."

The Prime Minister rose and crossed to a sideboard set with a full tea service alongside several crystal decanters.

"I hope you don't mind if I have a spot of whiskey?" the prime minister asked.

"Of course not, sir."

The Prime Minister plucked a ring of lemon peel from a small glass bowl, placed it in one of the tea cups, and added freshly-brewed Earl Grey. After pouring himself a finger of Scotch, he returned to his seat, and handed the tea to Sir Gregory.

"Cheers!" the prime minister said, raising his glass.

"Cheers," Sir Gregory repeated, sipping at his cup.

"I have a surprise for you, Sir Gregory," the prime minister said, suddenly becoming cold.

"I'm sorry, sir. What?" Sir Gregory said, his voice slurring slightly.

From behind the prime minister, a door opened. Frank Deal walked into the room.

"What is he ..." Sir Gregory couldn't finish his question. The drug infused into the lemon peel had already taken effect.

A second later, Sir Gregory passed out, his chin resting on his chest.

"What happens now?" the Prime Minister asked. "I don't want him harmed."

"He won't be," Deal said, two members of his Blue Team already carrying Sir Gregory out of the room. "He'll wake up in his own office with no memory of the last hour. Other than a lingering headache, he'll suffer no long-term effects at all."

The Prime Minister looked with disgust at Sir Gregory – a man who once held his respect. "Good. I want him in fine fiddle to stand for treason before the eyes of the entire country. You will keep me informed. Personally."

Deal, with an unconscious Sir Gregory strapped carefully on a gurney, boarded a helicopter that rushed them to the roof of Oxford's Aeronautical Engineering building. Inside, Bubba waited with Zach and McWilkinson for Agent Deal's special delivery.

Thirty minutes after leaving Number 10, Blue Team members unloaded Sir Gregory and carried him inside.

"Once we get the codes, how long will it take to stop the drones?" Deal asked Bubba.

As Deal and Bubba followed Blue Team down to the lab, Bubba explained the next steps.

"Up to thirty minutes. There are two possibilities. First, if the drones are flying on a preset course to a set target, we'll have to find the GPS satellite carrier waves and upload the codes onto those signals. That's complex and will take time. Second, and this is much more likely, they will use long-range FM transmitters to control the drones manually. This would give them complete flexibility in choosing targets of opportunity. But these same FM signals are their Achilles heel. To broadcast up to a hundred miles they will need a lot of watts and tall antennas. Drones operate on a narrow frequency, so finding signals that strong should be straightforward. Once I find the frequencies, I can easily transmit the codes directly to the drones and take over control. And, I can even trace the signals back to the launch sites."

"I'll have Blue and Red teams standing by with helicopter transport to take down the terrorist cells. We can't use MI5 assets yet.

We don't know if Sir Gregory has associates embedded inside his agency," Deal explained.

"Agreed. But we must work fast," McWilkinson added. "I just heard from one of your technical experts who is monitoring social media. In the past hour, rumors of a major event have appeared on several websites and social media pages. In the past twenty minutes, those rumors have begun to spread like wildfire."

"That can't be good," Zach said.

"I talked with analysts in Washington, as well. They are convinced of an attack taking place today," Deal said, a hard edge in his voice. "This has to work. And it has to work right now."

FIFTY-ONE

Sir Gregory sat up in his office chair, suddenly aware that his intercom was buzzing.

"Yes?" he snapped, irritated at the intrusion.

"Sir, the Prime Minister's office just rang. He's had to postpone your tea this afternoon."

Gregory looked at his watch. It read 3:02 p.m.

"Yes. Fine. Please tell the PM's office we will look forward to next week, then," Sir Gregory replied.

Turning around, he looked through the massive bullet-proof windows that framed most of East London. The late afternoon sun glinted off the Thames River. To the north, Westminster Bridge spanned the water from the London Eye on the east to Westminster Palace, Parliament, and Big Ben to the west. The bustle of traffic and hurried crowds of tourists flowed along and across the river, bringing the city to life.

Vibrations from his personal cell phone suddenly interrupted the MI5 Director's musings. He wasn't expecting a call.

"Yes?" Sir Gregory said, swiping open the phone.

"I want an update," Margie Franks' voice barked, without further greeting.

Sir Gregory hesitated. The Directors never called his personal number.

"Who is this?" Sir Gregory asked suspiciously.

"Just who the hell do you think it is, you uptight English ass!" Franks shot back.

A call to his cell phone went against protocol.

"How did you get this number, madam?" Sir Gregory asked.

"I tried the satellite phone, but it was dead. Check it."

Sir Gregory retrieved the miniature satellite phone he carried in his pocket at all times.

"It must have malfunctioned. I charged it just this morning," Sir Gregory responded, confused.

"Fine. Fine. We don't have time for this. What is the status of your mission? I'm in the room with the Directors. We may need to change targets."

Sir Gregory still hesitated. His long experience in the intelligence services made him cautious.

"Where are you calling from?" Sir Gregory asked.

"Santiago, of course. Trace the call if you want. But do it quick," Franks barked, impatiently.

Sir Gregory knew he couldn't do that. Red flags would go up all over MI5 launching an immediate investigation into who had hacked the Director's secure cell phone.

"Alright then, Margie. We are at one hour and thirty-seven minutes until the drones are launched. Six armed drones will begin attacks as soon as they arrive on target."

"Six!" Margie shouted. "That's not enough!"

"It will be," Sir Gregory responded confidently. "And more importantly, the special FBI team is still here in the UK chasing our little terrorists all around the countryside – just as you wanted. Is our main objective still on track? My family's oil company has spent billions gearing up for this."

Franks didn't answer for a few seconds. Sir Gregory assumed she was verifying information.

"Yes. It's a go. Now that we have the preliminaries finally ironed out, the Directors want the codes to the drones. We have some special targets that need elimination. Send them to this number now," Margie Franks demanded.

"This is unexpected. Why do you want control of the drones at this late hour?" Sir Gregory asked.

"Because I want them. And because I can throw you to the wolves with a phone call. Play ball, Gregory, or get the fuck off the field."

When The Cause approached Sir Gregory years before, they made it perfectly clear that the rewards for uniting with them would give him power and wealth beyond his wildest imagination. But The Cause also expected nothing less than complete obedience and loyalty. His choice was clear.

"Transmitting now."

A few seconds passed in silence.

"Received. Where is your first target?" Franks asked.

"You know I don't have that information," Sir Gregory replied, his suspicions once again piqued. "The Wolf chose the targets. Call him."

An uncomfortable silence settled over the conversation. Sir Gregory began to pace back and forth behind his desk still holding his phone to his ear. As the seconds ticked by, a cold knot of stress formed in his gut. The call didn't make sense. In the two years since he joined The Cause, no Director had ever broken protocol. Now, in the last minutes before the operation that would make him the most powerful man in all Britain, Margie Franks wanted to take control of the drones?

Suddenly, he knew. The call wasn't real.

Without saying anything else, Sir Gregory hung up. With a trembling hand, he picked up the satellite phone. Turning it over, he slipped off the back cover. The battery wasn't dead – it was gone.

It took every ounce of self-control he had learned as an intelligence officer not to panic. Somehow, someone had fooled him into giving up the codes that controlled the drones. More importantly, his cover was blown.

Sir Gregory straightened his classic striped tie, took a few deep breaths, and thought about his next move. Once outside MI5 headquarters, he would drive himself home, pick up his emergency cash and passports, and disappear.

Options for escape ran through his mind as he walked to his office door. He would have to appear calm and perfectly normal so his assistant didn't become concerned. Pausing to take one more deep breath, he grabbed the doorknob, pulled the door open and stopped dead.

Instead of the bright light of his outer office, he faced a blank wall covered with something like dark grey carpet.

Astonished beyond words, Sir Gregory touched the obstacle that blocked his way. He tried pushing on the soft carpet, but found it absolutely rock-solid.

Now questioning his sanity, Sir Gregory stepped back from the door, turned, and began lowering himself into one of his leather armchairs. But as he did, the chair disappeared into thin air. Like a bad cartoon character, the highest-ranking intelligence officer in the country fell to the floor, landing hard on his backside.

After a moment to recover, Sir Gregory sat up only to see the entire room fading into nothingness before his very eyes. He found himself in a perfectly square room with carpet-covered floors, walls, and ceiling.

Then, a door opened to his left and Officer Eva McWilkinson stepped inside, followed by FBI Agent Frank Deal.

"Sir Gregory. You are under arrest for espionage and high treason," McWilkinson announced.

"Wha...What?" Sir Gregory stammered.

"You heard the lady, Gregory. Stand up," Deal ordered.

Outside the door, two young men laughed uproariously.

FIFTY-TWO

"Target 1 confirmed for drones A, B, and C," Tony said into the headset microphone. "Five minutes to attack point. I will open fire on the London Eye. Drone B will loiter over the northeast corner of Jubilee Park to ambush people running away from the gunfire. Drone C will do the same over the Dungeons of London Building."

In his headset, Tony heard the pilots of drones B and C confirm the attack profile.

Standing 443 feet high, the massive Ferris wheel on the south bank of the Thames River was the most popular tourist attraction in the United Kingdom. Over three million visitors a year from all over the world rode inside sealed and air-conditioned glass pods that offered stunning views of historic London. The Wolf chose his initial target for shock value. Each pod held thirty-five passengers. The miniguns mounted under the drone would shred one pod after another, slaughtering the trapped and helpless tourists inside. Then, as panic on the ground mounted and people scattered, the other two drones would pounce. Essentially, everyone visiting the huge observation wheel would die in a deadly crossfire.

"I have the London Eye in sight," Tony reported. "Two minutes."

"Bubba!" Deal shouted. "What's the status on those codes?"

From outside Ali's hyper-sophisticated holographic simulator room, Bubba called, "I have telemetry data on all six drones. Three are already over the city. Three more are ten minutes out. Initial data indicates the first target is the London Eye."

Deal joined Bubba and Zach at Bubba's workstation. McWilkinson followed behind and forced Sir Gregory onto his knees with his hands tightly handcuffed behind his back.

On Bubba's screen, they could see six red lines converging on central London. In just minutes, the leading three drones would meet close to the Thames River.

Bubba's fingers danced over the keyboard as incomprehensible lines of codes rolled down one side of his screen.

"Zach, use that joystick to your right," Bubba said without looking up. "In a second, your screen should show a view from the drones' forward-looking cameras. When it does, you'll have control. Fly those things into the river."

"You want me to do it?" Deal offered.

"I got it. Just like the game Combat Patrol, right?" Zach said, sitting down and taking hold of what looked like a gaming joystick.

"Almost. Almost. Almost," Bubba chanted, quietly.

No one moved a muscle as the red lines drew closer and closer to the now-obvious target. Deal considered having McWilkinson order an evacuation of the London Eye and Jubilee Park, but decided against it. The order would be too late, anyway.

With all eyes on the screen, McWilkinson knelt behind Sir Gregory, drew her weapon and held it against the back of the traitor's skull.

"You should know, Sir Gregory," McWilkinson hissed quietly. "If those drones kill anyone, I'm going to make sure your life ends here and now. So, if you can help, do it now."

"You wouldn't dare," Sir Gregory replied, summoning his courage.

Deal looked away from the screen long enough to add, "If she doesn't, I will."

The London Eye turns so slowly that passengers step on and off the attraction without the huge wheel coming to a stop. One revolution of the wheel allows sightseers thirty minutes to take in the panoramic views. But none of the excited riders could see the three deadly black drones approaching.

Drone A, piloted by Tony, flew around Big Ben, its eight propellers making only a soft buzzing sound. Although large for a drone, it flew high and quietly enough to avoid drawing attention from the ground. As the drone passed over Westminster Bridge, Tony issued his final orders.

"Thirty seconds. Drones B and C report. Are you in position?" Tony asked in his headset as the massive white Ferris wheel grew bigger on his screen.

"In position and holding," Drone B's pilot reported.

"In position and holding," Drone C's pilot added.

"Hold your fire until I engage the second pod."

The terrorist leader moved his small joystick to the left, causing the drone to move out over the river. As it grew closer to its target, Tony could see individuals standing in the glass-enclosed pods pointing at the sights and taking pictures. He wanted to get close enough for his victims to see the instrument of their destruction.

As he moved the weapon into range, Tony silently prayed again for the strength to do what had to be done. He knew that after today's attacks, his enemies would have to live with the unrelenting terror of sudden and unstoppable death from the air, just as his own people did at home. That was enough.

Approaching the massive wheel slowly, Tony finally saw a few tourists notice the drone. At first, they just pointed or took pictures, fascinated with seeing new technology up close. But then, after he flew closer still, they noticed the minigun, its barrels pointed menacingly in their direction. One by one, people in the pods began to panic. Tony tried to imagine the horror of suddenly realizing you are utterly trapped, hundreds of feet off the ground, and facing certain death. He watched as the horrified passengers ran from one side of the pod to the other, like a flock of sheep trapped in their pen with a ravenous wolf.

The terrorist stopped the drone in midair thirty yards from the pod that had reached the top of its travel. He reminded himself that what the minigun lacked in accuracy, it more than made up for in firepower. All he had to do was pull the trigger and "walk" the line of red-hot tracer bullets from one target to the next.

Tony counted down in his headset. "Firing in five, four, three, two, one."

The minigun's barrels spun up to speed. A half-second later, hundreds of steel-jacketed rounds shot across the short distance to the target. Sparks erupted from metal beams while, inside the pods, people ran to the far side of their glass death trap. They screamed and huddled together against the glass. But there was nothing they could do.

After only a couple of seconds, the 7.62 mm rounds began to chew into the observation pod. Razor-sharp shards of glass rained down onto the ground below. Inside, people screamed at the drone as if their voices alone could stop the onslaught of bullets.

Tony noticeably cringed at the bloody carnage just a second away.

Then, the firing stopped.

The next second, the drone inexplicably flipped over and dove at full speed into the water of the Thames.

"No!" Tony shouted. Then into his microphone he bellowed, "Fire! Fire!"

But the guns on the other two drones remained silent. Moments later, Tony watched helplessly as drones B and C turned and plunged into the river just a few yards from where his own drone had disappeared.

Instead of wails of death and destruction, cheers arose all around the London Eye. Except for a few minor cuts and scrapes suffered by those in the single pod hit by Tony's drone, nobody had been injured.

Tony desperately searched for the location of the last three drones – but their tracks had completely disappeared from his computer display. It didn't take long for him to realize that all the attack drones had fallen out of the sky. His operation, the Wolf's operation, had failed.

Still reeling from the unexpected disaster, Tony was about to pick up his telephone when he saw the door to the barn slide open. A rectangle of light pierced the darkness for a moment before the door slid closed again. Instead of his phone, Tony grabbed his 9mm pistol and stood up from his worktable.

"Who is there?" the failed terrorist called out.

"The Wolf is displeased," a voice said from the darkness.

"The failure was not my fault," Tony replied, moving away from the light of his computer.

"I don't care."

Tony backed away from the voice. "Leave me alone!"

"No."

With nowhere to run, Tony fired three shots, roughly in the direction of the voice. Now panicked, he took one step backward – only to feel the barrel of a gun pressed against his back. At that moment, he knew he was about to die.

Falling to his knees, Tony looked up toward heaven.

"Allah ak..."

The assailant shot Tony in the head before he could finish his prayer.

"Yeah. Yeah. Whatever," the killer said, standing over the corpse.

The Wolf, Randall Snow, waited patiently for the call confirming Tony's elimination. Afterward, he dialed Margie Franks' number.

"The drone operation failed," Snow reported.

"We expected it might. Deal and his people are good. But the operation fulfilled its purpose by keeping Deal's team occupied. Has security been maintained?" Margie asked.

"Of course. I guess I'll just have to choose a few new true believers for next time," Snow said with a chuckle.

"Good. And where is Deal's team now?"

"Still in Oxford. Probably congratulating themselves." Snow replied. "And they have Gregory."

"Well, shit! How did that happen?" Franks demanded.

"No idea. But I assume that's how they got the codes to the drones," Snow responded.

"Doesn't matter. It's too late for anyone to stop us now. Just make sure Sir Gregory doesn't have a chance to talk," Franks ordered.

"I've already assigned my best asset. "

FIFTY-THREE

"What do we do with him?" McWilkinson asked, still pointing her gun at Sir Gregory's head. "I can't take him back to MI5 until we know if others are involved."

"What do you say, Gregory? How deep is The Cause into UK security services?" Deal asked, almost sarcastically, leaning down to look into Sir Gregory's face.

Sir Gregory met Deal's eye and laughed. "Wouldn't you just love to know."

Deal grabbed Sir Gregory's hair and in one lightning move lifted the traitor's head and slammed a knee into his nose. The Brit bellowed in pain as blood erupted from his face.

Deal grabbed Sir Gregory's hair again and lifted his head so he could look into Deal's eyes.

"I would indeed like to know," Deal snarled. "And I want to know everything about the other operation you asked the fake Margie Franks about. Now, I recommend you begin talking while your face is still recognizable."

Holding his nose and trying to stem the tide of blood still streaming from his nostrils, Sir Gregory looked at the MI5 officer. "Officer McWilkinson, you cannot allow this man to torture me!"

McWilkinson stood from the chair she was sitting in next to Bubba and Zach and silenced Gregory's bravado with a vicious downward jab into the man's face.

"The hell I can't. You better be forthcoming with Agent Deal immediately. Because if you don't tell him everything, I'll fly you down to your special facility in Angola. Since you were the one that convinced the government to open such a place, you also understand what they do there."

"You wouldn't," Sir Gregory said, his voice breaking.

McWilkinson didn't respond. Instead, she motioned for Bubba and Zach to follow her out of the room.

"You scared the crap out of him with that reference to Angola," Zach observed. "It must be a pretty bad place."

McWilkinson gave a small grunt. "You Americans have Guantanamo Bay. That's a luxury resort next to the hellhole Sir Gregory created in Africa. He actually hired Liberian cannibal warlords to extract information."

"You're kidding!" Zach exclaimed.

"I wish I was," McWilkinson responded with disgust. "But it exists. After less than a day in that camp, everyone talks. Everyone."

After McWilkinson and the others left the room, Deal gave Sir Gregory a minute to recover before asking, "Shall we continue?"

Even with his nose broken and a massive bruise forming over the right side of his face, Sir Gregory managed a chuckle.

"I'll be happy to tell you everything I know," he croaked. "But it will be of no use. It's far too late now. Once it's done, every security service in the world will be occupied, I'll be released, and you...you will be utterly embarrassed by your own blindness."

Deal said nothing before smashing his fist into Sir Gregory's already broken nose.

After the Brit stopped moaning and gasping, Deal growled, "Specifics! Now!"

Sir Gregory put up one hand in a weak sign of surrender.

"Alright! Stop! I'll tell you what I know. Just a few months ago, an American salvage dealer discovered a lost nuclear bomb off the coast of your state of Georgia."

"*What?*" Deal cried, shocked.

"I thought you'd find that interesting," Sir Gregory said, enjoying Deal's reaction. "I don't know his identity, but instead of informing the authorities, the gentleman offered the weapon for sale on the black market. My colleagues acquired the bomb with little real effort."

The Cause and Margie Franks with a nuclear weapon! Franks had attempted to use such a device before – and nearly succeeded destroying the U.S. Capital. If she pulled the trigger before, she wouldn't hesitate to do so again.

"Where is it now?" Deal asked, trying to remain calm.

Sir Gregory spit some blood and mucus on the floor. Even he could see his options slipping away. And Eva McWilkinson had been right. He was intimately acquainted with the horrors inflicted on prisoners at the Angola facility. He knew, without a doubt, he wouldn't last two hours in the hands of his own carefully selected interrogators.

"Well?" Deal demanded. "You're out of time. Talk."

Sir Gregory's eyes flashed about, searching in vain for a lie to mislead Deal's investigation. It didn't take long for him to realize he would do anything to avoid being questioned in Africa.

"It's in the Middle E…"

With little sound other than a sickening wet slap, a bright red hole appeared on Sir Gregory's right temple. His head fell to the side and he slumped over his bent legs – dead. Only after the sniper bullet found its mark did little shards of glass from the laboratory window make a soft tinkling sound as they hit the floor.

Deal instantly drew his weapon and threw himself behind a desk. Instead of further shooting, the lab turned as silent as it had been before the kill shot.

"Eva!" Deal shouted. "Sniper! Stay in the hall!"

"Copy that!" McWilkinson shouted back.

Deal cautiously looked around the corner of the desk. Roughly estimating the angle between a single hole in a lab window and Sir Gregory, he could make out several rooftops that would provide a perfect position for a sniper.

"I can't see anyone from here!" Deal called. "I think they got what they wanted."

McWilkinson pushed the door to the lab open far enough to see Sir Gregory laying with his head in a pool of his own blood. She didn't have to ask if he was dead.

Amina Kent walked out of the administration building across the street from the lab with her disassembled sniper rifle tucked inside a light pink leather backpack. With a cell phone in her hand, she looked like any other student, casually mingling into the early evening crowd on Oxford's sidewalks. She was several blocks away by the time she heard the first sirens in the distance.

A few minutes later, Amina found a secluded bench just outside a small park and called the number Snow had given her to report on the job.

"This is Amina 1810 in Oxford."

"Report," someone said on the other end of the line.

"Sir Gregory is dead," she said simply.

"Hold," the voice said.

Amina checked her lipstick in a small mirror while she waited patiently. After thirty seconds, a female voice came on the line.

"Sir Gregory mentioned you. He said you were his best operative. And coming from him – that's a hell of a compliment," Margie Franks began.

"Great," Amina said, all but ignoring Margie's remark.

"Do you think he talked?"

"I neither know nor care. You pay. I kill. Simple as that," Amina replied, sounding bored with the conversation.

"Damn! You're a stone-cold bitch, aren't you?" Margie replied.

"Yes, I suppose. Just doing my job, you know," Amina replied, replacing her lipstick in her backpack.

"Oh, don't get me wrong. I admire women with brass balls. Why didn't you kill Frank Deal too when you had a chance?" Margie asked.

Amina looked at her phone, exasperated. "I wasn't hired for *that* job. If you want him dead, you'll have to pay up. No freebies. I *thought* I explained how this works."

"Fair enough. Maybe later. But since you've proved useful, I have a different target for you. How fast can you get to the UAE?"

FIFTY-FOUR

"Oh my god!" Bubba exclaimed, after Deal shared Sir Gregory's revelation about a rogue nuclear weapon.

"You have to be kidding!" Zach cried.

"I am not. Eva, is there anyone at MI5 you can trust to run down something on this?" Deal asked.

McWilkinson stood quietly. Sir Gregory was just too high in the government to totally trust anyone that worked for him. She couldn't risk making things worse by tipping off a mole about the information Sir Gregory had just revealed. She had to put aside the deep ramifications for British security caused by Sir Gregory's treason while she worked on how to respond to Deal's question.

"No," McWilkinson finally responded. "I'm afraid there's not. We'll have to rely on your, I mean U.S., intelligence resources."

"I checked with my boss already," Deal replied. "They have nothing on a broken arrow."

"A what?" McWilkinson asked.

"It's what we call a lost nuclear weapon – a broken arrow," Deal explained. "All we have is Gregory's last words. He was about to say

'Middle East.' But that's useless. Even our most advanced satellites and human intelligence sources can't hope to locate a single bomb somewhere in the entire region. What else do we have?"

Nobody spoke as they thought through possibilities. Suddenly, Zach jumped out of his chair.

"Geez. It's right in front of our faces! The mess Ali is in. The nuclear weapon must have something to do with that. I know it!"

"Yes!" Bubba agreed. "Ali told us all about the tensions between Oman and the UAE...not to mention the Iranians. Here, take a look at this."

Bubba pulled up a map on the big monitor at the end of the laboratory displaying the Persian Gulf in high definition. Iran appeared at the top of the map separated from the UAE and Oman by a narrow, curving bit of water called The Strait of Hormuz.

"Certainly, the three countries, Iran, Oman, and the UAE are close to each other," McWilkinson observed. "But I can't see how detonating a nuclear bomb would be of use to any of them."

Deal rubbed his chin a moment before saying, "I agree. It wouldn't. Accusations would fly and probably cause an all-out war between the countries. But that's looking at it from the wrong perspective. The bomb wouldn't be used for or against those countries. The Cause would only use it for their own benefit."

"Ah! I think I see it now," McWilkinson exclaimed. "I've struggled with Sir Gregory's motivation for some time. But no longer. His family owns Britain's largest oil drilling company. A Middle-Eastern conflict would cause oil prices to rise significantly. But that's not all. If, by working with The Cause, they could somehow completely shut off the supply of oil coming through the Strait of Hormuz, his company's oil would become as valuable as gold itself.

The bomb isn't going to be used to start a war. It will be used to stop nearly every drop of oil coming from the entire region."

"How would they do that?" Zach asked.

Bubba zoomed in on the map of the Strait of Hormuz. Several small islands sat in the middle of the waterway, halfway between Iran to the north and the UAE and Oman to the south.

"Here," Bubba pronounced, circling the largest island with his cursor. "Greater Tunb. It's three miles wide and three miles long. A nuclear blast here, depending on its yield, or power, would create an area so hot with radiation, nobody would be able to pass by for decades."

Deal looked at the map, considering Bubba's theory. "Why not one of these smaller islands? There's several scattered around the Strait."

Bubba answered, "Simple. The more ground to absorb radiation, the longer the Gulf stays bottled up. If they blew the thing in the water, currents would disperse the radiation almost immediately."

"What's the connection to Ali's situation, then?" McWilkinson asked.

"Someone has to take the blame," Deal said. "The added turmoil, confusion and resulting conflicts would only serve to further hamper oil exports from the entire Middle East. And nobody would think to blame an outside conspiracy like The Cause."

While the others wrestled with the ramifications and viability of their theory, Bubba turned to his computer. After running several simple searches, he compiled a list of lost nuclear weapons that might have been recovered and sold to The Cause.

"I think I know where the bomb came from," he announced. "And the news isn't good."

"Explain," Deal said.

"A salvage operator generally searches for and recovers lost vessels and cargo. In 1958, a mid-air collision between a Stratojet bomber and interceptor jet on a training mission caused the bomber to eject a Mark 15 nuclear weapon into the Atlantic Ocean off the coast of Georgia," Bubba explained, bringing up photos of a Stratojet and Mark 15 bomb on the monitor.

"Why's that bad news? Other than the obvious, of course," Zach asked.

"A Mark 15 is a powerful two-stage thermonuclear device. Detonation on a small island like Greater Tunb would not only destroy the island, but throw nuclear debris into the atmosphere. Prevailing winds in the Persian Gulf would carry the radioactive fallout across parts of Saudi Arabia, Kuwait and Iraq. Perhaps as far as Syria and Israel. It won't just shut down shipping, it will crush oil production for years. Not to mention immediately killing thousands of people, and sentencing maybe hundreds of thousands more to slow painful deaths from radiation poisoning and cancer."

"And send the world's economy into a tailspin," McWilkinson added. "Wars would break out over limited resources. I can't even bear to imagine the evil that could enter our world. God help us all!"

They all realized that the use of one nuclear weapon, one, would jeopardize the life every human on earth.

Deal looked again at the map and the round island that sat in the middle of the Strait of Hormuz like a bullseye.

FIFTY-FIVE

Dr. Dave Knox didn't like boats. As an aeronautical engineer he had designed and flown the most advanced aircraft in the world. He never became airsick or worried about falling out of the sky. But boats made him sick. And small boats were the worst.

Dave held on to the side of the metal shipping container for dear life. The rusty little cargo transport that plucked the container off the wharf in Oman was designed for work along the coast. Using it in the middle of the Persian Gulf caused it to roll and pitch, even in the night's light chop. More than once, he heaved into the water while the three-man crew laughed and scoffed at him in their incomprehensible dialect.

Dave just ignored the crew, taking macabre solace in the fact that they would all be incinerated in just a few hours while he jetted back over the Atlantic in the comfort of a well-appointed private jet. But before that could happen, he had a job to do.

Checking their location on his GPS device, Dave could see they would be docking at their destination, Greater Tunb Island, in approximately two hours. The almost perfectly round island sat in the dead center of the Strait of Hormuz. Iran took control of the island in the early 1970s and maintained a small force on the otherwise uninhabited, desert island – mostly to maintain their claim and provide a refueling point for their fleet of small attack craft. He didn't like to even imagine the punishment Iranian authorities would inflict on him if they caught him smuggling a nuclear bomb into their territory. The thought alone made him shiver in the warm night breeze.

He only agreed to accompany the bomb to its target after paid sources within the Iranian military had guaranteed the safety of their route to the island. Of course, those sources had no idea what would be offloaded onto the shore. They believed a major oil company hired Dave to set up monitoring equipment to keep tabs on outbound oil shipments by competing companies.

The moonless night sky provided little light as Dave removed the padlock and pulled open the doors to the cargo container. With his security guard standing nearby to ensure the crew didn't suddenly get curious about their obviously illegal cargo, Dave stepped inside and turned on a powerful flashlight.

Even though he had worked on the bomb many times, Dave always found the mere presence of the device deeply unnerving.

Shaking off his raw fear of the weapon's devastating potential, Dave unscrewed a few retaining bolts with a small electric screwdriver and removed the nose cone. Inside, he located the metal tube containing the cylindrical plutonium arming plug. With extreme care, Dave removed the critical plutonium from the tube. With the plug removed, Dave found the lever he and his team installed to open the trap door at the bottom of the tube. Moving the lever upward opened the end of the tube. Then Dave re-inserted the plutonium cylinder and slowly pushed it down the tube until it seated into the uranium core. A satisfying, but frightening, 'click' told him the plutonium was secure.

The bomb was now alive.

Dave quickly reassembled the nose cone and stepped back. Even though he knew the bomb could not explode until the shaped TNT charges around the core ignited, sweat still poured down his face and neck. The old bomb sat at the bottom of the Atlantic Ocean for more than sixty years, and despite his best efforts to update its safety mechanisms, there had been only so much he could do.

After taking a few deep breaths to calm his nerves and steady his hand, Dave unlocked and opened a square access panel on the side of the bomb's casing. Inside, a small square metal box with a single red LED light and a simple toggle switch sat securely riveted to a steel bulkhead. The deceivingly plain little device was actually a modern detonator. Once activated, a call to the detonator's special number from a satellite phone anywhere in the world would ignite a massive nuclear explosion.

Dave paused to gather himself before continuing.

To activate the detonator, all he had to do was push the toggle switch back and forth two times. The task could not have been simpler. But the consequences of making a mistake would be catastrophic. As a security measure, if the toggle was thrown only once, the weapon would detonate in exactly one hour. If someone manipulated the switch more than twice, the bomb would explode immediately. After admonishing himself for being nervous, Dave reached inside and pushed the switch back and forth. Once. Twice. A moment later, the red light on front of the box turned green.

Dave's hand shook a bit as he closed and locked the access panel. Though fully aware of his actions and why he undertook this mission, he couldn't shake the strange feeling that threatened to overcome him as he stood next to the bomb. It wasn't fear. Or guilt.

It took him a minute to put a finger on it. He felt utterly alone.

He, and he alone, would do this nearly unthinkable act. Few men in history had been responsible for death and chaos on this scale. Was he a psychopath? Or was he just pragmatic about the state of the world?

He fully understood the enormity of his actions. He knew the destructive power of the bomb and he had carefully calculated its blast radius. The explosion would destroy Greater Tunb Island and vaporize every human inhabitant. But that was only the start.

Strong northwesterly winds, called Shamal Winds, would carry radioactive fallout over the northern Gulf and into the oil fields of Kuwait and Iraq – shutting them down for years. Crucially, the radiation from the blast would render the Strait of Hormuz, and perhaps the bulk of oil fields in the Middle East, totally useless.

In the end, he told himself it didn't matter. He had just prodded a sleeping monster to life and nobody on the ship, including him, could disarm it now. And afterward, he would enjoy riches and power beyond his wildest dreams.

Anyway, every man has a price.

Dave plucked out his satellite phone and called Santiago. Margie Franks answered immediately.

"Our baby is alive," Dave reported.

"You sound nervous," Margie responded. "Is there a problem?"

"No. But perhaps you'd like to change fucking places with me and see how you feel?" Dave responded.

"No thanks," Margie said, flippantly. "How long?"

"We'll be there in an hour. Weather has delayed us. I'll keep you informed," Dave replied.

"Just make it happen."

"You'll know when it does. Believe me," Dave answered, before closing his phone.

FIFTY-SIX

Ras Al-Khaimah
UAE

A gentle breeze lifted sheer white window coverings into the room as Agent Stella Sims opened the sliding door to a wide balcony. For the past thirty minutes, she had been in deep discussion with Deal back in Oxford. The look on her face betrayed the gravity of their conversation.

"Are you okay?" Sarah asked, immediately aware something was wrong.

"Yes and no," Sims replied, trying to hide her concern. "Michael, would you pick up the phone and ask Ahmed to come in please."

Michael could see Sims meant business and did as she asked. Less than a minute later, Ahmed appeared in the apartment.

"How may I be of service?" he asked, in his usual deferential manner.

"I've just received information your government needs to hear. I assume you are the person I need to speak to?" Sims asked, looking Ahmed in the eye.

Ahmed barely hesitated before responding.

"I am indeed with the UAE Security Operative, as you suspected, FBI Special Agent Stella Sims," Ahmed replied, dropping any pretense of being a simple servant. "I am at your service. Shall we sit?"

"I prefer to stand. Let's dispense with the formalities," Sims suggested, not at all surprised Ahmed knew exactly who she was and who she worked for. "This is urgent."

"Then it is best you proceed. Do you feel comfortable discussing this matter with Mr. King and Ms. Marshall present?"

"They are part of my team. So, yes."

Ahmed looked at the young couple and raised an eyebrow, but simply said, "Then please go on."

"I just got off the phone with Special Agent Frank Deal. He's in charge of our unit. Currently he's in Oxford. Just hours ago, he and MI5 officers successfully stopped a multi-pronged terrorist attack."

"Yeah!" Michael blurted, pumping his fist in the air, unaware of the much more dangerous plot Deal had just reported to Sims.

"Yes, good news. But we're going to have to wait to celebrate," Sims added solemnly. "There's more. Without going into detail right now, those attacks, although complex and well planned, were only a diversion to keep our team in England. We now know about a much more serious threat. The main attack, if you will. And it involves a nuclear weapon."

Ahmed didn't lose his cool detachment when he asked, "I am well aware of your team's expertise with WMDs. This is disturbing information, to be sure. But what has it to do with my country? Do you believe this nuclear device is a danger to the UAE?"

"We don't know yet. But I've been tasked with finding out," Sims answered. "The question is whether the UAE will cooperate with us. I feel fairly certain His Highness will agree, but we don't want to overstep," Sims explained.

Suddenly, the door to the apartment opened and Ali walked inside, tossing his traditional robes on one of the low soft couches in the center of the room.

Ahmed turned and bowed deeply. "My sheik. Welcome home."

"Thank you, my brother. The answer to your question, Stella, is yes. Your help, and that of your entire team are most welcome."

"Thank you, Your Highness," Sims answered formally. "Do I understand that Ahmed is your brother?"

"Indeed, he is. There is a long tradition of trusting only family members in this part of the world. Now, what's this about a nuclear weapon?" Ali asked.

Sims explained what Deal learned in Oxford.

"Could this have anything to do with the controversy between my country, Oman and Iran?" Ali asked. "And by the way, thank you for the information about the Iranians from earlier."

"That's a distinct possibility. Agent Deal, MI5 officer Eva McWilkinson, and the rest of our team have developed a theory that you need to hear."

Ali motioned everyone into seats. This time, Sims didn't protest.

"Alright Stella, please tell us about this theory," Ali prompted.

Sims outlined the scenario Deal and the rest of the team had uncovered while Ali sat quietly. If the possibility of a nuclear weapon on the doorstep of his country frightened him, he didn't show it. In the last twenty-four hours he had confidently and effectively taken over the sheikdom of his emirate and shouldered the responsibility of quelling the crisis between his country, Oman, and Iran. He reacted like a seasoned leader.

"Agent Deal, Bubba and Zach will remain in England to assist with rounding up the terror cell responsible for the attack there and rooting out Sir Gregory's accomplices. Although, Agent Deal expressed his willingness to come here immediately if Your Highness requested his presence," Sims said, finishing her briefing.

"I'm perfectly comfortable as long as you are here," Ali responded. He then turned to Ahmed.

"Is the SO in possession of any information that would either confirm or refute this theory?"

"No, my sheik. As you know, the Security Operative has increased patrols near our shores to deter the Iranians from any overt act against us. But we have not approached the Tunb Islands since they were taken by the Iranians fifty years ago. If the target of this attack is Greater Tunb, then is it not the Iranians who will have to deal with it?" Ahmed suggested.

Ali took a moment to explain to the Americans how the Tunb islands once belonged to his emirate, the RAK. In an act of aggression in the early 1970s, Iran invaded the islands, hoping to create a chokepoint in the Strait of Hormuz. Ali's great grandfather gave up the islands peacefully for two reasons. First, the islands were desolate and offered no useful resources. Second, western countries guaranteed the Strait would remain open for international shipping, thus effectively countering any benefit the Iranians hoped to gain by occupying the otherwise worthless island chain.

"Let's assume for a moment there is a nuclear bomb on the way to Greater Tunb. As Stella told us, this device weighs in excess of three tons and is more than ten feet long. How would it be transported?" Ali asked the group.

Ahmed spoke first. "The Iranians have a small airfield on the island, but it is used only to transport military troops and supplies. They also have several anti-aircraft batteries. Air transport of such a weapon to the island is out of the question."

"So, it would have to go by ship of some sort," Sims concluded.

"Yes," Ali agreed. "But the Strait is one of the world's busiest shipping lanes. Everything from massive oil tankers to tiny fishing vessels ply the waters day and night. Even if we had the resources, it would not be possible to stop and search them all."

"Until some ship or something approaches the island," Sarah said.

Sarah's simple, but brilliant, insight rang true with everyone in the room.

"Can U.S. satellites provide us a picture of the Strait and its shipping lanes?" Ali asked.

"It can do better than that," Sims replied. "I can request access to imagery and plots of courses and speeds that should pare down the number of suspect vessels. With a nuclear threat out there, we'll have as much coverage as we need. I'll get on that now."

Sims left the group to arrange the satellite overflights.

"That's good," Michael said. "But once we have identified a bunch of ships that *might* be carrying the bomb, we need a way to pick out the right one. And, I might have an idea how."

Ali looked at Michael and asked, "What do you suggest?"

Michael smiled. "Your drone. The long range one you brought along with us from Oxford. It can easily get out to the islands. And with a high-def camera on board, we should be able to get pictures of high enough quality to pick out the right boat or whatever. Plus, the Iranians won't pick it up on radar."

"Yes!" Ali said. "And I can increase our chances further. I'll also mount a radiation detector. An old nuclear weapon will leak enough radiation to be easily identified. Perfect. I'll need some help. While Stella arranges the satellite coverage, Sarah, Michael and I will prepare the drone."

"My sheik, may I be excused?" Ahmed asked. "I would like to have our analysts look at effects on the country should the worst come to pass. It is only prudent."

"Of course, my brother. Please proceed as you see best," Ali responded.

As Ahmed left the room, Sims put her hand over her phone and looked back at the group.

"Move fast, guys. Agent Deal believes we have hours – at best."

FIFTY-SEVEN

Dave Knox listened with growing alarm as the engine on the coastal transport ship sputtered and coughed. For the past thirty minutes, their progress across the Strait of Hormuz had slowed to a crawl. As plumes of grey smoke appeared over the deck, the boat came to a complete halt. Dave quickly made his way to the rear of the tiny transport to assess the situation. He found two crewmen crouched inside the engine compartment, covered with grease and sweat, cursing at the engine in their native language. Their useless anger at the old engine irritated Dave. To him, mechanical devices possessed a life of their own. And like any living thing, they needed proper care and attention and not abuse.

"What the hell is going on?" Dave shouted into the cramped space below the deck.

In response, one of the crew hit the engine's intake manifold with a huge wrench, threw his arms into the air and shouted some unintelligible explanation.

With no way to respond to the irate crewman, Dave ran to the pilothouse. He found the captain of the boat slumped in a battered chair next to the ship's controls, casually smoking a cigarette. When he saw Dave at the door, the captain brushed ashes from his grimy t-shirt and sat up slightly.

"No problem! No problem! We go five minutes," he said, flashing a smile through deeply stained teeth.

"We have to go *now*!" Dave said, pointing at the watch on his wrist.

"No problem! No problem!" the captain repeated. "Five minutes. No problem!"

Getting nowhere, Dave called to his bodyguard.

"Tell him to fix this boat now. And give him a good reason to get off his ass," Dave ordered.

The bodyguard shrugged, unslung his Uzi assault rifle, and pointed it at the captain. The message got through. The man jumped to his feet and scampered toward the stern.

"No problem! No problem! Five minutes!"

A few minutes later, the engine coughed twice and came back to life.

Dave slumped against the side of the cabin, nearly exhausted. Checking his GPS, he saw Greater Tunb was still almost ten miles to the east. At their decreased speed, he estimated it would take another two hours before they came within sight of the island. At least they would be approaching the shore under the cover of darkness.

Not for the first time, the genius aerospace engineer and physicist wondered how he came to be on a broken-down ship, carrying a fully-armed nuclear bomb to an Iranian-held island. Yet, here he was. To help his mood, his thoughts turned to his escape plan.

Once they pulled the flat-bottomed boat onto the shore of the island, the crew would simply place the container with the bomb on the beach. A mile back out to sea, he would be picked up by helicopter and whisked across the Gulf to Bahrain, where he would board a plane and detonate the device.

About three hours from that moment, he would be thirty thousand feet over Africa, sipping vintage champagne and watching the world descend into uproar and confusion on never-ending news feeds.

Dave stepped back on deck and tried to dry his soaked shirt in the slow hot breeze. The sweat on his back came from the coiled tension in his gut, not the heat of the Middle East.

FIFTY-EIGHT

As Dave plowed slowly across the Strait of Hormuz, Amina Kent stepped from a chartered jet in Ras Al-Khaimah. Dressed in the latest Paris fashion, Amina confidently presented her counterfeit Kuwaiti passport to a deferential and distracted customs agent, more concerned with ogling the beautiful girl than making sure her credentials checked out.

Amina became concerned when she found several serious-looking military police officers securing the airport entrance. She knew the brewing crisis with Oman and Iran had triggered enhanced security all over the UAE. But a broad smile and flirtatious glance their way melted the soldiers' tense suspicion. One of the guards even stepped forward to open the door for her.

The ease with which she gained access to the UAE, even in a time of crises, didn't surprise Amina whatsoever. She effectively used her stunning beauty and natural charisma as her greatest asset. Doors just seemed to open for her wherever she went. Nobody ever suspected that the stylish young girl, who looked like a model for Vogue magazine, made a fortune killing other human beings.

Amina paused outside the airport. For a moment, she looked out across the parking lot to the empty desert and allowed memories of her childhood to creep into her head. She remembered the day when she was about seven, peddling cheap trinkets to tourists on the sidewalks of Cairo next to her mother. Even dressed in rags, her long shiny black hair and wide-set, haunting eyes attracted attention. And on that day, too much attention. She had been chewing on a piece of stale pita bread when, suddenly, rough hands snatched her from the sidewalk and threw her into a dirty blue van. She still remembered her mother's screams fading into the distance as the van sped away.

For the next seven years, she was bought and sold like livestock. Then, at age fourteen, she stole a knife from her current owner's kitchen. When the sick pedophile threw her on his bed for his usual sadistic games, she sliced open the fat pig's carotid artery. After watching him choke to death on his own blood, she calmly showered off and escaped into the night. Eventually, she became a ghost, moving around the world without any official identity.

Now, while she occasionally took contracts on females, she looked forward to killing men. Both types of jobs were profitable. She just got more personal satisfaction from watching a man die. Preferably slowly.

Taking a deep breath, she shook off the memories and hailed a cab. She didn't have any time to waste. She had a job to do in the city center and her contract required it to be completed in the next few hours.

The taxi took Amina into Ras-Al Khaimah and dropped her off in front of the same glass twin towers where Sims, Sarah, and Michael were meeting with Ali. Stepping from the cab, Amina looked at her watch. Her contact should have been waiting for her arrival.

While she waited, Amina tied a black and red scarf around her head in the Arab fashion and put on a pair of large Gucci sunglasses.

"Ah! Ms. Kent! Thank you so much for coming!" Ahmed said, emerging from the heavily-guarded entrance to Ali's building. "It is such a pleasure to have you in our country!"

Ahmed took Amina's rolling suitcase in hand and led her to the front doors. When one of the guards stepped forward, Ahmed shooed him away with a flip of his hand.

"Ms. Kent is a guest of His Highness," Ahmed explained, leading the girl inside.

"Thank you," Amina said, flashing the guard a smile.

When they were well out of earshot of anyone, Ahmed pulled a white key card embossed with Ali's royal seal from his pocket.

"This will give you access to the entire building. Ali is on the top floor with an FBI agent and two younger members of her team. There will be a car waiting for you on the other side of the building for...afterward," Ahmed said.

After a pause, he stressed, "*Do not fail*. My brother is unfit to lead our emirate. My grandfather should have seen this. At least your employers had the wisdom to place me in charge."

"I could care less about your reasons or theirs. I've been paid handsomely already. So, calm down. Go to your office and make a long telephone call or have a meeting. You'll need an alibi. Just stay out of my way. What about security?" Amina asked.

"You are cleared as a personal guest of Sheik Badran. If you are stopped, show that card," Ahmed answered, trying to overcome his nerves.

Amina noticed Ahmed's eyes shifting from side to side.

"Go!" Amina ordered.

Ahmed nodded, and slinked away, already imagining how satisfying it would feel to be called "Your Highness."

Amina turned and took the elevator to the top floor. When the doors opened, an immense guard dressed in a black suit stepped forward.

"Good afternoon," Amina said, coolly presenting the card Ahmed provided. "His Highness is expecting me."

"Please remove your head covering and glasses," the guard requested.

"Of course! I'm so sorry," Amina said, slowly unwinding the scarf and gently shaking her hair so it fell over her shoulders.

Amina looked into the guard's eyes and removed her glasses and opened her bright red handbag.

"Oh, dear!" Amina said, putting her hand inside the purse.

"What is it Ma'am?" the guard asked, leaning forward to see.

"This," Amina said, calmly, pressing the purse into the guard's chest and pulling the trigger of a small silenced semi-automatic pistol three times.

Amina had to jump out of the way when the man's dead body fell forward, threatening to crush her into the opulent hall carpeting. Without hesitating, she threw the handbag to the side, opened the door to Ali's apartment, and stepped inside.

She found herself in a short entry hall. Pressing herself against the wall and holding her weapon in front of her, she moved inside. A glance around the corner provided her with a glimpse of the brightly-lit apartment, floor-to-ceiling windows and expensive furnishings. But her attention was drawn to a blond-haired woman seated on a couch, engrossed with an open laptop.

Amina waited, using all her senses to detect whether anyone else was in the room. With no one else present, she stepped out of the alcove, her gun leveled at the other woman.

"Hello," Amina said.

Sims looked up from her laptop to find a gun pointed at her head. She didn't recognize the other woman, but from Zach's description of the girl that tried to kidnap him, she had a good idea of the intruder's identity.

Sims stood slowly and raised her hands. She didn't have a weapon, so she tried to stall.

"You're Amina Kent," Sims said.

"Why, yes. Yes, I am," Amina replied, stealing quick glances around the apartment but keeping Sims covered. "And you are?"

"Special Agent Stella Sims, FBI. What are you doing here?" Sims asked, not taking her eyes off the assassin.

"Where's the prince?" Amina asked.

"Oh, I see," Sims said. "How did you get in here?"

"His brother let me in," Amina answered, simply. "Now, enough girl talk. Tell me where he is, or I'll just kill you and find him myself."

"I don't know..."

Amina fired, the pistol making an evil spitting sound that got lost in the huge penthouse.

Sims crashed to the floor, blood splattering over her still-open laptop and the white couch.

Sarah left Ali's personal workshop near the rear of the massive flat. Halfway down the long hallway, she heard Sims speaking to another woman. She couldn't make out what they were saying, but she could tell something was wrong.

When Amina pulled the trigger, Sarah froze.

A gunshot?

Sarah almost ran forward, then stopped. *Should she run back to the workshop? Or see if Sims needed help?*

Then she caught a glimpse of Amina Kent turning toward the hallway.

What is she doing here?

Sarah knew that if she tried to get back to the workshop, Amina would see her before she could get that far. Instead, Sarah stepped into the kitchen area to her left. Inside, she scanned the countertops for a weapon. The only thing within reach was a heavy stainless-steel pepper grinder.

In a flash, Sarah grabbed the makeshift club and knelt just inside the doorway.

She had no idea what she was going to do, but she had to do *something.* Sims could be hurt, even dead, and Michael and Ali had no idea they were in danger.

Amina turned toward the hallway, intent on finding Ali. She moved swiftly, but silently into the hall, hunting for her prey. At the doorway to the kitchen, she paused and glanced inside. She saw and heard nothing. But something wasn't right. *A fragrance that shouldn't be there.*

The assassin stepped into the cold, quiet kitchen. Highly-polished quartz countertops and stainless-steel appliances reflected the light from the cloudless sky and glittering Gulf waters outside. Then she saw it, in the glass of an oversized refrigerator — the distorted reflection of someone kneeling.

But she was too late.

Sarah swung the pepper grinder with all her might into the Amina's shin.

"Aaaaaaa!" Amina screamed, the intense pain making her lose her grip on the gun.

In a flash, Sarah jumped up, grabbed the gun, and shouted, "Michael!"

Even as tears streamed down her face, Amina lashed out with her other leg, trying to make contact with the scared girl, awkwardly holding the gun out with two hands.

"Sarah?" Michael called.

Amina knew she was out of time.

"Another time, bitch!" Amina spat, quickly recovering, and running out of the apartment.

Michael found Sarah still shakily holding Amina's gun. He gently took it from her hands, engaged the safety switch, and took her in his arms.

When Ali ran by, Sarah shook out of Michael's embrace and raced from the kitchen. She and Michael found Ali holding Sims' head in his lap, pressing his torn shirt against Sim's shoulder.

"Is she…?" Michael asked, unable to complete his question.

"No. But she needs help. Right now," Ali replied. "Push the red button on the phone!"

Moments later, the room filled with black-uniformed security guards and medical personnel.

Ali wouldn't leave Sims until a helicopter arrived on the roof just above his apartment. Ali ordered his personal royal doctor to stay at her side and keep him informed about her condition.

Re-entering his apartment, he found Michael and Sarah sitting close to each other on a couch, well away from where Sims had been shot. They looked at him, leaving no doubt about what they wanted to ask.

"The doctor believes she will be fine. He called it a "through and through" wound to her left shoulder. She lost a lot of blood, but…." Ali said, relief in his voice.

"Did they find the girl?" Michael asked. "Sarah said it was Amina Kent, the same girl that tried to turn Zach over to terrorists."

"Unfortunately, no. Somehow, she bypassed all our security."

"Tell everyone looking for her that she'll have a limp for a few days," Sarah said. "And a nasty bruise on her right shin."

"How did you know to strike her on the shin?" Ali asked, impressed with Sarah's bravery.

"Self-defense class," Sarah answered. "If she had been a guy, I'd have aimed higher."

"We have distributed her description to every law enforcement agency in the country. We'll just have to let them do their job," Ali said. "We have work to do here."

Michael rose from the couch. "We need to call Agent Deal first. But I'm ready to get back in the workshop and finish up rigging your drone."

"I already contacted Special Agent Deal," Ali replied. "He has asked you two to stay here and provide assistance. Michael, I'd appreciate your help with the drone. Deal provided the code to Stella's computer, and he is transmitting the satellite images. He asked if Sarah would monitor sea traffic around Greater Tunb. When he heard of Stella's injury, he decided to come here as quickly as possible. He and the rest of your team will arrive in five hours. But that's well after when he believes the bomb will detonate."

Ali and Michael left Sarah with Sims' laptop. The program tracking vessels in and around the Strait of Hormuz provided a detailed picture of the entire region. Each vessel on the screen was accompanied by an inset with its speed and course. Choosing a ship with the cursor produced a course projection in the form of a red line. With another click of the mouse, the satellite zoomed in on the chosen ship.

Sarah methodically examined ships and boats that maintained a general heading toward Greater Tunb Island. As darkness descended, the satellite automatically switched to infrared mode, which allowed Sarah to continue monitoring the sea, but cut down on the detail she was able to see when she zoomed in on a particular target.

Thirty minutes later, Sarah became convinced she had looked at every possible ship, boat, barge or fishing scow that might be headed to Greater Tunb. Nothing.

Then it hit her. If she concluded nothing in the Strait was currently moving toward the island, there was only one other possibility.

She aimed the satellite camera at the island itself.

FIFTY-NINE

The old coastal cargo ship's flat bottom ground onto the rocky beach of Greater Tunb with an unsettling groan. Dave Knox stood next to the pilothouse while the ship's captain expertly placed the bow far enough onto the beach to allow his cargo to be unloaded without the ship becoming trapped in place.

Despite the captain's assurances that the Iranians rarely patrolled this part of the island, Dave looked inland, half-expecting to find soldiers waiting to arrest him and the entire crew. But the only thing he saw was a stretch of empty beach with dark desert beyond.

"Captain!" Dave called into the pilothouse. "How long will it take to offload the container?"

Not getting a response, Dave climbed the short ladder and found the captain talking to one of his crewmen in a low voice. When he saw Dave out of the corner of his eye, the fat, grimy owner of the ship began shouting in Arabic. The other man nodded and jumped from the pilothouse.

"Yes! Yes! No problem!" the captain said, turning to face Dave. "That man lazy. We unload cargo here on beach as you say. Yes?"

Dave had to set aside his revulsion at dealing with the disgusting ship's captain.

"How long to offload the container?" Dave asked again.

The captain smiled through his yellow teeth and said, "You come! I show you. No problem!"

Pungent body odor threatened to make Dave gag as the captain squeezed past him and dropped to the deck.

Dave followed along as the captain ambled to the bow where the shipping container sat still firmly locked to the deck. Overhead, the crane remained stowed.

"Captain! What's going on? This must be done now!" Dave demanded, tapping his watch with his finger.

Instead of answering, the captain spun around with a wicked curved dagger in his hand and a derisive sneer on his face.

Dave was about to shout for his bodyguard when shots rang out at the stern of the boat. He turned in time to see one of the crewmen scream and topple headlong into the shallow water below. When more automatic weapon fire erupted at the other end of the ship, Dave instinctively ducked and threw himself against the pilothouse bulkhead. For the next fifteen seconds, the night filled with the loud chatter of automatic weapons fire.

Then, someone cried out in pain and the shooting stopped.

Dave stood and looked back toward the stern. When his guard didn't appear, he feared the worst.

"Your big man dead. You open container now," the captain demanded, pressing the point of his dagger into Dave's back. "If you wish to live more."

With his automatic still tucked into his shoulder holster, Dave just raised his hands and nodded. He couldn't possibly get to it before the captain gutted him like a fish.

"Go now," the captain ordered, allowing Dave to pass by, the knife now resting over Dave's kidney.

After taking a step forward, the captain snatched the gun out of Dave's holster and tossed it into the water. Now completely unarmed, the loathsome ship's captain threatened Dave's entire operation with nothing but a rusty knife.

"Okay. Okay!" Dave said, walking to the container's heavy metal doors.

"You open now," the captain ordered, pressing the dagger harder into Dave's spine.

Without another word, Dave picked up the heavy padlock and entered a long string of numbers. When the lock snapped open, Dave grabbed the handle of the door and pulled.

The captain peered around Dave into the darkness. With the knife still held against Dave's back, he pulled a flashlight from his pocket.

The beam of light landed directly on the nose of the Mark 15 nuclear bomb.

The captain's mouth dropped open. Whatever he thought may be in the container didn't compare to what he actually found. Moving the light down the side of the bomb, he could clearly see the square stabilizing fins. Shocked to his core, the captain took a step backward.

That's when Dave struck. Lifting his arms, he threw an elbow into the captain's face. The man screamed and dropped the knife as blood erupted from his nose.

Not hesitating, Dave landed another punch to the captain's face. Now staggering backward, the captain couldn't react as Dave picked up the dirty knife.

"No! No!" the captain shouted.

But Dave wasn't listening. He coldly slashed the knife across the captain's round belly, opening a deep bloody gash.

"Please!" the captain begged, falling to his knees. "Please no!"

Consumed with rage, Dave plunged the knife into the captain's neck, viciously twisting the blade as it pushed through bone and cartilage.

"No problem," Dave snarled, yanking out the knife and stepping back to watch the captain fall to the deck.

For a minute, Dave stood triumphantly over the body, blood still dripping from the knife in his shaking hand. He felt like an animal, completely consumed by the bloodlust still pumping through his veins.

When the adrenalin finally began to dissipate, Dave calmed down. He had to find a way to finish the operation.

Running to the back of the boat, he found his guard's body draped over a railing. Across the deck, the second crewman lay dead, an old AK-47 assault rifle still clutched in his hand. Now alone, Dave had no choice but to offload the bomb himself and pilot the boat off the island.

Back at the bow, Dave used the crane control panel to swing the lifting arm directly over the container. After climbing to the top of the metal box, he attached lifting straps to the crane's hook. Now all he had to do was release the mechanisms holding the container to the deck and lift it onto the beach.

Kneeling to release the first hold-down point, Dave found a heavy-duty combination lock placed through the bolt. It would have to be removed before the bomb could be lifted off the deck. Checking the other three hold-down points, he found they were all secured with identical combination locks.

And he had just killed the only man who knew the combination.

Beginning to panic, Dave desperately searched the ship for something he could use to break or cut through the locks. Bolt cutters, hacksaw, even a heavy sledgehammer might work. But he found nothing.

"Well, shit," Dave spat.

Nearly exhausted, Dave sat down on the deck, his back leaning against the cargo container. He needed time to think.

He knew it didn't matter if he detonated the device while it was still on the ship. The effect would be exactly the same. But he also had to get away. That meant convincing his extraction team to pick him up at the island and not after he reached a safe distance out to sea.

Dave opened his satellite phone and spoke with his team leader. The helicopter crew flatly refused to approach the island by air. The Iranians maintained a well-known no-fly zone three kilometers around the Tunb Islands which they enforced with a battery of anti-aircraft guns.

Finally, Dave convinced them to send a fast cigarette boat to the island from a marina in Dubai – seventy miles to the south. But even at top speed, Dave couldn't expect to be extracted for the better part of two hours. Until they arrived, he would be alone, just hoping the Iranians didn't choose that particular night to drive down the beach.

While he waited, Dave did what he could to ensure his operation would go forward even if someone discovered the boat after he left.

After tying whatever he could find as weights to the dead bodies still onboard, he rolled the dead men one-by-one into the water.

Then, Dave opened a hatch and dropped into the engine compartment. With the knife he had used to slice open the captain's throat, he cut the rubber fuel line leading to the engine's fuel pump and tossed the knife into the darkness.

While gasoline dripped into the bottom of the boat, Dave climbed back on deck and sat down to wait. The operation had nearly cost him his life. Nearing the end of his physical and mental endurance, Dave decided that Margie Franks and the rest of the Directors of The Cause owed him. Big.

And, one way or another, they would pay up.

SIXTY

Sarah found Ali and Michael in the workshop, testing the gimbal mechanism that allowed a high-definition camera mounted under Ali's drone to swivel and tilt in all directions. Ali used a small control stick attached to a laptop to manipulate the camera in every direction. As he did, a view of the lab appeared on the screen in front of him.

"I think I found the ship," Sarah announced, a bit breathlessly.

Ali brought the camera to a halt.

"That's great!" Michael exclaimed.

"Where?" Ali asked.

"I looked for every kind of ship or boat headed anywhere near the island. When I didn't find anything promising, I looked at the island itself and saw this," Sarah explained, turning the open laptop in her hand around for Ali and Michael to see.

All three looked intently at the image. The satellite's infrared camera revealed a small cargo ship with its bow planted on the eastern side of Greater Tunb Island. They could just make out a single shipping container still in place below a crane. It looked like the crew intended to offload the container directly onto the beach.

"Nice work, Sarah!" Ali commented. "You would make an excellent analyst."

"It looks like the engine is nearly cold," Michael observed. "There's not much of a heat signature coming from the engine compartment. It's been on the beach for a little while already."

"What's this little white spot?" Sarah asked. "A person?"

Ali looked closely at the image.

"Let's put it on the big screen. Maybe we can get a bit more definition," Ali suggested, taking the laptop from Sarah and casting the image onto a 75-inch monitor mounted on the wall.

"No doubt about it," Michael said, squinting at the image. "That's some guy sitting with his back against the cargo container."

"What do you think he's doing?" Sarah asked. "I don't see anyone else on board."

"No idea," Ali replied. "But we can sure find out. Let's launch the drone."

Michael remained quiet a moment, which drew Sarah's attention.

"What's wrong?" she asked.

"I hate to say it," Michael said. "But if there's an actual nuclear bomb or whatever in that container, it's already in place. We may not have enough time for the drone to fly all that way."

Ali knew he was right. Even at top speed, it would take over an hour for the drone to fly from Ras Al-Khaimah to the island. But he had an idea.

"Michael, help me with the drone. I believe we can cut down on the flight time. Sarah, would you stay here and monitor our progress? Let Agent Deal know what we are doing. And, if you don't mind, let me know if Stella's condition changes?"

"Sure," Sarah replied. "But maybe you better tell me what you have in mind. Where are you and Michael going?"

Ali pointed to Greater Tunb. "There."

"The hell you are!" Sarah exclaimed. "I don't want you guys anywhere close to a nuclear bomb!"

After Ali explained his plan, Sarah grabbed Michael's shirt and pulled his face down to her own.

"Don't you dare take any foolish chances!"

Michael smiled and put his hand on the side of Sarah's face.

"I won't. I promise."

Ali made a quiet call on his phone before leading Michael to the roof. After placing the drone down a moment, Ali removed a small remote control from his pocket and pressed a button. To his right, a set of clamshell doors began opening on a box-like structure Michael hadn't noticed before. When the doors opened fully, a sleek futuristic-looking helicopter emerged from the building, riding on a robotic platform. When it arrived at the center of the roof's helipad, rotors automatically unfolded above the helicopter's cockpit and the engine began spinning up to speed.

"Hell yeah!" Michael cried, profoundly impressed.

"Yes, quite the toy," Ali replied, smiling.

"Bubba's going to kick himself for missing this!" Michael exclaimed.

The gleaming dark gray helicopter crouched on the helipad, slightly nose-down, like a big cat coiling its muscles to leap at its prey. A dark glass windscreen wrapped around the cockpit, giving the craft a slightly evil appearance. Above, high-tech rotors barely made a whisper in the air.

"How fast is she?" Michael asked as they picked up the drone.

"Fast cruise is 160 mph," Ali replied. "But she'll go faster."

"Where's the pilot?"

"You're looking at him," Ali said.

As Ali and Michael climbed into the air over the Strait of Hormuz, Sarah reported what had occurred in the past hour to Agent Deal.

"They did what?" Deal shouted. "Who the hell authorized them taking off, by themselves, into the Persian *goddamned* Gulf?"

Deal's outburst didn't faze Sarah in the least. Men often overreacted before the reasonable part of their brains kicked in.

"I suppose Ali did, sir," Sarah answered. "He is the sheik of this part of the UAE after all. And, isn't *finding* the nuclear bomb the first priority? Ali has his own helicopter. They left a few minutes ago. Like I said, they're just going to launch a drone to check out the ship."

Sarah listened to silence over the phone. She didn't know what to expect next.

"Alright. Alright. Ali's move is rash, but given the circumstances, probably for the best."

"What do you mean, sir?" Sarah asked, hearing the deep concern in Deal's voice.

Deal explained how relations between the UAE, Oman and Iran had deteriorated in the past few hours. Negotiations ended after Iran and Oman accused the UAE of mobilizing its military. Despite flat denials by the UAE, the Omanis moved a battalion of armored vehicles into the area around Khasab, where Ali's family held the rights to oil reserves. In response, the Iranians began rattling swords by sending fighters over the Strait of Hormuz, nearly piercing Omani airspace. Even a perceived intrusion into the territory of any of the three antagonistic nations would ignite a devastating war.

"So, if Ali had ordered a military helicopter or patrol boat into the waters around Greater Tunb, the Iranians would have attacked," Sarah concluded.

"Yes. And any intervention by the U.S. Navy would have drawn immediate condemnation, if not overt threats, from Russia, China and others. This whole thing is a powder keg and the fuse is lit," Deal said.

"Then they better be careful," Sarah replied, with more confidence than she felt.

Michael turned to Ali shortly after taking off. "How long before we can release the drone?"

Ali checked their position. Before departing, he had entered a waypoint on his navigational computer a mile from the grounded cargo ship.

"Twenty minutes, forty-two seconds," Ali responded. "But I'll try to cut that down a bit."

Michael could feel the aircraft accelerate. On the heads-up display that appeared to float just outside the visor of his helmet, he could see their airspeed increase from 160 to 170 mph.

"This helmet is cool," Michael said. "We look like badass fighter pilots with these things on."

"Yes, we do, don't we?" Ali responded with a chuckle.

Ali truly appreciated Michael's ability to remain relaxed. They were flying at top speed toward an enemy island where a nuclear bomb may be waiting to detonate. They both had every right to be deeply anxious, if not terrified. Plus, while Ali was there to protect his country, Michael volunteered to come along just because it was the right thing to do.

A few minutes passed in silence before Ali asked, "Would you mind going back and getting the drone ready? We'll be on station shortly."

"Roger that," Michael said, unbuckling and slipping between the seats into the passenger compartment. "By the way, I can't fly a helicopter and I'm not checked out on your drone so…"

"No worries, my friend," Ali responded, hearing the concern in Michael's voice. "I'll fly the drone while the autopilot holds us in a hover."

"That's a relief," Michael responded before turning back to the drone.

Time passed quickly as Michael doubled-checked the drone's electrical charge and did a final test on the camera and Geiger counter.

"We're five miles from the island. I'm dropping down to one hundred feet to avoid Iranian radar. Hold on," Ali said.

Michael held onto the back of a heavily-padded passenger seat. When Ali dived toward the ground, Michael felt weightless for a second, like an amusement ride that unexpectedly goes into a free fall.

As soon as they returned to level flight, Ali had Michael open the wide side door. The helicopter became motionless and Michael picked up the drone.

"Ready?" Michael asked.

Ali picked up his laptop, flipped up the control stick and initiated the camera.

"Launch on my mark. Three. Two. One. Launch!"

Michael shoved the big drone out the door and watched it fall, ungainly twisting and rolling toward the water. For a second, he thought it would crash. But in an instant, its eight propellors came to life, steadying the pilotless aircraft. Then it silently leapt forward and disappeared from his line of sight.

"I'm sending the signal back to Sarah. She can relay it to Agent Deal," Ali reported.

Michael stood behind the pilot's seat and watched the view on Ali's screen.

The drone's camera showed the darkened waters of the Strait flashing by just fifty feet below. When Ali lifted the camera's lens a bit, the island of Greater Tunb came into view.

At first, just a low dark mound on the horizon, barely discernable from the surrounding water, the island quickly grew on the screen as the drone approached.

"Michael, would you please check the radar and see if we have company of any kind?" Ali asked.

Michael climbed into the co-pilot's seat and looked closely at the radar screen. Ali had showed him what to look for, even though the symbols on the screen were fairly self-explanatory.

"No aircraft within a hundred miles. Several surface contacts, all moving slow. Wait! There's a small contact heading directly toward the island at high speed. Looks like seventy knots plus," Michael reported.

"That's too fast for a patrol boat. Must be a recreational speed-boat," Ali responded.

"Well, we're going to see it in a second on the drone's camera if it stays on course," Michael reported.

"I'm approaching the beached ship," Ali said. "We'll know if we have a problem in a few seconds."

SIXTY-ONE

Dave Knox heard the cigarette boat's engines long before he could see it approaching in the darkness. Standing, he straightened his clothes and made sure he had his satellite phone safely tucked into a zippered pocket.

Somehow, he had shepherded a nuclear bomb from the Persian Peninsula, across the Strait of Hormuz, and placed it onto an island controlled by the Iranians. Now, in just minutes, he would be spirited off the disgusting old boat and back to his life of luxury, wealth, and privilege.

Dave took a deep breath, allowing himself to revel in his accomplishment. Once he initiated a nuclear blast and closed the Persian Gulf, he would be heralded by The Cause and his personal fortune would increase at least tenfold.

Then he heard something else. A strange hum coming from somewhere above.

Looking up, he thought he saw a shadow pass overhead. Confused, he twisted around. Nothing.

But the hum didn't go away. Instead, it became louder. He could even hear it over the growing growl of the cigarette boat's big V-8 engines. He knew something was wrong, but he didn't have time to worry about it. His ride home was slowing down to come alongside.

When the long white speedboat bumped up against the side of the container ship, Dave forgot everything else. He ran to the railing and climbed down. In seconds, they reversed away from the island, and in a sweeping turn, sped off into the night.

Dave slumped into a comfortable passenger seat, pulled his satellite phone from his pocket and dialed Santiago.

"I'm away. I'll initiate as soon as I'm in the air," he said.

"How long will it be now?" Margie Franks demanded. "You're behind schedule by almost two hours."

Dave laughed into the phone.

"Let me put this in a language you will understand. It goes boom when I decide it goes boom. So, until then, *go fuck yourself.*"

Ali and Michael watched the unidentified man on the boat look into the air for the drone. Then the boat Michael saw on radar arrived. The man turned and jumped into the long, sleek craft that immediately blasted back out to sea.

"Whoever that was is gone now. Let's take a closer look at that container," Michael suggested.

"Agreed. We have good shots of his face anyway. Deal can figure out who he is later," Ali said, sending the drone as close as he dared to the rusty old cargo container.

"At first glance, it looks innocent enough," Michael observed. "And it's obviously still attached to the deck."

"Yes, but it appears someone was about to unload it. The crane arm is above the container and lifting straps are already attached. Maybe there was a malfunction," Ali offered.

"Hold on. Zoom in on the place where it's attached to the deck," Michael said. "Look there! Those are some big padlocks. Why would someone padlock a container to a ship?"

"Only if they were transporting something of great importance," Ali concluded. "Let's look at the Geiger readings."

Ali brought up the graph showing the amount of radiation leaking from the container on his screen. What he saw made his blood run cold.

Michael looked at the screen but couldn't decipher the numbers that appeared along the bar graph. But the look in Ali's eyes told him all he needed to know.

"Bad?" Michael asked.

"Yes," Ali said as he pulled up various published scientific charts of radiation levels.

"This is normal background radiation," Ali continued, pointing at a horizontal blue line that squiggled along the bottom of the graph generated by their Geiger counter. Then, pointing to a red line halfway up the graph he added, "And this is the reading coming from that container."

Michael looked where Ali indicated. "Is it dangerous?"

"The radiation leaking from the container isn't enough to be dangerous. The problem isn't the radiation. The problem is that it matches exactly a shielded combination of uranium and plutonium," Ali explained.

Michael didn't have to guess what that meant. Any doubt that a nuclear bomb rested in the container evaporated.

They found it.

Michael called Sarah and reported, as calmly as possible, what he and Ali uncovered. Though shaken by the thought of her boyfriend hovering so close to a nuclear weapon, Sarah managed to patch Michael and Ali through to Agent Deal.

"We're still an hour out of Rah Al-Khaimah," Deal said. "What's your status?"

Michael recounted their flight to the island, launching the drone, and the man they saw escaping by speedboat. Meanwhile, Ali sent the radiation readings they collected to Bubba's laptop.

After a moment, Bubba joined the conversation.

"The readings match a Mark 15 thermonuclear bomb from the late 1950s. The mystery of the lost nuke of Tybee Island has been solved," Bubba reported.

"What do we do, Boss?" Michael asked.

"We have to assume whoever was on the boat is still in control of that bomb. We also have to assume that since he didn't detonate the damn thing while on still on board, he will wait until he is well clear of the area before doing so. The problem is, we don't know when that will be."

"Can it be destroyed or disarmed?" Ali asked.

Bubba answered the question. "Destroying it with a cruise missile or some other explosive would throw deadly radiological debris into the air. The effects, both long and short term, might be even worse than an actual nuclear detonation. Plus, I'd have to say that anyone clever enough to smuggle a nuclear bomb into Iranian territory would make it extremely difficult, if not impossible, to disarm."

"Bubba and Agent Deal?" Michael asked. "What if it detonated under water instead of on land?"

"Hold on a second," Bubba said.

"Bubba's doing some calculations," Deal reported. "But in short, still bad, but manageable."

Bubba got back on the radio. "As I thought, the effects depend on depth. Of course, the deeper, the better. Water has a much higher density than air, so it contains the explosive effects. Underwater shock waves would be a problem for fish or submarines in the immediate area, but studies show that surface waves would be more like a bad storm than a tsunami."

Ali's fingers flew over his keyboard, bringing up nautical maps of the Gulf around Greater Tunb Island. The deepest part of the Persian Gulf was only five miles due east of the island. But maximum depth was only about three hundred feet.

"At that depth, and with the power of the weapon, I expect a column of water at the surface – maybe four hundred feet. Effects on land would be minimal. But you wouldn't want to be on a boat right over the detonation site," Bubba concluded.

"We don't have time for more analysis," Deal interjected. "We have to get that bomb under water if we can. And right now. Ali, what's the carry capacity of your aircraft?"

Ali turned grim. "Not even close. I can have a heavy lift helicopter here in an hour, maybe two at best."

Everyone turned silent. Options to keep the Middle East, and maybe the world, from descending into economic chaos and military confrontation were quickly slipping through their fingers.

Suddenly, Michael sat up in his seat. "Get me down there!" he blurted.

"What?" Deal demanded. "Why?"

"Look, the bomb's already on a boat. Let me pull it off the beach, drive it out into the water and sink the whole damn thing! Ali can pick me up."

"We don't know how much time we have," Deal said.

"Yeah, then why are we wasting time!?" Michael insisted. "It's simple. We leave it where it is to blow the shit out of everything. Or we move it."

"Damnit!" Deal shouted, angry at his lack of options. "Go!"

SIXTY-TWO

Ali didn't hesitate. The helicopter's nose dropped and he accelerated toward the grounded ship.

In the few minutes he had left, Michael called Sarah and told her what he was doing.

"No! Hell no, Michael King," Sarah cried. "You can't risk your life like that. Please!"

Michael didn't know what to say and felt bad for putting this burden on her.

"I'll be fine. A lot of people could die. Anyway, it's just a short boat ride. Ali will have me back there in an hour," Michael said with all the confidence he could muster.

"I love you. Please come back," Sarah pleaded.

"I love you, too," Michael replied. "I'll be back soon."

"I meant *now*, you big idiot!" Sarah said, crying.

"I know. Soon. I promise."

It didn't take long for Ali to hover over the stern of the cargo vessel. Michael grabbed a walkie-talkie from the helicopter's emergency kit and tossed a rope ladder out the side door. After throwing Ali a wave, he carefully climbed down the ladder as it twisted around in the rotor wash.

Michael jumped the last few feet onto the deck and immediately ran to the ship's pilothouse. To his relief, he found the key still inserted in the ship's ignition. Turning the key made the control panel come to life.

Michael had experience driving small boats on local lakes in the United States, so the ignition and throttle wouldn't pose a challenge. He didn't waste time figuring out any other controls. Pushing the 'start' button, he listened to the engine whine and turn before it coughed to life.

"Alright, baby! Here we go," he said out loud, before slowly pulling back on the throttle lever.

The engine revved, spinning the propellors in reverse. Ever so slowly, the ship began to squirm backward across the rocky beach. A few more seconds and he would be fully afloat.

Then the engine coughed twice and quit. Michael found himself in near silence, the boat's flat bow still partially lodged on the beach. He pushed the start button again, but the engine remained silent.

"Shit!"

Michael told himself to calm down. The fuel gauge indicated the boat still carried over half a tank of gas, so it had to be a problem with the engine itself.

Picking up the walkie-talkie Michael quickly reported to Ali. "Engine quit. I'm going to check it."

Opening the hatch to the engine compartment, Michael smelled the strong distinct odor of gasoline. If he knew anything about engines, he knew they didn't run without gas.

Michael jumped down into the dark cramped space and used a flashlight laying nearby to inspect the engine. The electrical connections looked good, so he pulled the fuel line off the fuel pump. Expecting gas to run out of the rubber tube, he was surprised to find the other end of the rubber line hanging free in his hand. Someone had obviously cut it cleanly in two. Looking down, he found a curved dagger with drying blood all over the blade.

Someone didn't want the boat to move away from the island.

With sweat breaking out on his head in the hot, humid air, Michael knew he didn't have time to search the ship for spare parts. And he didn't have a way to splice the fuel line back together well enough to hold while he piloted the ship. Then, he remembered his uncle's old fishing boat.

On a deep-sea fishing trip on the Gulf of Mexico, the boat had developed a leak in the main fuel tank. Michael had worried they would be stranded at sea waiting to be rescued by the Coast Guard. But his uncle told him something he had always remembered.

"Classic boats are great. But never take them out to sea without a backup plan."

His uncle had opened up the engine compartment, flipped a butterfly valve and switched to an auxiliary fuel tank, allowing them to safely return to shore.

"If anything qualifies as a classic, it's this piece of floating crap," Michael thought.

He didn't have to look too long before finding the emergency fuel tank. Using the bloody dagger, Michael sliced off a long length of fuel hose from the main system, connected it to the engine's fuel pump and plunged the other end into the auxiliary gas tank.

Back in the pilothouse, Michael took a deep breath and turned the engine over. Thirty seconds later, the old engine sprang back to life. Throwing the throttle into reverse, he backed completely off the beach. Once away from the island, he checked the compass and spun the wheel to the left, bringing the ship around to the correct course.

Slowly, the boat pushed its way through the water, gathering speed at an infuriatingly slow pace.

"I'm underway," Michael said into the radio. "I had a little problem with the fuel system, but it's okay now."

"Well done! You are on the proper course," Ali replied. "Are you at maximum speed, my friend?"

"Yeah, looks like this is it."

"Understood," Ali replied, doing his best to sound reassuring. "I'll stay with you."

"I'm fine. Stay a few miles away, you know, just in case," Michael said.

"No, my friend. I will stay above you. My country has diverted all traffic away from your destination coordinates. I only hope we acted in time."

"You and me both, brother. You and me both."

SIXTY-THREE

Dave Knox stood inside the cockpit of the cigarette boat, watching the dazzling lights of Dubai approach. The driver informed him they would be at the marina in ten minutes. From there, a car would take him directly to the airport, a short fifteen-minute drive from the Al Zora Marina.

Dave looked at his watch. In less than an hour, he would be twenty-thousand feet in the air. He would love to see the fireball, but he would be flying West, safely away from the nuclear firestorm he would leave behind.

As Dave's boat sped across the water, Deal's plane touched down in Ras Al-Khaimah. Ali had alerted UAE security forces and a helicopter whisked him, Bubba, and Zach to the roof of Ali's building. They found Sarah sitting nervously by herself in Ali's apartment, glued to a screen showing Michael's progress toward the deepest part of the Persian Gulf. She didn't even get up to greet her two friends.

They could all see her agonizing over her boyfriend's fate. Now was not the time to try and comfort the strong young woman.

"How far is he from the destination?" Deal asked.

Sarah didn't take her eyes off the screen. "Another three miles. But the *piece of shit* boat won't go any faster. At this speed, it will take thirty-three minutes to get there. Then he has to find a way to sink the boat. So, forty, forty-five minutes until Ali can pick him up. Ali is going to stay directly above to make sure Michael can get away as quickly as possible."

"Understood," Deal said.

The FBI agent knew he could do little else at this point except monitor Michael's progress.

Damn! These kids all have brass-freaking balls!" Deal thought to himself.

Bubba and Zach sat down quietly next to Sarah. All three watched the dotted red line crawl slowly across the screen toward a blue triangle that indicated where Michael needed to sink the ship.

On board, Michael held the old boat on course. With the throttles wide open, he had nothing to do except look out over the black water. The only thing he could see clearly through the windscreen was the corroded blue cargo container – no more than twenty feet away from his face.

Trying to take his mind off the fact he was all but sitting on top of a nuclear bomb, Michael turned his mind to sinking the boat. He realized he didn't have any idea how to do such a thing. Though old and rusty, the ship still had a steel hull. He needed help.

"Ali," he said into the walkie-talkie. "Get our team on the line and ask for advice on how to sink this thing."

"Calling now," Ali responded.

Bubba, Deal, and Zach took the call.

"Ali, is your helicopter armed at all?" Deal asked.

"Negative. This is just a civilian passenger model," Ali responded.

"See if Michael has seen any other cargo on board," Bubba said. "Maybe there's something he could combine with gasoline to make an explosive."

When Ali responded that the only cargo was the bomb, the room fell silent. They had to think of something or the bomb would explode above water – with nearly the same devastating effect as if it were still near the island.

"This may sound weird," Zach offered suddenly. "But in one of my history classes, I read about whiskey smugglers in the 1930s who installed seacocks in their ships. If they were going to be caught, all they had to do was open a big valve and the ship would sink in just minutes. The crew of Michael's ship had to be smugglers. I mean, they smuggled a nuclear bomb."

"Can't hurt to check," Deal agreed.

After hearing Zach's suggestion, Michael tied the wheel in position with a piece of rope and began searching for a way into the bilge space below the lowest deck of the ship. He finally found a manhole-sized hatch held closed by a metal bar locking mechanism mounted in the deck.

It only took a moment for him to throw the handle and pull open the heavy metal hatch. Almost immediately, a foul stench of fish, rotting food, and human waste assaulted his nose.

Putting aside his revulsion, Michael laid on his stomach and stuck his head into the hellish black hole. Shining the light along the bottom the bilge, he saw nothing but the filthiest water anyone could possibly imagine.

Then, his light flashed over a circular handle sticking up out of the muck. It could only be one thing — the seacock.

"I got it! I got it!" he shouted into his radio. "Tell Zach he's a genius!"

Dave Knox climbed onto the dock at the Al Zora Marina near the fabulous city of Dubai, where two men, dressed in identical black suits, greeted him formally and led him to an enormous black Rolls Royce town car. Inside, he found a strikingly gorgeous young woman who held out a chilled glass of NV Krug Champagne. Long black hair flowed over her shoulders, and her red, perfectly-applied lipstick matched her fashionable lightweight red overcoat.

Dave accepted the champagne and took a seat across from the girl.

"And who might you be?" Dave asked, wondering if one of his fellow Directors had been thoughtful enough to provide him with a plaything for his flight back to Chile.

The girl looked back at Dave through dark, wide-set eyes and flashed a devilish smile.

"I'm Amina Kent. Margie Franks offered me a ride," Amina Kent replied.

"A ride?" Dave asked. "And that's all?"

"Oh, no, Dr. Knox. She also asked me to be sure you didn't get cold feet about completing your mission or decide to make some sort of demand on the other Directors before you detonate your little bomb or whatever."

"I think I understand," Dave said, lifting his glass and smiling. "Margie has nothing to worry about. We'll be in the air in a few minutes. When we reach twenty-thousand feet, I'll make the required call."

"I know you will," Amina replied, pulling a silenced pistol from her jacket.

"No need for threats," Dave said, smiling. "We're all friends here."

"No, we are not friends. But if everyone behaves themselves, we can have a pleasant and profitable ride to the other side of the Atlantic."

Dave held out his hand and took the glass from Amina. "A little later, I'd like to talk with you about something I may need."

Michael returned to the pilothouse and checked his position with Ali. He would be in position in fifteen minutes. For the hundredth time, he pushed on the throttle lever forward. It just didn't seem possible that the boat could move no faster.

Suddenly, the engine barked. Looking back toward the stern, he saw a cloud of black smoke belch into the air. He stood still, listening for another warning sign.

Thankfully, the engine continued its slow, uneven growl, as it pushed the ship forward. But Michael knew something was wrong. Perhaps the engine had swallowed something into one of its cylinders. Whatever it was, it wasn't good.

"We might have another engine problem," Michael related over the radio. "It's okay now, but we could be in for total engine failure before long."

"Understood," Ali said from the cockpit of his helicopter. "Ten minutes out. I shall pray for the engine. May I suggest you check to be sure the seacock valve in the bilge operates smoothly."

"Couldn't hurt," Michael replied. *Except that it smells like hell's outhouse down there.*

Back in the bowels of the ship, the vile smell of the bilge took Michael's mind off the nuclear bomb above his head – at least for a minute.

Trying not to gag and vomit in the greasy sewage challenged Michael more than locating and testing the seacock valve. Probably the only thing on the entire ship maintained properly, he found the round handle moved smoothly. He even made sure he felt a slight inflow of seawater at his feet before closing the valve again.

Now he knew. If the old boat made it to the deepest point of the Gulf, he could actually sink the whole damn thing without much trouble at all.

All he needed was time.

Michael looked at his watch.

Five minutes to be exact.

Dave and Amina alighted from the Rolls Royce, still holding their champagne flutes, and walked briskly to the open door of a white and gold executive jet.

As soon as they were on board, the pilot appeared in the passenger compartment.

"We're cleared to take off now. If you'll take your seats, we'll get in the air. I understand you wish to get underway immediately, so, if it's alright, we'll delay taking your dinner order for a few minutes."

"Thank you, Captain," Dave replied. "Please take off."

"Yes, sir."

"How will we know it worked?" Amina asked.

Dave pointed to the flat screen television mounted on a bulkhead at the other end of the cabin.

"There won't be anything else on that thing."

"How long?" Amina asked.

"Oh, ten minutes or so," Dave answered, swallowing the remainder of his drink.

"All stop!" Ali shouted over the radio. "You're there!"

"Thank god!" Michael replied, pulling the throttle back to neutral, cutting the engine, and leaping from the pilothouse.

He knew he had to move fast. Up to now, all he could do was wait. Now it was up to him.

Michael sprinted from the pilothouse and dropped to the next deck down barely touching ladder. When he reached the entrance to the bilge, he dropped into the water, ignoring the stench. Finally reaching the seacock, he paused to remind himself to turn the valve all the way open. Then he would have to make it back to the ladder before the space filled with seawater.

He took one deep breath and turned the handwheel hard left. His hand moved like a machine, opening the valve until it hit its stops. Water immediately surged through the opening.

Michael couldn't believe how fast the water flooded in. In seconds, it was nearly at chest level. He waded back toward the ladder, water climbing to his shoulders and then to his neck. Just a few feet from safety, the inflowing sea swept him off his feet. With one last lunge, he just managed to grab onto the ladder.

The water rose faster and faster, lifting Michael toward the opening above. He knew if he let go of the rungs, he would be swept into the bowels of the bilge. Using all his strength, he climbed upward, finally hauling himself onto the lower deck even as water shot up through the bilge hatch.

Not wasting any time, he splashed through the fast-rising water and climbed up to the main deck. To his relief, he saw Ali's chopper already hovering above, a rope ladder hanging out of the side door.

Although exhausted, Michael snagged the end of the rope ladder out of the air and steadied it enough to get a foot into the first rung. As soon as he did, Ali began moving away from the fast-sinking old cargo ship.

Looking down, Michael watched water shoot out of the hatch he had just climbed through. The stern of the ship already sat very low in the water. It seemed like only seconds before the back of the ship was under the water, the bow now pointed at a forty-five-degree angle into the sky.

Michael climbed higher as Ali continued to fly away toward the South.

Finally, the rest of the ship slipped below the surface – taking the nuclear bomb to the bottom of the Persian Gulf.

"Go! Go!" Michael shouted as he pulled himself into the cabin.

Instead of answering, Ali accelerated the helicopter to top speed.

"Lady and Gentleman, we have reached twenty thousand feet," the captain announced to his only two passengers. "We'll be taking your dinner orders now. Thank you for your patience."

Amina pulled an open bottle of champagne from an ice bucket the attendant had just placed next to her seat and poured herself a glass.

"Now?" she asked.

"Yes," Dave replied, pulling the satellite phone from his pocket. "Now."

SIXTY-FOUR

The cargo ship sunk into the darkness stern-down, the weight of the engine dragging the ship deeper and deeper. When it slammed into the seabed, the metal hull partially collapsed, sending shockwaves through the rest of the ship. Bubbles from trapped air emerged from all over the upper decks.

Just before the bow settled into the sand, the now-weakened metal fittings holding the shipping container in place snapped. Inside the container, enough trapped air remained to lift the metal box and the bomb inside off the deck. For a moment, the container snagged on the crane arm just above. But then, it slid around the crane and rose again, as if the bomb inside wanted to explode in open air.

If it did, the nuclear fireball would be uncontained by the vast waters of the Gulf. Everything The Cause planned for and wanted would happen. The world would have to confront the consequences of a nuclear detonation at the center of its most volatile region.

Then, the lifting straps Dave Knox had attached to the container went taught. For a second, the container looked like a rectangular metal balloon, prevented from floating away by the crane arm. After remaining above the ship for a few seconds, the weight of water seeping inside finally overcame the lifting power of the air and the bomb slowly descended back toward the ship.

Suddenly, in a blinding light, the ship simply disappeared, blown into atoms by the Mark 15 thermonuclear bomb it once carried on its deck.

In milliseconds, a massive bubble took the place of the ship and nearly a mile of seawater. Expanding faster than the human eye could comprehend, the bubble burst through the surface of the Gulf and rose five hundred feet into the air.

Shockwaves in the water moved at hypersonic speed, forming waves at the surface that struck distant shores like hammer blows. Thankfully, the great measure of destruction had been absorbed by the water. The waves maxed out at only ten feet, expending their energy on mostly empty beaches.

Except for a distant mysterious rumble, the nuclear blast barely raised an eyebrow in the surrounding countries.

Of course, the explosion was detected by every developed country that monitored seismic activity.

Ten miles from ground zero, the shockwave hit Ali's helicopter from behind. Both Michael and Ali were thrown forward in their harnesses and Ali had to wrestle with the controls while the fast-moving air swept past his aircraft.

"They did it!" Michael exclaimed. "They actually did it!"

"Let's see," Ali said, slowing down and turning back toward the explosion.

In the distance what looked like a giant glowing ball of water and steam hung in the air. But even as they watched, the glow faded and ball collapsed in on itself. In just seconds, the view through the windscreen returned to normal — a dark sky hanging over the glinting water of a darker sea.

"Let's go home," Michael said, tired to the bone. "I've seen enough."

"Yes, my good and special friend. Yes. It is time to go home."

EPILOGUE

Two Weeks Later

Michael and Sarah relaxed together in a double-wide lounge chair on the balcony outside Ali's apartment. A gentle breeze blew in from the sea while they sipped Mai Tai's prepared by the sheik himself. For the past two weeks Michael, Sarah, Zach and Bubba had all been Ali's honored guests. Despite their protests, Ali insisted on pampering his new friends, making sure they lacked for nothing.

And, for the past two weeks, Sarah had not let Michael out of her sight. After barely avoiding being vaporized by a nuclear explosion, Michael didn't mind the attention.

The couple turned around to see one of the glass sliding doors to the interior open. To their delight, Stella Sims walked slowly through the door, one arm encased in a black and chrome splint. The Sheik of the RAK Emirate walked next to her, gently holding on to the other arm and fretting over every step she took.

"Agent Sims!" Sarah cried, jumping from her seat.

"I think you can call me Stella now," Sims said, a bit weakly.

Michael stood and pulled another oversized lounge chair close to theirs.

With Ali and Sarah's help, Sims lowered herself slowly onto the soft warm cushions.

A few seconds later, Bubba and Zach emerged from inside, each carrying a cold bottle in one hand and arguing over which country made better beer, America or Great Britain.

"I'm glad to see you two haven't suffered from the past crisis," Sims commented.

"Dumbass here still thinks American beer is better than a British ale!" Bubba complained, with a wide smile on his face.

"Oh, so now you *like* England, do you?" Ali asked. "I was given to understand it didn't suit you."

"Well, a man can change his mind, can't he?" Bubba responded. "Anyway, any country that can pour me such a fine malt product is okay with me!"

"Oh my, god!" Zach said, sitting down at the foot of Michael and Sarah's seat.

"You two are worthless," Sarah said. "You didn't even ask how Stella is doing."

"We saw her inside," Zach objected.

"I'm fine, Sarah," Sims said. "A few weeks in this thing and some physical therapy and I'll be back to work."

"And you shall recuperate here," Ali added, more stating a fact than asking.

"I can't think of a nicer place," Sims replied, taking Ali's hand in her own.

Bubba, Zach, Sarah, and Michael exchanged knowing looks. Something was obviously going on between the two.

"Where's Agent Deal now?" Bubba asked.

"Back in Spain looking for a lost nuclear bomb from the 1960s," Sims replied. "He got pulled off the project last year when The Cause first started causing trouble. Since what happened here a few weeks ago, the agency has suddenly become much more interested in getting it back."

"Was he able to identify the man we saw on the cargo boat?" Michael asked.

Sims nodded. "Yes. Dr. Dave Knox. He is one of the scientists that stole the black project technology last year from Area 51 and gave it to The Cause. Unfortunately, he took off in a private jet just before the bomb exploded. We lost him. By the way, what's the latest on the effects of the explosion?"

Ali explained that the nuclear detonation initially led to a flurry of accusations between his nation and Iran. But scientific analysis of the radiation output conclusively proved the uranium used in the bomb came from the U.S. And the deterioration of the atomic isotopes proved the bomb had been manufactured in 1956.

Backed into a corner and unwilling to admit that one of their lost nukes wound up in the hands of terrorists – or in this case The Cause – the U.S. informed the world that it had lost a submarine in the Gulf many years before. The explosion had been nothing more than an accident and the U.S. agreed to pay for any damage.

"We are still in negotiations with the Omanis and Iranians over my family's oil rights, but tensions have thankfully eased. Everyone involved would rather sell oil than risk a war that would cost more than any of us could ever recoup from the oil fields. In other words, peace is far more profitable than war," Ali concluded.

"Makes sense to me," Michael said, stretching his arms over his head and relaxing back into his chair.

Santiago, Chile

"The Middle East should be a burning wreck, and you sit there, you smug asshole, grinning like an idiot!" Margie Franks bellowed at Dave Knox. "You failed!"

Dave just sat back in his conference room chair and put both hands behind his head. "Did I?"

The ten other Directors didn't interfere with the escalating conflict between Margie and Dave.

"We spent a quarter *billion* dollars on this operation. Perhaps you'd like to explain to the Directors just how this was a success," Margie shouted.

Dave rose from his seat to address the gathering of billionaires.

"First, let's look at the value of our holdings in North American and South American oil production and refinement operations."

A screen lowered from a panel in the roof. Using a remote, Dave brought up a graph of valuations in the areas he discussed since the nuclear explosion.

"As you can see, we have gained nearly ten times our investment in the project just from decreased confidence in the Middle Eastern oil supply. Theirs is worth less, so ours is worth more. In addition to that, after Sir Gregory's untimely demise, the value of his company took a nosedive. We picked it up at a big, big discount. Of course, threatening to reveal his role in the terrorist attack in London made the rest of his family more, uh, willing to sell."

Dave changed the screen to depict another graph.

"Since the explosion, the value of our holdings in military armaments has increased three-fold. The detonation of a nuclear weapon has caused almost every nation to increase its military spending."

"Finally, our politicians have received numerous requests from overseas interests to join our little endeavor. Our willingness to take whatever action is required to increase our wealth and influence has not gone unnoticed."

The other Directors looked back at Franks. Dave Knox, Ph.D. had outthought her at every turn.

"Oh, and one more thing," Dave said. "I want your seat at the head of the table. We took a vote. And I'm afraid it was unanimous."

"He's right, Margie," Alexander Monroe added. "Perhaps you should go ahead and relinquish your seat now."

Too incensed to heed Monroe's warning, Margie lashed out. "Bullshit! You don't have the balls to do my job, you stinking little turd!"

"Well," Dave said, shrugging, "after I personally delivered a nuclear bomb into the heart of the Strait of Hormuz under the noses of the Iranians, the UAE, and the American Navy, everyone here thinks I do possess the balls. So, please take Alexander's advice and step down. Now."

"Never," Franks answered, leaning over the table. "Not to you. Not to *anyone.*"

"Yes, well, I thought you'd say that."

Without warning, the door to the conference room opened and Amina Kent stepped into the room.

Margie looked up. "Who is this bitch?"

Without a word, Amina raised a pistol and shot Margie Franks in the exact center of her forehead.

Margie Franks died as she lived, with an arrogant scowl permanently plastered across her face.

"Thank you, Miss Kent," Dave said, without emotion. "Your payment has been deposited as you requested."

Amina nodded and stepped back out of the room.

Dave Knox walked slowly to the head of the table, kicked Margie's leg away from his chair and sat down.

"Gentlemen, our successful operations to date have reaped untold wealth and political power. But we have only just begun. Our cause is now ready for expansion, and I stand ready to lead us into the next era. My fellow Directors, to The Cause!" Dave said, taking Margie's untouched glass of fine bourbon from the table and raising it high in the air.

"The Cause!"